Soulless Creature

Marceline Ghanime

"Being with someone who has a lot of baggage, leads to inevitable damage."

DEDICATION

This book is dedicated with love and affection to my mother.

CHAPTER 1

"I'm going to teach you a little something, Lucy," Howard Brown yelled out, venom dripping from his voice as he slammed his leather belt against the counter. "I told you to fucking clean my room and change my bed sheets. So, why the hell is my room still messy? And why do I still have the same bed sheets?" He growled, clenching his jaw so hard that his teeth threatened to crack.

Lucy whimpered, backing away from the man she knew as her father. "I'm s-sorry. I just came from school and I-"

Howard immediately cut her off, his flaming eyes daring her to utter another word. "You had time before school, you lazy bitch." He tightened his grip on his belt.

Lucy did not bother to defend herself, for she knew that she'll get beaten up one way or another. The contact of the leather belt with her already bruised skin broke off Lucy's thoughts. She flinched, biting down on her bottom lip hard enough to draw blood. Forcing back the bitter tears, she refused to give him the satisfaction of screaming out; she always knew what that led to. More and more whipping.

Lucy sighed deeply, cringing at the sound of her father yelling out for her to hurry up and come down for breakfast. Today was her first day at her new school. Rolling her eyes, she put on her favorite blue shirt along with a pair of black skinny jeans. She quickly brushed her long, dark blonde hair, as she smeared red lipstick on and applied black mascara. She looked at herself in the mirror one last time before she ran downstairs to have her breakfast with her oh-so loving family.

She sat down with her parents and her brother, Chad. Chad was her older brother who, as a kid, also faced Howard's abuse. The only difference was that she still got beaten up up to this day. However, she no longer felt as affected as she used to. Lucy hurriedly gobbled her pancakes, avoiding any chit chat. "Look who's excited for school," Her father remarked mockingly.

"Trust me, I'm not," Lucy said bluntly.

Her father shook his head, scrunching his nose in disgust as he motioned to the shirt she was wearing. "That is one ugly shirt."

Lucy gritted her teeth. Before lashing out, she eyed Chad, wanting to leave right now. Getting up, she grabbed her bag and made her way to Chad's car. She stared out the window, taking in the beauty of Goldwallow, her hometown. The town was a maze of narrow streets decorated by linden trees. The houses were an astounding collection of different styles, such as Georgian-style houses. It was a small, cozy, and busy town.

She gave a long sigh as she entered her new school's dull hallway; *this is going to be a very long day.* She made her way to her locker and placed the books she didn't need inside of it. Checking her schedule, she smiled. 'First period: English (Miss Woods)'. She strolled through the hall as she looked around her school, trying to waste some time.

She accidentally crashed into someone. "Whoa! Watch where you're going you, you moron!" A girl in a tight, red shirt and a face caked with makeup squealed.

Lucy faked a smile and walked away, completely ignoring her. The girl's eyes widened, expecting some sort of a comeback. But Lucy didn't really want to waste any of her precious time.

Lucy felt someone gently tap her shoulder from behind. She turned around to face a short girl with wavy, brown hair and big, green eyes that felt so warm and friendly. Lucy smiled as the girl spoke, "Hey, I'm Amy and I just want to say that not replying to that girl was really a wise thing to do, because she's just not worth it." Amy blurted out, obviously feeling nervous.

Noticing how tense she was, Lucy stretched out her hand for Amy to take. "Nice to meet you. I'm new here. Would you show me around, if that's okay?"

Amy willingly nodded as she moved along next to her. She kept asking her random, silly questions like 'What's your favorite color?' and 'What music do you listen to?' According to her, that was how you got to know someone well as quickly as possible. She seemed really fun and bubbly. Lucy had a feeling that she'll get along fine with her. She didn't have much to say though, she certainly didn't want to tell her how her life at home was; she just didn't want to bring it up at all. She had simply registered in a new school because she felt like she needed a change in her life. Maybe here in a new school with new people, she'll actually feel wanted and truly content.

"This is English class by the way," Amy said, pointing at the fairly wide classroom. She has practically shown her all the classes that came in sight, and now they somehow reached the last one. Lucy spotted an alluring figure in the crowd, she squinted her eyes to get a better look at the boy who caught her attention.

She nudged Amy by her elbow. "Who's that?" She asked, pointing at the boy with the long, red locks and perfectly-toned body.

Amy bit her lip. "Mmm, he's new, but I heard rumors about him. He's some sort of a delinquent. I mean look at his long hair! But I bet he's not like any one of those delinquents that they're referring to. There's something real strange yet appealing about him, he seems different. I mean that's what everybody is saying, you know?" She paused as she rubbed the back of her neck. "We'll eventually find out for ourselves."

Lucy ran a hand through her hair as she stole another glance at him. He was handsome in a way she had never seen before, though there was something about him that could make you feel uneasy if you looked at him for too long. He then suddenly turned around and looked in her direction. And once he noticed her gawking, she felt a rush of heat course through her veins and a weird sensation shot through every inch of her body.

Their eyes met for a few seconds; his had an unusual dark glimmer in them that made it hard for her to break eye contact. It was as if they were piercing right through her soul and exposing her, but he was expressionless and immediately turned away. Lucy hadn't noticed that she was holding her breath the whole couple of seconds. She breathed out and mumbled, "Whoa." She felt her heart rate increase drastically. She could almost hear the wild, rhythmic drumming of her heart in her ears. The hair on the back of her neck stood straight up. *That was super odd*, she thought to herself as she shook her head, ignoring what she had just encountered.

The bell suddenly rang, making her jump. "I'll see you after class at the cafeteria!" Amy yelled as she made her way to her math class.

Lucy took a seat next to the window as she waited for the whole class to be filled. She saw many new faces enter through the door, some pretty, and some plain ugly. The girl she bumped into today sat down at the back. *She's in my English class, great just great.*

Just when the teacher was about to begin her lecture, Mr. Hot-Yet-Brooding entered the class and everyone stared at him, taking in his attractive features as the sound of ongoing whispering filled the room. He didn't even look around, didn't even care that he was the center of attention. He just took his seat which was across Lucy's and glared, obviously annoyed by the constant staring. Lucy took a deep breath as she bit her lip, *this is going to be an interesting class.*

Lucy tried as hard as she could to pay attention to Miss Woods, but all she could think of was how hot the boy sitting across from her was. *Get a grip girl, he's just a guy,* she mentally scolded herself.

She buried her face in her hands as she breathed in, calming herself down. "Would you please pay attention?" The teacher yelled at Lucy, making her jump in her seat.

She stuttered. "I-I I'm sorry, I um...have a slight headache." Miss Woods glared at her, seemingly unfazed by her excuse as she placed her square eyeglasses on top of her damp hair.

The boy across from Lucy's seat suddenly stood up and said, "I need to leave..." His deep voice made Lucy shudder; it was mellifluous to her ears even though it was rough.

The teacher sighed deeply. "No you're not! Class is going to end, so you can wait."

The boy huffed as he cleared his throat. "But..."

The teacher glared, causing the vein on her forehead to protrude as she flailed her arms in the air. "No buts, now sit down Drake Reid!"

He sat down, obviously agitated. Lucy swore she saw the edge of his wooden desk slightly crack due to the way he had thrust it with full force. *So Drake is his name, it really suited him.*

She stole a glance at him as she studied his features intently. He had mesmerizing dark, blue eyes that were outlined by long, thick eyelashes. He had a perfectly-formed nose, full, plump, soft lips, and gorgeous, fiery, red hair that will take so much effort not to run your hands through them. *Yep, he's most definitely out of this world.*

"Staring at others is rude." Lucy nervously gulped as her breath got caught in her throat, she slowly looked around the room as her eyes searched every bored face, but no one seems to be paying attention to her, not even Drake. *I must have imagined it, yeah that's for sure,* she thought as she bit her inner cheek.

The bell finally rang saving Lucy from getting crazy. She quickly got out of class to see Amy running towards her with a warm smile. "So how was your first period? Any good-looking boys in your class?"

Lucy nervously spoke, "Well yeah, but he's sort of the guy I asked you about earlier, the weird yet hot one."

Amy furrowed her eyebrows as she drew closer to Lucy. "Every girl in my class is talking about him; ugh, if I hear one more comment about that guy I'm going to lose it!" She added, "Besides he doesn't seem like he likes the attention, I mean look at him!" she gestured at him. He was sitting alone in the corner with his earphones in his ears.

Lucy's lips formed a tight line as she suggested. "I'm going to go talk to him, he's new I'm new..."

Amy grabbed Lucy's arm as she pulled her aside. "No way! He's creepy, you're staying here."

Lucy pulled her arm away from Amy's grasp. "Thanks for your concern Amy, but I'm really curious about him. I will be right back." With that, she made her way to the lone table.

She stood beside Drake's table as she cleared her throat. "Um...hi, I'm Lucy." Drake glanced at her as he eyed her from head to toe; he nodded giving her a faint smile. *That's it? Wow, he seems friendly.*

Lucy continued to speak as she sat down next to him. "So what brings you here? To this school."

Drake puckered his brow. "Is this your way of making a conversation? Cause it sucks baby."

Lucy's mouth was agape now. "Ouch. I guess you really deserve to be alone. Bye you douche." When she got up to leave, she was suddenly grabbed by Drake and pinned to the wall with his arms on each side.

He drew closer and huskily whispered as she felt his hot breath tickle her ear. "I've been called worse." He slightly pulled back to

10

look her in the eyes and added. "I advise you not to make friends with guys like me because guys like me can hurt you, real bad."

Lucy gulped, ignoring the warm tingles that ran through her entire body as she nervously yet boldly replied. "For your information, I don't get hurt easily."

His lips twisted into a smirk. "Ah, you're one of the feisty girls. Good for you." He gently lifted her chin with the tips of his fingers, making her meet his gaze as he spoke in a hushed tone. "Here's a thing you should keep in mind, 'looks can be deceiving', so do not be fooled by my charm." And as soon as those words left his lips, she wasn't able to suppress the bolts of electricity that shot through her body. Her heart wildly pounded against her chest and she couldn't help but feel tempted by him. The sound of his husky yet seductive voice was enough to make her legs go limp.

He then suddenly chuckled as his eyes darkened. "And baby, I think you should move away from me now before I do something to you that's somewhat dirty." *What the hell?*

Lucy's cheeks were flushed red as she pushed him away with full force. She wanted to shout at him and attack him with cruel words but nothing came out. So, she just hurriedly walked away, avoiding everybody's lingering stares and most definitely avoiding him.

"Are you serious? What a jerk!" Amy squealed as her mouth hung open after hearing about the intense conversation Lucy and Drake shared.

Lucy shrugged. "I know, but it's not like it really affected me or anything."

Amy pressed her lips in a tight line. "Yeah right." Lucy huffed while Amy suddenly nudged her, motioning for her to look ahead. "Look who's hanging with Mr. Draky over there!"

Lucy whipped round to face the scene that had caught her friend's attention. And there he was surrounded by that fake girl whom she previously bumped into, and a bunch of other girls that were practically drooling over him. Lucy shook her head. "Ugh, he's not even pushing them away like he did to me!"

Amy suppressed her giggle as she placed her hand on her lips. "I thought you weren't affected by him whatsoever."

Lucy gave a shocked expression. "Am not! It's just that...never mind, forget it."

Amy rolled her eyes at her. "Trust me I think he's somewhat giving them attention so that he'll have some fun, you know cause they're bitches duh, and you went as a friend and acting all innocent... "

Lucy was about to say something when Amy shushed her to continue, "Like I said he wants some fun, you do know what I mean now do you?"

Lucy glared at her as she flailed her arms in her face trying to make a point, "I don't need an explanation! I don't care about him, and I most certainly don't care how he has his so-called 'fun'!"

Amy bit her lip. "Sure, now let's get ready for our next class."

The classes went by swiftly, as quick as a snap. Lucy thanked God it was over for she couldn't tolerate any more school drama. Amy said her good byes as she gave Lucy a warm bear hug, and went to get her car to drive home at last. Lucy simply stood there, waiting for her older brother to come pick her up. She knew how to drive of course, but did not have a car of her own yet. Her parents weren't that rich like Amy's and she really didn't want to get a job just yet. Lucy paced back and forth impatiently as students left one by one, leaving her there with a few teens and a couple of teachers. *Where is Chad? He's really going to pay for this.*

All at once, Drake appeared and passed by her as he made his way to his car – oh wait – his motorcycle, a Harley Davidson, what a beauty.

He noticed her gawking at his baby, so just before he woke his motorcycle to life, he mockingly asked, "Aww, you were waiting for me? Well, here I am."

Lucy rolled her eyes as she crossed her arms and sneered. "Ha-ha you're so charming. For your info, I'm waiting for my brother."

Drake wiggled his eyebrows as he placed his helmet on his head, buckling the strap around his neck and securing it tightly. "How about I give you a ride? I know it'll be your dream come true."

Lucy approached him and looked him straight in the eyes. "Look here Drake, I don't need your ride and you're certainly not like any of my dreams-"

He cut her off as he drew nearer to her face, causing the motorcycle to slightly bend to her side, and stated in a rough tone. "You're absolutely right. I ain't no pretty dream love, I'm your worst nightmare." After saying that, he immediately revved up the engine and drove away with full speed, making Lucy's hair fly and tangle up.

She combed her hair with her fingers, adjusting it as she cursed under her breath. "What a jerk," She murmured, but still she couldn't shake the feeling of attraction away. There was something about him that intrigued her and pulled her to him. It was like he was an unpleasant magnet drawing her into his engaging yet wicked world. She breathed in as she tapped her foot against the ground, obviously irritated by the long wait. *I should have accepted his ride*, she grinned like a Cheshire cat but then rubbed her temple, shrugging off such thoughts.

After a few more minutes, Chad finally arrived. He had a stern yet worried look on his face as he told Lucy to get in the car. "What took you so long?" she asked in an aggravated manner.

He closed his eyes shut as if considering and then spoke, "Well I don't know how to say this sis, but our parents got in a fight and things aren't so pleasant back there. Plus there was traffic and..."

Lucy raised her brow and bit her nail. "There's something you're not telling me Chad. What is it? Tell me."

He exhaled as he ran a hand through his hair and stated with concern, "Mom is bruised all over."

Lucy placed her hands against her cheeks in shock. "What? Is it dad again? What the hell is wrong with him?"

CHAPTER 2

Lucy stormed into her house as she slammed the door against the wall and yelled, "Mom? Where are you?"

Chad replied instead, "She's in the kitchen."

Lucy nodded. "And where's the 'father'?"

Chad's nostrils flared as he inhaled deeply. "He's in his room drinking, that's what he's good at."

Lucy rubbed her face and ran towards the kitchen to check on her mother. She had bruises on both her arms and a couple of cuts on her face. Lucy shrieked. "Shit!" She approached her mother, Natasha, to get a better look at her wounds. She examined them by lifting her mother's arms and checking her left and right cheeks. "Whew, at least they're not deep, it'll be okay."

Her mom sobbed as bitter tears made their way down her dry face. "He had to dear. He was drunk."

Lucy straightened up, furrowing her brows. "He had to? Are you out of your mind? You don't have to tolerate his immature and irresponsible habits. Leave him."

Her mom widened her eyes at her as she placed her hand on her chest. "Don't talk like that about your father. He's under pressure!" Words wouldn't come out of her mouth, she just watched her mom sit there and talk nonsense. "We should respect him. He's the man of the house," Her mother blabbered.

Lucy spoke mockingly, her fingers trembling. "You know what? Respect him yourself. I'm outta here!" With that, she hurriedly made her way upstairs to her room, leaving her mother alone in her gloomy kitchen. She was sick and tired of her dad who constantly kept treating everybody like trash, and she was mostly sick and tired of her mom who kept sticking up to him. *I'm going to run away.* She prepared her bag whilst blasting some loud rock music on, so that they would think she's having an emotional outburst and not plotting her escape or something. Once she got it all ready, she placed it under her bed and made her way to her father's room. No way was she going without facing that animal.

She opened the door without a thought to see him slumped against the pillows. He was surrounded by a couple of empty vodka bottles, and in his hand, he held a half empty whisky bottle. *He quit drinking, such a pathetic liar.* She made her way to him and crouched next to him, so that she'd be at the same eye level when speaking to him. "You are a complete pig who only cares about his self-desires. That's all I have to say to you."

He hiccupped as he lazily opened his eyelids. "What-was-that-you-said?"

Lucy rolled her eyes and got up to leave, but he roared from behind her. "Come here young lady, that's no way to talk to your-your-father!" She ignored his stupid attempt at a comeback and went to her room.

Chad knocked at her door before he entered. "I'm sorry you have to face these things every time Lucy, but sometimes you can't control it," he said, his hands tucked in his pockets.

Lucy turned around, not wanting to face him as she felt a tear trickle down from the corner of her eye. "You don't have to give me a philosophical lecture, Chad. I get it." He wore an apologetic look on his face, then hopelessly shrugged and walked away.

It was 1:30 am, she hurriedly got out of her covers, revealing her dressed self and placed her bag on her left shoulder. She silently opened her bedroom window and climbed down through it. It wasn't that high and she was somewhat athletic, thus it was easy for her. Once she got close to the ground, she jumped and landed on the flower bed just below her window. She got up and wiped the dirt off her butt as she readjusted her bag on her shoulder, and made her way in the dark.

She was walking and walking to who knows where. She thought she'd go to Amy's but she didn't want to bother her with her drama. Besides, she wasn't that close to her. She knew that what she was doing was childish, but right now, all she wanted was to get her mind off of things. Just when she was about to stop and take a breath, she heard a noise coming from the alley ahead of her. She sneaked her way to it and stopped to slightly tilt her head and see what's going on; Lucy was curious. What made her freak out as soon as she saw the dreadful scene in front of her was the figure hovering above a dead person on the ground. She could spot those red locks anywhere, it was Drake. A sudden sense of fear ran through her nerves like the chill of an icy wind. *What the hell is going on?* She gradually backed away gulping, but accidentally tripped over a used tire near the bins. This tiny minor accident was going to make her wish she had stayed in bed.

Oh boy, she thought to herself as she panicked and tried to run away before he actually found out that she had witnessed that awful scene. But just as she was about to flee, she felt a cold, strong arm grab her by her waist and pull her close, not allowing her to move and make her escape. Drake covered her mouth with his rough hand as he violently slammed her against the brick wall and drew nearer to her. She squirmed in his grasp but he was too strong for her to make him back off. She could feel his warm breath fanning across her face as he spoke tensely, "I'm going to let you speak now...if you dare shout or try to run away, I'm going to make you regret the second you planned on doing so."

Lucy instantly nodded her head, her heart hammering against her chest with every single second that ticked by. An uncomfortable premonition of fear permeated her senses. She most certainly did not want to get on his nerves. "Good girl," Drake sneered.

Lucy's eyes were widened as she took in his agitated features, his jaw was tensed and his eyes were so dark, no one would even notice they had a shade of blue. His lips slightly parted and he asked in a low tone, "What did you see? Tell me."

Lucy gulped anxiously, trying to form words. "N-nothing I swear-"

He cursed under his breath, irritated. "I'm going to pretend you're not lying right now, if you supposedly did not see anything then why the hell are you here at this late hour?"

She bit her lip as she blabbered nervously, "I-I- ran away from home and this is none of your business. I said I didn't see anything and I'm not lying. Besides, what are you scared about huh? Did you kill the poor man? Shouldn't we call for help?" She breathed in heavily, hoping she did not push it. He smirked. *Wait, did he just smirk?* Lucy had a puzzled expression on as she fiddled with her earrings with trembling fingers.

He drew even closer to her face if that was possible and looked intently into her bright blue eyes. "First, I did not kill him and second, he clearly needs no help for he's fuckin dead as you can see, and third-" he stopped and licked his lips, "-third, you are coming with me."

Lucy narrowed her eyes, ignoring the lump that was forming in her throat. "Wait, how did he die? What happened? Aren't you going to tell me?" She argued, ignoring the last part that he mentioned.

Drake softly traced her cheek with his finger, sending tingles throughout her entire body as he glared. "You ask way too many questions, so how about you just shut up and be grateful."

Lucy's mouth fell open with shock and annoyance. "Grateful? Why the hell should I be grateful?"

The corners of his lips lifted in a smirk. "Well, I did spare your life now, didn't I?"

"What-" She asked, cutting him off.

He placed his finger on her lips, shushing her. "And I'm going to give you a place to stay, so you owe me princess."

Lucy furrowed her eyebrows. "Who said I wanted to go with you? And worse, stay at your apartment, alone with you? I prefer to be killed." She crossed her arms, fuming with anger. "And how about you stop pinning me against walls, do you have a problem?" She said bluntly.

He then suddenly lifted her up with his muscular arms and carried her on his shoulder as he firmly held her by her legs.

She smacked his back with her fists as she pleaded loudly, "Put me down! Where are you taking me? I don't want to be a collection of your dead zombies!" The putrefying stench of rotten flesh engulfed her. She felt her heart clench when she briefly eyed the lifeless body, before turning away.

He chuckled. "That's funny babe, but no. How about you just lower your voice and be a good girl."

She gave up as she spread her arms down against his back, too tired to try to change his mind. He finally put her down once he reached his motorcycle. Lucy panicked; no way was she going to ride this thing to who knows where. She slowly began to back away while he was busy turning his Harley on with his keys. "Stay right where you are Lucy. Even if I can't see you, it doesn't mean I can't hear your stupid heels click," He exclaimed.

Lucy stopped dead in her tracks as she fidgeted with her fingers nervously. "I um…wanted to ask you-"

He approached her, impatiently waiting for her question to be blurted out. "What is it? You're starting to get on my nerves."

She took a deep breath, ignoring the terror that held her in a vice-like grip. "What about the dead man? We can't just leave him there!"

Drake ran a hand through his hair, disheveling it. "Really? Then how about you go and bury him in a sweet little grave with sweet little flowers and give him your sweet little prayers. Wouldn't that be sweet?"

Lucy was simply shocked. *How can he be cool about this? This is no joke.* Just as she was about to reason, he spoke again with a frown, "I don't want my fingerprints to be on the dead body. Soon the police will know about this man and would want to fuckin know how the hell this happened. And if you want to volunteer in being one of the suspects, then go ahead babe, he's all yours."

Lucy swallowed back her words as she rubbed the back of her neck. She took a long, deep breath, forcing herself to be strong. *What is that boy hiding?* She shut her eyes very tight, she would know what he was hiding and she would certainly know what exactly happened to that poor dead man. She'll just have to play it smooth.

Her hair flapped dramatically in the wind as it brushed roughly against the nape of her neck. *How do I get myself into these situations?* She asked herself, clamping her eyes shut.

"Hold on tight Lucy! You're riding a motorcycle, it's not a roller coaster ride so you're not supposed to flail your arms, for God's sake." He was obviously agitated for she felt his muscles tense against her arms that were clutched around his torso securely. She held her bag firmly against her, not wanting to lose it as the ride went along.

"I'm not flailing my arms. I just don't really want to um...touch you." She bit her lip.

"I know you're attracted to me, you just have to accept reality and try to control your hormones." He shouted out smugly over the noisy sound the motor was making. She could see his stupid smirk in the rear view mirror practically haunting her. She felt her cheeks flush with embarrassment as she hid her crimson red face further away behind his back, thanking God she wasn't standing there in front of him.

"You're wrong, I'm not attracted to jerks like you. Ugh, you're so conceited." She yelled in his ear, wanting him to hear every single word, but that didn't seem to make that smirk of his vanish. Instead, he flashed another arrogant wide smile, showing off his pearly white teeth.

"Keep telling that to yourself. I'm sure it'll help with the control of your horm-" She cut him off as she harshly slapped his back from behind, wanting him to shut that blabbering mouth of his. He winced with *pain?* She wasn't sure, he did not give her the reaction she aimed for but at least she did stop him from completing his inappropriate statement.

"If you playfully hit me once more – because dear, if that was a hit you need a whole lot of practice, as I was saying, I will literally speed up real fast and make you regret what you did."

She didn't answer him for she didn't even have the time to do so, he just increased his motorcycle's speed without waiting for her to reply. She clutched him even tighter and buried her head against his back. His scent enveloped her, it was the scent of his fresh cologne that filled her nostrils, intoxicating her. She couldn't help but want more of him. *He smells so sexy,* she immediately shrugged it off, she shouldn't be thinking that way about him, especially after what had just happened.

She felt a rough jolt when the motorcycle made a stop near a tall, neat building. *Whew, that was over,* she sighed. Even though she really liked motorcycle rides, nothing with him was likable.

"Hop off," He exclaimed as he stretched out his hand for her to take. She huffed as she took it and was gently pulled off his

Harley, she was now standing on the ground facing his oh-so charming self.

"Is this where you live?" She asked as they made their way through the entrance.

He rolled his eyes. "Of course, where'd you expect me to take you?"

Lucy shot him a glare as she crossed her arms. "You don't have to be mean about it." A yawn forced itself out of her mouth as she rubbed her drowsy eyes. He ran a hand through his hair and cleared his throat. "You're obviously sleepy, so let's get you to bed."

His apartment looked cozy. She stood by the plain white door, looking around, taking in every single detail. Two grey English roll arm sofas were situated around a coastal coffee table. White rod pocket curtains were swept aside to reveal a slider window. The white walls were simple, unadorned. She sat her bag down on the ceramic floor tiles as she forced her eyes open.

"There's the bathroom so that you can change," He pointed to the door across him. "But if you want to change here, I don't mind really," he winked at her, making her blush.

She grabbed her clothes from the bag and stormed straight to the bathroom without another glance at him. She searched for a key to lock the door but there was no key lock.

"Drake! The door doesn't have a key lock!" She yelled as she brushed off a wisp of soft hair from her eyes.

"Is there supposed to be a lock to the bathroom door? Come on, I live alone I don't need it," he chuckled, approaching her. "Besides, don't you trust me yet? I won't peek, only if you want me to." He licked his lips, enjoying her anxious expression.

"Are you insane? Of course I don't trust you!" She blurted out. He placed a hand on his heart and feigned a pained expression. "That hurts." He added, "Just get in there and change, would you?" He rolled his eyes as she slammed the door.

She stripped down to her underwear and wore her pajamas. *That dead man did not have any vast wounds, trails of blood, nor did he have a visible mark of a gunshot. Maybe Drake didn't really kill him, but still, why would he be so defensive about it and obviously bothered that I was there? What didn't he want me to see?* Lucy wondered as she straightened her top and looked in the mirror. Her hair was a total mess. She ran her fingers through it, trying to put it back in place as she tugged a couple of strands down.

"Nice pajamas, Hello Kitty turns me on," He joked as he burst out laughing, obviously entertained. Lucy furrowed her eyebrows, ignoring his silly comment. "Where do I sleep?"

He smirked, studying her pleasant features for a minute. "Next to me of course."

Her eyes widened as she protested, "No way!"

"Fine, you sleep in my bed and I'll sleep on the couch or on the floor," he rolled his eyes as he took his shirt off and stripped down to his boxers.

"Ah! What the hell are you doing?" She squeaked and hastily covered her eyes.

"I'm obviously getting ready for bed. Haven't you ever seen a man in boxers only?" He mocked her and laughed at the way she reacted. "You're blushing." He drew nearer to her as he softly brushed her cheek with his finger, sending shivers down her spine. He squinted at her through hardened eyes.

She gulped, not liking the fact that he was half naked and so dangerously close to her. *Oh dear Lord*, she bit down on her bottom lip as she stared at his well-built muscular body. He had perfectly-sculpted packs. She tried to mask her emotions in order to appear unaffected.

A sinister smirk tugged at the corners of his lips, casting a spell of desire to whoever looked his way.

She licked her lips slowly, not realizing that she was holding her breath. Lucy reluctantly made her way to his bed. "I'm going to go to sleep." She was too tired to bother talking. She just wanted to get some sleep and figure out everything later, well, tomorrow. Closing her eyes, she wondered why she wasn't that afraid of him.

CHAPTER 3

Lucy woke up to rub her eyes due to the annoying, illuminating rays of sunshine that made their way through the half shut blinds. She sat up straight as she stretched her arms and neck, and slowly fluttered her eyelids open. At first, she was slightly confused as to where she was, but then it suddenly clicked and hit her in the head like lightning. She was in his room, in Drake's room.

She immediately looked around and her eyes spotted a sleeping figure on the floor. He was lying on his tummy with his arms and legs spread against the white sheets. She got up and crouched beside him, staring at him awkwardly. His long hair fell across his face, and it took her so much effort to not reach out and brush them away in order to give her more access to his beautiful face. But she wouldn't dare. *He's so peaceful in his sleep. Then again, everybody looks peaceful in their sleep somehow.* His chest rose and fell as he rhythmically breathed, his lips slightly parted.

She felt like such a stalker. She desperately wanted to know how his warm, strong arms would feel around her and how his tempting, plump lips would feel like...she shook her head to shrug off such silly imaginations. Just as she was about to get up, she heard him softly murmur in his sleep, "I don't want to leave, I-I didn't mean to be so careless." Lucy furrowed her eyebrows and leaned closer to him. *What does he mean by that? Is he scared of something? What is that boy hiding?* And when she leaned even closer, his eyes shot open and he burst into laughter. "I got you good."

Heat rushed into Lucy's cheeks as she bit her lip in embarrassment, but then quickly replaced it with a frown. "Were you awake this whole time?" she gulped.

Drake pressed his lips together to suppress the laughter. "Nah. You woke me up when I felt you approaching me, so I thought, why not play a prank on her? Have a little fun in the morning."

Lucy rolled her eyes playfully. "Don't you have a time of day when you're not so – well, how do I say this – an ass?" She crossed her arms, irritated.

His lips pulled up in that cocky smirk of his that always made a chill run down her spine. She cleared her throat. "By the way, we need to talk...you know about the-" She said, but was cut off by Drake.

"I think we should start with you, what were you doing so close to me?" He got out of the covers, revealing his half naked self. He looked straight into her eyes, amused by her embarrassed expression.

She twirled a hair strand around her finger nervously as she looked down, not knowing what to say. What was she doing so close to him anyway? Didn't she know he'd haunt her about it for the rest of her life? "I um...wanted to see if you were awake."

His brows rose up. "Right, I'm just going to pretend I believe you, because we both know you were checking me out, just like you do in class."

Lucy's mouth fell open. *Why is it that he always seems to know? Does he really...well, stare at me too? Wait, I don't care if he does, he's a jerk, yes, a jerk.* She stood up. "Well, if you don't want to talk, I'm going to get my bag ready and leave. I don't have to be here any longer-" He placed his finger on her soft lips, shushing her. He looked at her intently as his eyes glistened; she had never seen them this bright or that blue before, in other words, she had never seen this shade of blue before. They were electric. "We will talk. Get dressed while I make breakfast," He huffed.

Lucy cleared her throat. "You cook? You really are full of surprises." She mocked him, surprised at the revelation.

He drew nearer to her, and slightly brushed his lips against the skin just below her ear, teasing her. He whispered softly yet seductively in her ear. "If you think I'm full of surprises, wait till you see what I can do to you and how I can make you feel."

A rush of desire coursed within her as soon as those sexy words came out of his lips. She wasn't able to control the warm, pleasant tingles that shot throughout her body. Lucy backed away as much as she could until her body was pressed against the wall and she could no longer back any further. Her cheeks were now flushed entirely and she couldn't hide it from him. This seemed to please him for he had a lopsided grin tugging at his lips. He then gradually made his way out of the room, leaving her feeling embarrassed and flushed, alone.

I am not affected by him, she kept saying to herself, repeating it over and over again.

Lucy sat at the table as she watched him crack five eggs into the frying pan. She stared at his toned chest and his six perfect packs. His muscular arms flexed each time he moved to either get salt or pepper. He was striking, simply striking. "What are you thinking?" Her conscious snapped at her, waking her up to reality. *Breakfast, I was having breakfast, right.*

Breaking the silence, he asked, "So what do you want to know?"

"Um…why were you there? I mean what were you doing?" She slurred.

He placed her plate in front of her and sat down across her. "Okay, I was, well, I was taking a stroll since I couldn't sleep, so I heard a noise and I went to check it out. I saw a man lying lifeless on the ground and then...you came along," He said.

Lucy narrowed her eyes at him, cocking her head to the left. "Really? That's the lamest thing I've ever heard."

He just shrugged his shoulders, not seeming to care whether or not she had believed him.

Oh, I'll know exactly what happened that night, but I'll just let it go for now. She got her bag and placed it on her lap. She rummaged through it, searching for her phone until she grabbed hold of it. She removed the silent mode and noticed that she had eighteen missed calls from her brother and her mom, and some messages from both Amy and her brother. *Oops, I'm in deep shit,* she thought as she opened each message.

"3:00 am

Where the hell are you Lucy? Call me to come get u!

-Bro-"

"3:45 am

Lucy! Your mom and I are worried sick about u! Don't do this, think of mom.

-Bro-"

"10:21 am

Hey, I wanted to say that there's a party tonight at Drew's place. Would u wanna go with me? Please. Pretty please. A lot of hot guys are gonna show up ;) so we'll have fun! Msg me back.

-Amy-"

The messages went on and on. Lucy sighed deeply; she had to text them back.

"To: Bro

I'm on my way home."

Drake wanted to give her a ride home, but she preferred to walk her way since she really did not want him to know where she lived. Besides, she still didn't feel like she could really trust him, there was something brooding about him. His presence screamed "danger", he was not your normal teenage guy. He had such an angelic face though, and all she wanted to do was get to know him and be close to him. She shook her head, she certainly did not want to think about that condescending man right now.

She stopped to rest a little and placed her hands on her hips, breathing heavily. *I better tell Chad to come get me.* She dialed her brother's number as she placed her cell against her ear, waiting for him to answer her call.

"Lucy! Where have you been? I was just about to call you-"

She cut him off. "Chad, I need you to come pick me up and we'll talk about this later please," She begged. Hanging up, she sent him her location.

After a few minutes, Lucy saw Chad's car burst out of nowhere and was hastily parked with two wheels up on the sidewalk. She knew immediately how furious he was. She sighed, preparing herself for the fight of the day. She sat in the front seat and bit her lip, not wanting to discuss anything whatsoever.

Chad furrowed his eyebrows, his nose flaring. "You have a lot of explaining to do."

She ran a hand through her hair and made up a lie. "I um...went to a friend's house. I wanted to just get away from all the drama. It's not fair, Chad!"

He rubbed his temple, irritated. "Couldn't you at least have told me where you were? I mean it wouldn't have killed you!"

She wore an apologetic look on her face. "I'm sorry, I um...forgot – I mean, I wasn't thinking...look I'm fine. It was just a sleepover at my friend's place, she's in my class." Making Drake a girl is not the best thing she had ever thought of.

He seemed to calm down as he grabbed the steering wheel, stepped on the gas pedal with full force, and drove them out of here.

As soon as she stepped inside her house, her mother ran towards her with flailing arms. "Oh my baby! I was so scared that something bad might have happened to you!"

Lucy hugged her mom back as she felt her ribs being squeezed tightly, making it difficult to breathe. "Mom I'm okay, really."

Her mom let go to look intently at her daughter's face as if she hadn't seen her in a year. "Don't you ever flee like this, you hear?"

Lucy nodded, remembering to ask, "Mom, how are your wounds? How are you feeling?"

She shook her head, sharing a warm smile with her daughter. "I'm fine. I'm just really glad to see you."

Lucy couldn't help but feel an ounce of guilt forming in the pit of her stomach. "I'm sorry," she whispered as she reassured her that she wouldn't leave her in such a state ever again.

Out of the blue, Lucy's cell vibrated in her pocket, she swiftly took it out to see another message from Amy. *Darn it, I forgot to text her back.*

"12:30 pm

So is it a yes? U going?

-Amy-"

Oh yeah, the party. Lucy clicked her tongue, tapping out a reply with her thumbs.

"To: Amy

I dunno yet, I'll text u later."

Would my parents even agree to this? I did run away and I skipped school. School. I wonder why Amy didn't bother asking where I was.

She made her way to the living room to face her mom and brother as she replayed the words she'd use. "Mom, I wanted to ask you if it was all right to go to a party tonight. Um...everyone at school would be there and I promise to be safe-"

Her mom interrupted her. "I don't know if you deserve it, but since I'm a good mother, I'll let you go. But don't you dare think I'm easy. I just trust you. So be careful and have fun. Oh, and don't come home late."

Lucy tried to take in what her mother just said. *She let me go? That was fast. Oh well, better not jinx myself.*

She gave her mom a quick hug as she tenderly wrapped her arms around her. "Thank you so much. I won't let you regret your decision."

Chad rolled his brown eyes at his sister while her mom giggled. Lucy grabbed her phone and texted a "Yes I'm going" to Amy. Instantly, her friend replied back.

"12:45 pm

Yay! I'll come pick you up and we'll go to my place and get ready for tonight. We are going to look gorgeous! Speaking of gorgeous, your brother Chad is a babe. I met him earlier today. Anws, see u.

-Amy-"

Met my brother? What did Chad say to cover my back today? Aww, I owe him big time.

It was around 6:30 pm when Lucy waited impatiently for Amy to come. She had worn a purple shirt with black shorts, and on her shoulder hung her matching black purse. "Where is she?" She murmured grumpily to herself. Just as she was about to pick up her phone to dial Amy's number, she heard a loud honk outside.

"Where have you been? I thought you weren't going to come." Lucy shrieked.

"Oh, don't be silly." Amy rolled her eyes at her.

Lucy bit her lip, asking curiously. "How did you get to meet my brother?"

Amy stared ahead as she drove. "Well, he stopped by at school today. He talked to the principal and I happened to be there, so once he mentioned your name, I asked him why you didn't show up... and he told me."

She leaned in, interested. "What did he tell you?"

Amy wrinkled her eyebrows. "Well duh, he said that you have family arrangements you needed to attend and you had to skip school, what else would he say?"

Lucy nodded as she mentally giggled to herself, her brother was a genius. "Yeah I did, I was just making sure he said the truth."

Amy shook her heard in mockery. "Right."

"Whoa! That looks great on you!" Amy hopped up and down in excitement as she scrutinized the way Lucy looked in her dress. It didn't actually fit on her and was sure it would fit on Lucy since she was incredibly thin.

"Really?" Lucy asked as she twirled in her short, tight, black dress and stared at herself in the mirror.

She bent her head to the side, taking a better look at it. "I think the red one suits me more." The red one was simple yet elegant, it brought color to her face, and it clung to Lucy's slim figure like a second skin.

Amy drew closer, tapping her finger against her lips. "I think you're right, go with the red one, red is hotter. I'll go get dressed in my other black dress."

Lucy put on her makeup as she covered her lips with red lipstick to match her dress and drew a perfect winged eyeliner. As for Amy, she had full makeup on, obviously to get attention.

"We look great Lucy!" Amy squeaked with joy. She most certainly loved parties and of course, the boys there.

Just as they were about to head outside towards Amy's car, Lucy's phone beeped. She opened it and read it nervously.

"8:00 pm

See u at the party babe. I hope you're wearing something hot for me ;)

-Unknown-"

Lucy gulped and bit her nail. *Oh great, he has my number.* She cursed under her breath. *This is going to be one hell of a party.*

"What is it Lucy? You suddenly freaked out just a moment there," Amy asked, concerned.

Lucy ran a hand through her hair, pulling at the ends. She couldn't possibly tell Amy the truth. She would just have to hide the fact that she slept over at Drake's and the fact that he is now actually stalking her somehow. "Oh, it's nothing, it was just my mom. Ugh, you know moms and their protection."

Amy pressed her lips together and nodded. "Whatever, now let's go."

As soon as Amy stopped to park her car, Lucy couldn't help but feel a little insecure about this. She suddenly didn't want to be at this party, especially because Drake would be there. *I don't know if I can tolerate him.* She sighed deeply, yet she couldn't help but slightly feel a little contented.

Amy and Lucy got out of the car to see a whole bunch of teenagers flooding Drew's place. He sure invited a lot of people. Amy motioned for her to go inside as they pushed their way through the crowd. The music was very loud, Lucy's ears began to drum as she felt her chest vibrate. The smell of booze engulfed her as it filled her nostrils. She never was a fan of booze and she certainly wouldn't be one tonight.

Amy yelled over the noise. "I'm going to get myself a drink, what would you like? I'll get one for you."

Lucy shook her head in a no. "I don't want to drink Amy-"

She cut her off, widening her eyes. "What? Are you serious? Come on, it's a party, loosen up a little."

Lucy rolled her eyes at her. "Fine, but not just yet, I'll get one later."

She looked around, her eyes searching for a certain figure. She couldn't seem to locate him anywhere. *Where is he? Wait, why am I searching for him again?* She sighed as she tapped her foot against the ground, waiting for Amy.

"Hey there," a random guy with a drink held firmly in his hand suddenly emerged out of the crowd and made his way towards her. He shot her one of his all-time smirks as he extended his arm for her to shake. "I'm Chase and yours?"

Lucy cleared her throat. "Hi, I'm Lucy." She shook his hand.

He grinned at her and asked sheepishly, "So, how come a girl like you is here alone?" He winked, making her roll her eyes at him. She hated when guys said stupid stuff like that.

"I'm waiting for a friend," she bluntly stated.

"Want to hang out with me? I'll show you some real fun." He licked his lips, his eyes darkening with lust.

Lucy furrowed her brows. "No thanks."

Chase was clearly annoyed at her. "You have a problem missy? I'm trying to be nice."

Lucy huffed, mockingly indignant. "Thanks for your 'niceness', but you can have some fun with another girl. Besides, I won't give you the fun you need."

Chase glared at her, his lips pressed in a tight line. "You should show some respect!" He flailed his arms in the air as his drink spilled on his black shirt. "Look what you made me do, you bitch!"

Lucy's mouth was agape now. She raised her hand and slapped him with full force right against his cheek, leaving a faint, red spot. She instantly noticed what she had done, so she swiftly moved away from him and squeezed herself against the crowd, trying to get away.

As she maneuvered away, she accidentally bumped against a strong chest. "S-sorry, I didn't see you th-" She stopped, noticing the familiar face. It was Drake and he was now smirking at her.

"Hey babe, you don't have to make an excuse to be in my arms, just say so next time." He laughed at his lame joke.

"Ugh! I'm so not in the mood for your jokes, Drake! So just move!" she yelled.

"There you are, you little bit-" Chase was cut off once Drake stood in front of him, eying him from top to bottom. "What did you say? Were you going to swear? I'm going to tell your mommy," Drake grinned mockingly then added, "But just after I finish you up."

Chase gulped as he tried to get a comeback. "I'm not scared of y-you!"

Drake smirked but it was immediately replaced by a frown. He drew nearer to chase and whispered in his ear, "I advise you not to mess with me, because I can literally end you." He emphasized the word "end". Fear was radiating off of Chase's body as sweat slowly trickled down his forehead. The color in his face suddenly faded, he turned very pale. Lucy had never seen someone get so frightened all of a sudden. She could even feel the dark energy coming from Drake. That made her shudder as she rubbed both her arms with her hands, trying to get rid of the unpleasant feeling. Chase gradually moved away as he struggled with himself, finding it hard to move. Lucy bit her inner cheek and tapped Drake's shoulder, wanting him to break eye contact with Chase and focus on her.

"Um...thank you for the help," she trembled, looking right into his eyes. They had an ominous dark color, and she couldn't seem to remove her gaze from them. They were mesmerizing.

"Forget it," he stated with no hint of emotion in his voice. *What was going on?*

Out of the blue, Amy strutted towards Lucy with a shocked expression. "I've been looking everywhere for you!" Then she stole a glance at Drake and seemed to have calmed down a little. "I mean I'll be in the room to the right if you need me."

Lucy rubbed her neck. "I'll catch up with you in a few minutes."

Drake puckered his brow once Amy left. "Oh, I'm guessing you're starting to like me, well, since you decided to stay with me."

She rolled her eyes. "Not even close. I just wanted to ask what the hell happened between you and Chase."

Drake licked his lips. "I just taught him a lesson, he was being a very bad boy."

Lucy clenched and unclenched her jaw. "I'm serious! You never give me answers!"

Drake narrowed his eyes at her. "That's because there are no answers! I just did what any guy would do. I thought you were thankful."

She broke eye contact. "I am but...never mind." With that, she began to walk away.

She felt a cold hand grab her by her arm and warm tingles shot down her spine. His touch was so alluring, she wanted him to touch her all over. *No, no, no, I'm losing it! What am I thinking?*

"Where are you going?" He asked.

"To hang out with Amy," Lucy replied as she pulled away from his grasp.

She couldn't wait to get away from him. He was having a huge effect on her. She wasn't the type of girl who squealed if a boy shook her hand or so.

Dreadful screams suddenly filled the room as shocked expressions lingered on every single face. As soon as Lucy found Amy, she was panicking. "Oh my God Lucy! This is awful, I'm so scared. We should get out of here!"

Lucy's heart hammered against her chest, trying to calm herself down. "What's going on? Why is everybody traumatized?"

Amy swallowed hard, breathing heavily. Her lips trembled. "My friend found a dead boy in the toilet just a couple of minutes ago. He was lifeless. Oh Lucy, it was horrible! I can't take it!"

Lucy covered her mouth with her hands as her eyes widened, her mind didn't seem to grasp such information. "Who is he?"

Lucy followed the trail of people who were standing right outside the toilet. She squinted her eyes at the body to get a better look as to who he was, since Amy had not answered. As soon as she did, a sob rose in her chest and threatened to break free as she drastically shivered all over. It was Chase.

CHAPTER 4

"Oh my God!" Lucy whimpered, covering her mouth with her trembling fingertips. She felt as if her brain needed to be rebooted, around her everything was fast-forward while she was motionless in the middle of it all. *How could this happen? Was it Drake? But he couldn't possibly have killed him; I was with him a couple of minutes ago...*Lucy breathed in as her eyes searched for Drake, she wanted to talk to him, she had to. She looked away from the terrified crowd, the sobbing faces, the boys who were calling the police, the shocked Amy, and her eyes landed on an unusually calm Drake who was watching from behind.

"Amy, I'm going um...to go talk to someone. I'll be right back, okay?" Lucy stated.

Amy immediately grabbed her by her arm. "No Lucy, let's just stick together till the police come."

"Amy, it's just a talk, I'll be back," she gave her a weak smile and made her way to Drake. He was staring at her in an emotionless manner as she got closer to him.

She stood right in front of him, studying his calm yet tense features. His eyes were dangerously dark and his lips were slightly parted as he stood there without saying a word to her. This was rather odd since he usually couldn't keep his mouth shut.

She cleared her throat. "You're taking this pretty easily, aren't you?"

A smirk tugged at his lips as he drew nearer to her so that their faces were mere inches away. "Do you want me to break down and cry? Cause baby I'm not the sensitive type. Besides, I don't care about him..." He rubbed the back of his neck and added. "People always die, accept it"

Lucy had her mouth agape as she gawked at him, trying to take in what he just stated. She pressed her lips firmly together, trying her best not to smack him. "You are cruel, Drake."

This somehow made him grin wider. He tapped his fingers against his chin as if wondering. "Have I ever told you I wasn't? I don't think so."

She furrowed her eyebrows, her jaw tensing. "You know what? I think you killed him." She mumbled in a low voice.

His grin vanished from his features and was replaced by a serious expression. "No baby doll, we both know you don't think that."

She dramatically flailed her arms in the air in exasperation. "Well, then, how come you're acting so calm and relaxed about this? Shouldn't you at least be scared of the killer or something?"

He ran a hand through his hair as he further disheveled it. He stared right through her curious, bright, blue eyes. "Like I mentioned, I. Don't. Care." He emphasized the last three words. He then proudly added, "And trust me, the so-called killer should be scared of me."

She gulped, an ominous feeling developing in the pit of her stomach. She was suddenly overcome with the urge to move away from him, she no longer wanted to confront him. Her pride, however, stood in the way. She certainly did not want to give him the satisfaction of running away, so she just shrugged away any unwanted feelings and sternly stood there.

Her actions shocked him when she drew closer to him, her statement bravely slipping past her lips. "Well, then, that killer is certainly a coward because I am not scared of you."

He leaned in as their noses slightly brushed, making her shudder. Her body drastically reacted to any slight touch of his. "I know you're not, because you're obviously into me."

She definitely wanted to kick him in the guts for making her blush profusely in a moment like this. "No I'm not, what makes you think I-"

He cut her off as he whispered in her ear, engulfing her with a tingling sensation. "Babe, if you weren't into me, you wouldn't be standing here talking to me while your friend is panicking and obviously in need of you."

She violently bit her lip. Her breath got caught in her throat. *He was right. He was absolutely right. Why am I standing here with him anyways? I know that he wouldn't give me the answers that I needed so why am I still here?*

She was about to say something but he quickly grabbed her by her waist to get a better hold of her, and stated in a very low tone, only for her to hear, "You're going to have to come with me."

She puckered her brow, confused. "What? Are you out of your mind?"

He rubbed his face with annoyance. "The police are going to be here any minute now. I think we better leave before this gets serious."

She rolled her eyes and mocked him. "Oh really? And why are you worried about the police? Shouldn't the police be scared of you as well?"

He clenched his fists as his eyes got darker, if that was even possible. He looked her in the eyes and she swore that she could feel him see right through her soul. "This is no time to joke. You are coming with me and that's final."

She was expressionless while she stared into his majestic eyes, searching for a hint of trickery. *Maybe if I did go with him, he'd actually give me some sort of information about what the hell just happened to Chase.* "Can I just tell Amy? I don't want her to freak when she knows I'm gone."

He looked away, gritting his teeth. "Okay."

She moved quickly, heading to face Amy. Amy looked calmer now and she was glad that her friend was regaining her composure. "Amy, I'm going to leave-"

"What? You can't leave! The police are coming and...it might get suspicious. You know what I mean, right?" She shrieked.

Lucy sighed, coming up with a lie. "I know, but I have to. My parents would be worried sick about me. Besides, I didn't either see or do anything about all this so I wouldn't be of much help anyways."

Amy shook her head in denial. "I don't think you should, Lucy."

She nodded, biting her nail nervously. "I know, okay, but-"

Amy didn't let her continue her sentence; she breathed in and let her head fall back. "I don't think the police would know who killed poor Chase anyways."

Lucy leaned in, curious. "How come?"

"Well, there are no marks, no bleeding, no nothing on the dead body. They won't get any proper clues, Lucy." She stated in a hopeless manner.

That weirdly rings a bell, but still, he could have been poisoned or something.

"What if it's on the inside, Amy? Poison or something." she stated out loud.

She shook her head, "Yeah, but still he wouldn't be in such a state. His body is in no normal condition, it's like he's been dead for a while now and the incident only occurred a few minutes ago."

Lucy nervously gulped as she wore an apologetic look on her face. "Well, do tell me what happens later on...I really have to go now." With that, she gave Amy a warm bear hug and left.

"The police cars are arriving, we can't leave now, we'll surely be caught Drake!" she exclaimed as she sneaked along with him. He didn't answer her but motioned for her to be quiet. He held her by her hand and hurriedly guided her further away from the scene of the crime. *Why didn't I run away from him when I was able to? Who am I kidding, he wouldn't have let me.*

How do I get myself into these things? She thought to herself as she nervously tugged at Drake's shirt.

"Would you stop pulling at my shirt? It's getting annoying." He quietly hissed, studying her anxious expression.

She was practically about to panic as she felt her heart dangerously pound faster against her chest. "I'm scared, Drake! I don't want to go to jail!" She wiped her sweaty palms down the sides of her dress.

He rolled his eyes, and quickened his pace in order to reach a certain spot, which was a little farther from Drew's place. He stole a look at Lucy, then sighed, "You're not going to go to jail, Lucy. So stop that already. You're with me, you shouldn't be scared."

She furrowed her brows and slightly stepped back from him, "You? That's exactly why I should be scared, but-"

Drake stopped dead in his tracks. He pulled her into a narrow alley just round the corner, pushed her against the wall, and stood right in front of her, face to face, then huskily said, "I thought you weren't scared of me."

She cut him off, ranting, "I'm not! And besides, did you have to push me against a wall to make your point? Jeez-"

She suddenly wished she could have taken her words back, for he certainly did not like her response one bit. His eyes oddly darkened, making the blue in them diminish as he heavily breathed in and out. "I have to make this clear, you shouldn't joke with me. You just don't want to mess with me."

She gulped as she fiddled with her fingers, trying to avoid his piercing eyes that seemed to do more than just stare. It was like they suddenly held a strange power that was too unfamiliar and rather peculiar. He was peculiar, yet she still couldn't brush the feeling of enticement away. He was luring her into his dark life which wasn't a welcoming place, but there was something about him that she couldn't get enough of. He was rather enchanting in his own ominous ways.

He felt the weird yet intense tension between them, so he cleared his throat, then started to move again. "Come on. We better get out of here."

She gradually walked behind him. She made an effort not to stare at his broad fit shoulders, and beautiful fiery red hair that waved gently against his back as he marched forward.

More police cars headed towards Drew's and loud honks were heard. Drake suddenly grabbed Lucy by her arm and pulled her behind and away from the sight of any police officer. Unfortunately, one of them did see their bizarre actions and motioned to the guy sitting beside him.

"Shit," Drake cursed as he quickly glanced around, trying to figure out how to get away without attracting more attention. He spotted a narrow bridge just ahead. He swiftly carried Lucy, placing one arm under her legs and the other supporting her back. He began to make his way to the bridge. He instructed her,

"Hide your face in my chest; you don't want them to see you now, do you?"

She didn't protest, for she didn't even have time to. This was all too quick. She buried her face in his chest and his appealing scent filled her nostrils. She didn't want to pull back ever, this was rather soothing. She just wanted to run her hands up and down his chest, and feel him under her touch. *Wait, what am I thinking? Really, now? When the police are about to catch us? Maybe he was right, I should control my um...hormones.* She blushed entirely and thanked God he wouldn't be able to see her flushed face; it would be too embarrassing. She shut her eyes and her grip on him tightened as he started moving faster and faster.

"We're going to have to jump. You ready?" he asked as he carefully put her down.

She had a puzzled expression on, her mouth buckling. "What? Are you crazy?"

He huffed, obviously annoyed. "There's no time for chit chat...choose; jump in or get caught?"

She nervously tugged at her dress and looked down the bridge. It wasn't a high jump, however, the flowing water didn't look too inviting; but she surely picked the first option. She inhaled a good amount of air and held it as she grabbed his hand and hurriedly jumped. At the same instant, the police car approached them and made a stop. Its lights flashed across the bridge, scanning it for two particular persons.

As soon as the cool water hit them, Lucy swam up to the surface kicking her legs in the water, urging her body on. She breathed in and felt her heart hammer against her chest. Drake swam closer to her as he murmured in a low tone, "Let's stay put for a while, suppose they're still out there."

She nodded her head and moved her arms around her, keeping herself above the water. "Drake...can I ask you something?"

He looked at her intently, urging her to speak, "Go ahead."

She licked her lips as she felt droplets of water trickle down her face from her soaking, wet hair. "Why are we hiding? I mean, why did we even leave in the first place?"

He lowered his head as if thinking of a suitable answer, and then gazed at her intently. "I didn't want you to have to go through such a terrible incident."

She puckered her eyebrow, not seeming to believe any word he just mentioned. "Are you kidding me, Drake?"

He chuckled and smirked wickedly. "I just wanted to see your expression, but unfortunately you got me."

She rolled her eyes at him. "Yeah, next time say things that aren't too hard to believe."

He drew nearer to her. He brushed off a wet strand of her hair, and gently placed it behind her ear, sending sparks of electricity throughout her body. "Are you saying that I don't care? That I'm just a wicked, careless person?"

She bit her lip. "Well, that's partly true but-"

Her breath got caught in her throat as he brought his lips to her neck and planted tiny, warm kisses against her wet, cold skin. He then instantly pulled away, not letting her enjoy the exquisite sensation that he had just engulfed her with. He whispered in her ear, making her shudder, "I do care. Otherwise, I would have drowned you by now, babe."

Her eyes widened and her mouth fell open. "Are you trying to be romantic? Cause this just sounded wrong."

He smirked as his eyes glinted in the moonlight. "I'm not being romantic. I just want to warn you, Lucy."

She leaned in and asked with curiosity, "Warn me from what?"

His eyes showed a glint of sadness while he forcefully mumbled out, "Me."

She simply stared into his sorrowful eyes. She had never seen Drake in such an emotional state. She felt the need to hold him and tell him that everything would be okay, but she wouldn't dare. *What was he hiding anyways? Why wouldn't he tell me? Is he a murderer? A drug addict? Is he in a mafia?* She let out a long, deep breath and pressed her lips together, not wanting to think of the worst. She'll just have to ask him herself when the time is right.

Just as she was about to open her mouth to speak, he cleared his throat. "I think we should get out of the water now."

She giggled, nodding. "Right."

He outstretched his wet hand for her to grab, and pulled her out. She stared at her soaking wet dress that was clinging to her body. She squeezed at its ends as she wrapped her fingers tightly around them, trying to get rid of the unwanted water. She took a glance at Drake, who was staring ahead. His wet shirt revealed every detail of his toned muscles that made it hard for Lucy to look away.

"Drake, um...I really have to go home." she blurted out as she got her cellphone and hastily shook it with her hand, getting rid of the droplets of water. Thank God, it's a waterproof phone.

"I thought you were running away from home, now you want to go back so badly?" he asked and crossed his arms.

"Well, things worked out and I have to go back-" she stopped, watching him take a step forwards.

"What happened anyways? You didn't tell me." he asked, curious.

She puckered her brow. "And I'm not planning to tell you now either."

The corners of his lips lifted into a smirk. "Oh, really now? And don't even think of telling me you don't trust me yet cause baby you certainly do."

She bit her lip and tried to think of a rational answer. "Well, I-I don't..." She looked away, knowing that her reply was partly wrong since she somehow did trust him as oddly as that sounds.

He sighed and rolled his eyes. "Don't deny it, you do, because if you don't-"

She cut him off. "I know, I know, because if I don't, I wouldn't have tagged along with you even though you somehow forced me to."

He licked his lips as he gazed at her. "First, I'm glad you admitted it, second, I didn't force you since I barely even threatened you, and third, when are you going to admit that you like me?" He winked at her slyly.

She narrowed her eyes at him, shaking her head. "I don't like you. Get over yourself."

He drew nearer to her and delicately touched her face with his fingertips, gently stroking it. Goosebumps formed throughout her entire body as his warm lips moved across her cheek and down her neck with his hot kisses. She went limp, her legs giving in. She couldn't control herself anymore for he had full control. She felt the urge to kiss him. She wanted to feel those lips of his against hers. *Oh, why am I thinking like this? This is not me; I'm not a desperate person.* He felt her shudder against him as he placed his hands against her hips; he wanted to get more access. His lips nudged at the sensitive area underneath her ear, making her heart beat accelerate. His touch burned her skin and his kisses were electric. He was addictive and she wanted him badly.

He then pulled away as he licked his lips and whispered in her ear, "Now, tell me you didn't feel anything."

She shivered, tingles running down her spine. She couldn't speak. *What is wrong with me?* She bit her bottom lip and looked into his hungry eyes. "I um...I-"

He cut her off, hushing her. "See, I knew it. I have a great effect on you."

She gulped, and then inhaled a good amount of air. "You d-don't."

He rolled his eyes as he took a few steps backwards, causing her to feel a little empty for she didn't want the warmth of his body to wear off. "Keep telling this to yourself baby, but we both know your body wants me."

She ran a hand through her hair irritatingly. He was somehow right. She walked besides him and asked, "What's your secret Drake? Spit it out."

His jaw tensed as he puckered his brow. "I don't have a secret, you like me so your body reacts to-"

She interrupted him, tapping her foot against the ground. "Ugh, that's not what I meant!"

He chuckled, "Let's go to my place."

Her eyes widened. "No way! I did it once, I won't do it again. It was a mistake."

He was expressionless. "You really just want to go home, huh?"

She nodded and felt his mood change. *What's wrong with this guy?* He confused her. At first, he was trying to get rid of her, and now, he's doing the complete opposite.

His voice had no tint of liveliness. "We'll take a cab because my motorcycle's at my place. And if you're wondering, yes, I did go to the party by foot."

Her lips formed in a tight line as she reached out to touch his arm, but he immediately pulled away. "What's wrong with you?"

He furrowed his eyebrows. "Nothing, just call a cab or something and make yourself useful."

She shook her head and dialed a number on her cell. She couldn't believe she was worrying about him, but she couldn't help but feel like he's missing something in his life. She sort of felt sorry for him.

"The taxi driver is on his way," she said and put her phone away.

He just nodded and stared at the dark sky above. She approached him and fiddled with her fingers. "I ran away because of my dad."

He seemed to come out of his trance as he immediately drew his attention to her and widened his eyes. He had a serious expression on while he clenched and unclenched his fists. "What happened?"

She lowered her head, staring at the ground. "He always gets drunk and ends up beating me or my mother... it's just tough Drake, I never got along with him."

The veins in his neck protruded and his nostrils flared with anger. He drew nearer to her, searching her gloomy eyes. "If he ever hurts you again, I'll kill him, Lucy. I swear it'll be the last breath he'd take."

Lucy had her mouth agape. "But he's still my father..."

His eyes darkened and his breathing quickened. "I don't fucking care. I'd kill a human who doesn't deserve to live, in a heartbeat!"

She backed away from him, a shocked expression lingering on her face. "Drake-"

He shushed her. "Babe, some people deserve to die so that others will live."

She wrinkled her eyebrows in confusion. "What do you mean?"

He gritted his teeth as he stated with no emotion. "Your father's soul should burn."

She suddenly wanted to flee, to run away from him and not turn back. He was truly a despicable person and she was officially afraid of him.

CHAPTER 5

What she thought of next was the lamest thing to do, but her
mind wouldn't function properly, so she simply ran. She turned
around without giving him a response to the cruel words he had
said, and ran away from him as fast as she could. She felt her
heart beat in rhythm with her feet against the hard ground. She
forced her legs to run faster as she sprinted to God knows where.
She just wanted to find a place to hide and make her call. She
breathed in and out heavily, trying to fill her lungs with the
oxygen needed as she gradually turned her head around to
check if she was being followed. No one was running after her.
She then stopped dead in her tracks and cautiously looked
around. She spotted an alley nearby, so she hurriedly made her
way there whilst grabbing her phone and dialing Amy's number.
Pick up. Pick up. Come on! She chanted in her head and paced
around impatiently, waiting for Amy to take her call.

"Lucy?" Amy asked over the line.

"Yes, it's me! Where are you? You're still at the party?" She bit
her nail, hoping that she wasn't.

"Well, we're going to leave in a few minutes I guess. The police
have already let some of us go after taking all our names and the
needed info since they had no trace of fingerprints or anything.
They're apparently going to get an autopsy done on the body."
She said in a low tone.

Lucy tapped her fingers against her chin as she contemplated. *It
couldn't be Drake, could it? Oh, who am I kidding? He might have
done it. But no fingerprints...I wonder.*

"Amy, I need you to come get me please. I mean, I don't want to have to tell my folks..." Lucy trailed off, knowing that Amy will understand.

"Are you in trouble? Besides, who did you run off with? Was it with Drake, the hot psycho?" She asked curiously.

"What?" *Although the description somehow suited him...*She snapped herself out of her thoughts, continuing. "Whatever, now can you come or what?"

"Where are you?" Amy sighed.

Her eyes scanned the area as she tried to figure out exactly where she was. Just as she was about to tell Amy that she wasn't that far from Drew's place, she suddenly felt a strong hand cover her mouth from behind. She dropped her cellphone with shock, trying to scream out.

"Shhh, it's just me." Drake whispered and slowly removed his hand from her mouth, allowing her to speak.

"Are you crazy? You scared the hell out of me! Get away from me." She shouted as she squirmed in his grasp. *How did he get here? I certainly did not see him chasing me.*

"Would you calm down please-"

She cut him off and kicked him right in the stomach. "I don't want to calm down! You're the killer, I know it!"

His jaw was firm and tense as he forced a smile out. He did not seem to be affected by her kick whatsoever. She certainly needed to do better than just that. "If you say that I'm the killer one more time, I'm going to-"

"Going to what? Kill me? Let my 'soul' burn or whatever?" She yelled as she felt salty bitter tears begin to trickle down her cheeks.

His eyes softened and his tense expression got replaced by a worried one. "Are you...crying? Please don't...I'm sorry." he whispered and cupped her cheek with his hand. He gently wiped away her tears with his thumb, savoring the touch of her soft, damp skin. *Did he just apologize to me?*

He rubbed his face, letting out a deep breath. "I'll call the cab off." He paused to pick up her phone and hand it to her. "Call someone to come get you; it's better than going alone in a cab so late at night...Bye." Turning around, he began to walk away.

"Wait!" She yelled and grabbed him by his arm. He slightly turned around to look her in the eyes. His icy, blue eyes were swirling with undecipherable emotion, she wanted to know so badly what he was thinking. She wished she could read that mysterious mind of his. He gently pulled his arm away from her grasp and continued to walk away without saying a single word.

"Don't leave. Where are you going?" She asked anxiously. *I ran away from him in the first place, so why do I want him here right now?* He kept walking forwards without even giving her a second glance. *Should I follow him? Maybe I should just let him go; I'll talk to him at school I guess.*

She huffed, watching his figure gradually disappear the farther he went. Her second thoughts were interrupted by the ringing of her phone.

"Hi." She hesitantly answered her call.

"Where the hell did you disappear to? I thought you were going to call again." Amy squealed.

"Sorry, I um...got another call." she lied.

"Okay, whatever. Where are you?" she impatiently asked her friend again.

Lucy told her friend exactly where she was. It won't take her long to get to her.

"Okay, got it. By the way, where's Drake? You were with him, right?" she asked curiously.

"I'll tell you about that later...and please hurry, it's kind of creepy here." she whispered, cringing.

After several minutes of waiting, Lucy got a text from Amy.

"12:05 AM

Meet me up just a little farther from the bridge, I'll spot you x

-Amy-"

She did as told and made her way towards that stupid bridge. She suddenly heard a car horn from up ahead and was certain it was Amy. She hurriedly ran towards her friend's car once she spotted it. *Thank God*, she thought and waved hello to Amy.

"You have a lot to tell me Lucy, so start talking." Amy demanded as she watched Lucy put her seat belt on, securing it.

"Yes, I did go with Drake and I'm sure you know this so far, but he had to leave. Something was up..." Lucy fiddled with her fingers, hoping to sound believable.

Amy eyed Lucy from top to bottom. "Why is your dress damp?"

Oh boy! She didn't know what to say but she had to think of something fast. "Well, um...I slipped and fell in a puddle of water."

Amy now had a frown on. "Seriously? Do I look that dumb to you?" She didn't let Lucy protest as she continued, "Look, I know he's hot and beautiful. I know he has a perfect body, a perfect smile-"

She immediately cut her off. "Your point?"

She sighed and swerved the car sharply to the right. "Well, he's a dangerous person, Lucy. I can feel his bad energy whenever I'm close to him. I don't know how you can't seem to feel it..."

Lucy exhaled and looked through the window, starting to get familiar with the place they were passing through. *Oh, you have no idea, Amy.*

As soon as Amy parked her car across Lucy's house, she hopped out and thanked God she didn't have to face anymore 'Drake' questions. She waved goodbye. "I'll see you at school tomorrow, okay? Drive safely! Nights."

"Sure." Amy shot her a warm smile, then swiftly drove away.

Lucy grabbed her keys as she gradually opened the front door. She entered silently, walking on her tiptoes. Her mother was sleeping on the couch with the TV on. Lucy quietly turned it off and took another look at her mother's sleeping figure. She looked very serene. She obviously was waiting for her to come home but sleep had taken over. She made her way upstairs to her room, and instantly took off her dress and threw it across her bathroom. She tied her hair in a low bun, removed her makeup, brushed her teeth, wore her pink pajamas and rushed to her soft, welcoming bed.

She sat up straight with her legs crossed as she held her cellphone in her lap, thinking. *Should I text him?* She bit her lip as she considered. *Maybe I will...I mean it's just a text, no harm done.* She went through her messages, searching for that unknown number. As soon as she found it, she added it to her contact list and simply named the contact 'Drake'. She let out a deep sigh while she typed.

"To: Drake

Hi I just wanted to say 'have a good night sleep'..."

She stared at the lame text that she had just typed. Her breath got caught in her throat as she sent it. *Please answer, please answer,* she chanted in her head. She decided to wait a little before she actually went to bed. Fifteen minutes passed, twenty five minutes passed, and no sign of any text from him. *What a jerk,* she huffed. She immediately went through his number and changed his contact name to 'poop', *yep, that'll suit you*. She held her head up high, feeling proud of herself for being such a badass and naming him as such. *Ugh, I really need to get some sleep.* She rested her head on her fluffy pillow. She felt her stomach twist in knots, she couldn't help but admit to herself that she liked Drake, even though she knew practically nothing about him. She wanted him to text her back so badly, she would somehow feel reassured that he was not mad at her or anything. *It's not your fault!* Her conscious butted in but she just ignored it since she did kind of feel guilty. She accused him of being a murderer several times, *but what if he wasn't?* She breathed in as she felt her eyes begin to slowly close, sleep overcame her and she drifted off.

A loud beeping sound woke Lucy up. She groaned and shut off her alarm. She stretched her arms as a yawn forced itself out of her mouth. She hated waking up in the morning more than anything else. She got herself ready by picking out a cute, striped dress with a matching bag, then made her way to the kitchen. Her father was seated at the table with a mug full of coffee in his hand. *Oh great,* she ignored his presence as she went over to her mom, who was busy washing the dishes. She kissed her mom on her cheek and went towards the door. Her father called, "I'm still waiting for an apology."

She stopped to turn around and look at him with disgust. "I will never apologize to you."

He furiously stood up, walked over to her, looked her in the eyes and yelled, "I'm your father and you should show some respect!"

She furrowed her brows. "Not until you act like a father because you're no father to me."

As soon as those words slipped from her lips, she wished she could take them back for he lifted his hand and slapped her hard against her cheek. She whimpered in pain. Lucy backed away from him as she hurriedly got out through the front door, ignoring his yells. She pressed her hand against her red cheek while getting in her brother's car. She muttered, "Please Chad, just drive!"

He did as he was told, stealing a quick glance at her. "He hit you, didn't he?"

She slowly nodded and looked out the window, not able to bear facing him. She forced herself not to cry, she could control it. She most definitely did not want to show any sign of weakness. Chad sighed deeply and placed his hand on her shoulder. "It'll be okay, Lucy. You're tough, I know it."

She stared into his eyes and gave him a weak smile. "Thank you."

She picked her bag up and entered her school's main door. She marched up to her locker to see Amy running towards her with her arms in the air. "There you are!"

She faked a smile, tucking a loose hair strand behind her ear. "Yep, I'm here."

After a couple of minutes, the bell rang noisily, reminding every student that it was time for class. "See you," Amy said as she disappeared with the other students. Lucy entered her chemistry class and her eyes landed on a familiar, stunning face. *He's in my chemistry class too? How the hell do they expect me not to flunk?* She looked down as she made her way to her seat, which was in front of his. She didn't want their eyes to meet at all, because she wouldn't even know what to say to him. As soon as she sat down, she felt his gaze burning into her back. She gulped and felt her whole body shiver. She breathed in and out nervously, trying to shake off the fact that he was right behind her. She felt his breath fan across the back of her neck and a rush of heat coursed through her veins. *This was hard, this was very hard for her. Why does he affect me so much?* The question played in her head over and over again.

She rested her elbows on the surface of the table and leaned her face in the cup of her hands, trying to avoid the closeness of his body. *That should do it*, she cleared her throat and focused on what the professor was explaining. Tap. Tap. Tap. She bit her lip and hesitantly turned around to face Drake. He had a huge smirk plastered on his face as he leaned in and huskily whispered in her ear, "I can see how you're struggling babe." She huffed, ignoring his embarrassing comment.

He then chuckled quietly, brushing his lips against the tip of her ear. "Do I make you nervous?"

She gritted her teeth, feeling her cheeks grow warm. "I really don't get you, Drake." She turned around quickly, ignoring what he had managed to say. *I truly don't get him, he really has major mood swings.* He didn't seem to get the message that she didn't want to speak with him since he tapped her shoulder once again.

His eyes were narrowed, rigid, and cold as he murmured, "What happened to your cheek?"

Oh great. How did he notice? She bit her lip, thinking of an appropriate lie. "It's nothing as you can see..." *Way to go Lucy, he's going to fall for it.*

He puckered his brow and clenched his jaw. "Tell me why it's red, Lucy. I'm no fool."

She fiddled with her fingers and her lips rose in a smirk. "I'm blushing, duh. Ha-ha..."

The muscles in his face tensed as he gradually got more irritated. He certainly was in no mood to take a joke. "Very funny. You have improved with those jokes of yours, but I'm not going to let this go, so I reckon you tell me what the hell happened."

A clearing of someone's throat caught their attention, it was Professor Smith. He shot them death glares as he spoke, "I've been waiting for you to shut up! So how about you just shut up! My class is no cafeteria for your chit chat, so pay attention!" Lucy sighed deeply, turning around to face her fuming professor. *At least I don't have to give Drake an answer now, well, for now.*

As soon as the bell rang, Lucy instantly fled away from the class for she most definitely did not want to face Drake's persistent questions. She made her way to Amy's class to wait for her to get out. Amy's face lit up once she saw her at the door. "Hey! You're here on time."

Lucy had a puzzled expression on. "Here for what?"

"I was just mentioning you to a new friend of mine," she slightly tugged his shirt as she pointed her finger at Lucy.

"So you're Lucy, I'm Josh," he outstretched his hand for her to shake.

She shook it and politely smiled at him as she took in his features. He had dark, chocolate eyes that matched his short, messy, brown hair perfectly. He wasn't that built but he was surely considered good-looking.

He flashed her a wide smile, showing off his dimples. "Well, can I tag along with you guys if that's no-"

Amy cut him off as she insisted, "Sure!"

Lucy rolled her eyes and silently walked beside Amy, who seemed to be drooling over Josh. A picture of some sort caught Lucy's attention; a red-headed girl was hanging the same picture on every wall. She squinted her eyes and drew nearer to get a better look. It was a picture of Chase and a short quote was scribbled on it saying, "You left too soon, we will always miss you and you are always in our hearts, RIP." She sighed, pressing her lips together. She didn't know him well and his first impression wasn't good at all but she couldn't help but feel sad for him. He was too young to die.

Amy later approached her and stood behind her. She eyed the picture. "He's gone, poor Chase."

Lucy nodded, then moved along with them to grab some food. She looked around the cafeteria to spot that bimbo sitting beside Drake, along with two other girls. *Ugh, I really don't like this girl.* She nudged Amy. "What's her name?"

Amy stole a glance at the blonde girl and rolled her eyes. "Her name's Rachel."

Drake didn't seem to give those girls any attention whatsoever. *Whew – wait, why should I care?* She glanced at him from the corner of her eye, studying the way he just sat there as if there wasn't anyone talking to him, in other words, flirting with him. She watched the way he took a huge bite out of his fresh, green apple, the way his deep, captivating eyes flickered, the way his fiery, red hair shone, the way he was looking right at her, *wait – did he just look right at me? Oh shit, that's embarrassing.* She gulped and quickly turned around.

Amy suddenly burst out laughing and then said in a low tone for only Lucy to hear, "Quick! Look!"

She immediately looked to see Drake standing up with his arms firmly at his sides. He was glaring at Rachel as he seemed to say something to her, which was unfortunately inaudible. Rachel later flipped her hair and click clacked away from him, yelling, "I don't need you anyways! You're just some loner!"

So he showed her who's boss, I'm impressed Drake. She giggled to herself, enjoying the scene that was just displayed in front of everyone. Amy said out loud for her and josh to hear, "No one has ever turned Rachel down, I now like that Drake guy no matter how um...odd he is."

Lucy smiled to herself, *I like him from way before.* Her thoughts were interrupted as she felt someone tap her shoulder. She shut her eyes tight once she considered who it might be, and when she turned to face an expressionless Drake, she congratulated herself.

He cleared his throat and breathed in. "I want to talk to you." he paused then added, "Alone."

She brushed a loose strand of hair off her face. "Um...I don't want to."

A smirk tugged at his lips as he shoved his hands in his pockets. "Yeah right, I saw the way you were staring at me. Your eyes practically bulged out of their sockets."

She lifted her head to meet his gaze and stood up. "So what?"

He drew nearer to her, feeling her shudder. "So what? You were so jealous Lucy. You did not see the look on your face." He caressed her cheek softly and she squirmed at his touch, unable to control the warm tingles that shot throughout her entire body. He whispered huskily in her ear, "A simple touch makes your body respond to me, imagine what I'm capable of making you feel babe. You have no idea. You'll beg for me to touch you, you'll beg for me to make you feel good." She couldn't help but feel the heat pool at her core. Her cheeks reddened; she was blushing furiously. She wanted him to stop talking.

"Okay! Okay! Let's go talk um...alone." She felt her whole body tense as she tried to shake off the feeling of awkwardness. She waved bye to her friends. "I'll see you guys later." Both Josh and Amy nodded, watching her leave.

Josh couldn't help but say, "Take care!" She gave him a warm smile whilst Drake shot him a dark glare, causing his muscles to coil with tension and making him want to swallow back his words.

She stood there in front of him, crossing her arms. "So, is it the cheek question again? Because I'm not going to answer it."

His gaze darkened as he seemed to get more agitated by the second. "I promise I'll understand."

She ran a hand through her hair, thinking this through. "I think you already know."

His jaw tensed as he lifted his hand to gently brush his fingertips up and down her cheek. "It's your dad, isn't it?"

She leaned into his touch, feeling the need to wrap her arms around him. He suddenly clenched his fists in anger as he stared straight into her eyes. His dark, fierce, blue orbs burned a trail over her face and she couldn't help but reach out to touch his soft yet cold face.

He stiffened at her touch at first but then he immediately wrapped his fingers around her hand tightly and cruelly insisted, "You have two choices, either you come live with me or you're going to have to mourn your father."

CHAPTER 6

Did he seriously expect me to choose one of those illogical choices of his? Who does he think he is? I choose what I want. The second choice is repugnant, I mean he talks about death like it is some game he mastered. Lucy simply stared at him in disgust as all those thoughts ran through her head, but then she finally managed to say something to him, "I'm not going to choose any of those two absurd choices!"

He breathed out heavily, rubbing his temple. "Am I not clear enough for you-"

She got even more irritated as she clenched and unclenched her fists. "Are you seriously going to argue with me? I mean you want to kill my father, that's not much of a choice, now is it?"

His eyes softened. "But he hurts you...all the time, so why pity him anyways?"

Lucy crossed her arms. "Because I'm not a monster like him. I mean who am I to decide whether he should live or die? I don't know if you get it because you talk about death so coolly."

Drake's face contorted with a venomous expression. He lifted her face up to meet his gaze. "Watch your mouth. You're crossing your limits."

She placed her hands on her hips, not caring about what he had just stated. "So you just go around threatening people-"

He cut her off, saying, "I do. Not. Threaten." He made sure to emphasize those three words, then added in a whisper that was almost for himself to hear, "You're lucky I even gave you two choices."

She ignored his hushed whisper as she drew nearer, and honestly asked him, "Why do you even care?"

His jaw tensed. "What do you mean?"

Lucy rolled her eyes. "You know exactly what I mean." And when he did not answer her, she further explained, "Why do you even care if I get hurt or whatever?"

Drake nervously ran a hand through his hair, thinking of a proper answer. "Well, what's so wrong with caring?"

He's avoiding my actual question. Playing dumb, I see. She smirked, then placed her hand on his chest. She slowly traced his muscles with her finger, startling him by her sudden touch. "Say the truth. Why me? I mean there are tons of girls you can hang out with and annoy, so why me?"

He stared right through her eyes as his pupils dilated, causing his dark, blue eyes to get even darker. He cocked his head to the side. "Are you somehow trying to be in control?" he chuckled. "Cause you need to do way better than just that."

She took a few steps backwards, almost stumbling. "I um-"

He placed his index finger on her parted lips, shushing her. "Save it." His gaze dropped to her lips and he said huskily, "If you want to touch my body so badly, all you have to do is ask. It's really simple, you know." He smirked, caressing her cheek softly.

She moved away from his touch, staring hopelessly at his strong features. "You are a prick."

Drake suddenly leaned in closer, causing her heart to beat faster. His face mere inches away from hers. He stared at her plump lips as he captured her face with his hands and smoothed his thumbs across her cheekbones. "Don't move."

Oh, trust me even if I wanted to, I just couldn't. She stiffened and looked away, not wanting to drown in those sexy, dark eyes of his. *Was he going to kiss me? Oh my God. Breathe, Lucy.* She shut her eyes tightly, feeling his cinnamon breath fan across her face. She wanted to taste him so desperately. Then he suddenly began to slowly back away, as if something just popped in his head. He whispered forcefully, "I um...have to go."

He has to go? Seriously? What is wrong with him? She felt empty as she watched him leave her standing there like an idiot. *I can't believe I wanted to kiss that jerk. He's simply playing with my feelings.* She shook her head and made her way to her English class. *I should calm down, English class is the only class left that I have with him.*

Lucy sighed deeply and hesitantly took her seat. The class was instantly filled. She waited for a familiar face to pop through the door but he never showed up. *Where did he go?* She tapped her foot against the floor, thinking of all the possible reasons. *Maybe he actually had a good excuse, I mean he probably remembered that he had something important to do, but still he wouldn't have left this way.* She shrugged her shoulders and pushed away thoughts about Drake.

Miss Woods placed her hands on her hips, staring at her students. "Who can give me a proper explanation to

Shakespeare's quote 'we know what we are, but know not what we may be.'?"

Lucy rested her chin on her palm, elbow on the table, and stared ahead. This quote oddly reminded her of Drake. The teacher huffed. "Anyone?" Once no one answered, she added, "Are you guys really this dumb?" *What teachers didn't know is that we're really too lazy to answer your questions that we couldn't care less about.* Lucy raised her hand, deciding to answer. Her teacher nodded in her direction, urging her on.

She cleared her throat. "Um...it means that we know what we currently are but we have no idea of what exactly we could become."

Miss Woods smiled as she said, "That's somehow a good explanation." She then picked up some papers from her desk and stated, "This will be your assignment for tomorrow." She began to distribute them till only one paper was left. She asked, "Does anybody know where Drake lives? And if it's close to your house – I need someone to give it to him. It'll be graded, so it's important."

Lucy bit her lip, thinking this through. This will be a perfect excuse for her to find out what he's up to. She stood up and boldly said, "I'll give it to him." *Oh, you'll have no idea Drake.*

As soon as Lucy got in her brother's car, she immediately asked him, "I um...was wondering; were you at home before you drove here?"

Chad shook his head in a yes and gave her a questioning look. She further asked as she rubbed the back of her neck, "Well, um...how's dad?" *I can't believe I'm asking about that jerk but I have to make sure of something.*

He wrinkled his brows, whipping his head towards her in astonishment. "Come again?"

She rolled her eyes. "Oh, just answer me!"

He sighed deeply and swerved to the right. "He's fine. Why?" *Whew, I'm glad that prick is still alive and breathing.*

She shrugged her shoulders. "Well, it's just a question."

He scratched the back of his head. "A very odd question, if I may add."

She pulled her knees to her chest and wrapped her arms around them. "Chad? I want to tell you that I'm going to take a cab later today. I want to pay a visit to a friend."

He puckered his brow. "What friend?"

She bit her lip as she recalled. "You know my friend whom I slept over at when I um...ran away?"

She fiddled with her fingers while he replied, "Oh yeah, I remember. I'll take you. Why go by cab?"

Lucy tapped her finger against her chin. "Well, I just want you to stop by her neighborhood, and I'll go to her place myself."

He nodded. "Whatever you say, sis."

Lucy was now standing in front of Drake's building. She did not want Chad to know his exact address because well, it'll just ruin everything. So once he drove her to his neighborhood, she continued her way towards the familiar building herself. She breathed heavily, suddenly having second thoughts. *What was I doing here anyways? Oh yes, the assignment. Good excuse, Lucy.* She ran a hand through her hair, fixing it as she marched in. She stood there silently in front of his door. With arms folded tightly across her chest, she swayed back and forth nervously. She chewed on her inner lip, urging herself to knock already. Lucy heard the jingling of keys from behind and slightly turned around to see an old man unlocking the door to his apartment.

He looked at her with an intense gaze as he spoke, "Don't even bother knocking."

She had a puzzled expression on. "Why not?"

He leaned against the wall, eying her. "That's because he's not home."

She felt upset. She expected him to be here. She couldn't help but ignore what the old man said and knock on his door. She waited but nothing. He really wasn't here.

She heard the old guy chuckle from behind; she clenched and unclenched her fists. "What's so funny?"

He rubbed his white moustache that somehow looked like a worn out broom. "You thought I was lying, and there you go. He's not here."

She sighed deeply in an agitated manner. "Well, do you happen to know where he is?"

He nodded his head, staring at his black boots. She impatiently tapped her foot against the ground. "Aren't you going to tell me?"

He stretched his neck as he suggested, "How about I get a cup of coffee and-"

She cut him off. "I'm sorry but I'm in a hurry, so if you can please tell me now."

He straightened up. "Well, since you said please." he paused then added, "He always seems to be out and about. He's strange. When I had a walk once, I accidentally spotted him in the woods just a few miles out of town...and I think he's there now."

She took a few steps forwards, interested in what he was saying. "In the woods?" *What was he doing in the woods? It's not that safe – but to leave school to be there, there's something up.*

He nodded. "I know what you're thinking, but don't follow him. I wouldn't do that if I were you. I suggest you wait."

She rubbed her temple in contemplation; she couldn't just sit here and wait. She'll have to go. She needs to find him, and find out what he's doing. "I know I shouldn't. I might even regret it, but I'm going." She shrugged.

He gave her an apologetic expression as his eyes softened. "You know what they say, curiosity killed the cat."

She shoved her hands in her pockets. "Well, I'm no cat." With that, she made her way out the building. Then suddenly someone tugged her by her arm; it was the old man again. She sighed, "What is it?"

He let out a deep breath. "Well, why do you want to know so badly?"

She bit her lip. "I won't say." *Well, I feel empty when he's not around. I want his closeness and warmness.*

He rested his hand on his cheek. "Oh, I think I already know. Anyways, here's my number." He handed her a piece of paper, then added, "I don't want to be the cause of something bad since I was the one who told you where he was. So just give me a call when-"

She cut him off. "Okay thanks." With that, she made her way out of town.

She walked and walked till her feet could no longer walk any farther. *Ugh, I'm such a grandma.* She urged herself to continue as she felt that she was getting closer. She paused, realizing that she soon was going to walk through the woods to probably God knows where. She took a long, deep breath and trudged along the soft yet damp moss of the forest path. She quickened her pace once she felt that this place lacked the feeling of security. Those tall, green trees were towering over her and she couldn't help but feel scared once she heard the snapping of twigs from behind her. She stopped dead in her tracks and breathed in, calming herself down, it's just a squirrel. She marched forwards as she felt the cool breeze sway her hair. The leaves were now rustling loudly.

After what felt like centuries, she gulped nervously once she suddenly heard low murmurs ahead. *This must be him, but he's not alone.* She got closer, making sure she did not make any sound. She hid behind a large tree that was not so close to whoever was speaking, since it was safer that way. She tried to focus on what they were saying.

"You're not the boss of me. You and the others banned me remember?" That was certainly Drake, she knew his mellifluous yet husky voice anywhere. She felt a shiver run down her spine as she leaned in to hear what the other person was going to say.

"You caused this on yourself, remember?" The other guy spat out.

She wanted to see that person's face but she wouldn't dare do so. She just sucked in a breath and wondered what Drake could possibly be banned from. *What the hell were they talking about?* All she had to do was simply keep listening.

"Do keep in mind what I had just told you. Don't make matters worse," the guy ordered. *Who is he? And what did Drake...do?*

"Whatever, I don't bloody care anymore. There's no use," Drake spat out viciously.

Lucy couldn't help but feel sorry for Drake as she twisted and turned behind the humongous tree. She bit her lip hard, thinking of what Drake could possibly be facing. She wanted to help, but he'll never accept her help and she knew it; he was just too stubborn. After those last couple of words, both of them went quiet. The guy seemed to have left or something since he said his goodbyes and began walking away. Well, that's what the sound of leaves crackling under someone's feet indicated. *Wait. Is Drake going to go back home um...my way? Oh shit, I better move away from here before he sees me.*

She quietly began to move as she tiptoed, avoiding any twigs or dried up leaves that might cause any unwanted noise. She even held her breath for a few seconds. And just when she thought she had made it, someone tugged her harshly by her arm, wrapping their fingers around it firmly. She suddenly clamped her eyes shut, knowing exactly who had caught her. She gulped and turned around to face a fuming Drake. His eyes were so dark almost black, his nose was flaring, and his blood was boiling with rage.

"What the fuck are you doing here?" he yelled at her as he tried so hard to control himself from bursting out in uncontrollable anger.

Color drained from her face. She couldn't speak; but she pulled herself together to try and form words as she stuttered, "I wanted to give yo-you the um...assignment for to-tomorrow."

He ran a hand through his hair, messing it up roughly. Fires of fury were smoldering in his narrowed eyes. Lucy took out the paper from her pocket and handed it to him with a trembling hand. His jaw tensed as his breathing got even quicker. "I don't fucking care about the assignment, Lucy. Now, answer me and tell me what you have heard from the conversation. How long were you standing here?"

She bit her lip anxiously and fiddled with her fingers, looking anywhere but his eyes. She couldn't make eye contact with him whatsoever. "I didn't hear anything important, I swear. I wasn't here for long, so I didn't even know what you and the other guy were talking about."

He licked his lips, pacing back and forth in his position. He certainly did not want her to know anything about the conversation. He took a few steps backwards from her and crossed his arms. "You shouldn't be here, you know? You should just stop interfering." he paused then whispered only for him to hear, "What if he had caught you?"

She creased her eyebrows. "What? I didn't hear you..."

He rubbed his temple over and over as he finally said, "Just leave. And next time don't follow me around, I repeat. Do. Not. Follow. Me." He made sure to emphasize the last four words.

Her heart hurt. Drake was never that disappointed in her. She approached him and stared intently into his cold eyes. "I want to help you."

He had a puzzled expression on as he chuckled darkly. "Help me? Really? I don't need help."

She nervously reached out to touch his arm. She gently stroked it up and down, trying to reassure him, but he directly flinched away from her touch. Her eyes became glazed with a glassy layer of unshed tears. "Please! You can't just shut everybody out. The world is not your enemy, Drake. So tell me what's wrong and I'll do my best to help."

He had a lopsided smirk on, which immediately disappeared as he took a few, slow steps towards her. He closed his eyes, breathing in, and then instantly snapped them back open to stare at her delicate face. He softly brushed away a strand of her hair and placed it gently behind her ear, causing warm tingles to run throughout her entire body. He whispered to her, giving her a weak smile. "You're so innocent, Lucy." She loved the way her name sounded on his lips. She wanted to touch those plump lips of his, and she did. She lifted her hand and gently rubbed his bottom lip with her thumb. His eyes widened at her, but then he quickly took her hand in his and lowered it to her side. "What are you doing?"

Her cheeks flushed red. She felt very embarrassed as she nervously stuttered, "I um...I-"

He cut her off, smirking smugly at her. "You want to kiss me that badly?"

Her mouth fell open and she furrowed her brows. "You're such a-"

He then suddenly smashed his lips hungrily against hers, not letting her say another word. Her heart was drumming against her chest as she tasted his soft, wet lips that were now tracing hers delicately. His hand softly cupped her face while the other was stroking the small of her back. She felt an electric current run through her body and goosebumps formed everywhere. She had never felt this way before, his kiss was passionate and intoxicating. She couldn't get enough of him. She wildly ran her hand through his long locks, gently twirling them around her fingers.

He deepened the kiss as he seductively bit her lower lip and nibbled on it, forcing a moan out of her lips. This made him smirk widely and pull her to him even closer. He wrapped his arms around her waist and pushed her up against a tree bark. She wound her arms around his neck; their lips still locked together. He then slowly pulled away to kiss her warm, delicate skin. He gradually planted feather kisses up and down her neck, leaving an igniting trace wherever his lips touched. Then he buried his face in her dark, blonde hair, breathing in her luscious scent.

Why can't we stop? And why do I want to do dirty things to him? Oh my God, I want him so bad. She dipped her head back to give him better access as she felt her legs go limp. His touch burned her skin, and she couldn't think straight anymore. She was simply melting with ecstasy.

Lucy took a deep breath. She tried her best not to look at Drake, who was busy kissing her neck all over whilst stroking her hair. "Dr-Drake"

He immediately pulled away, staring into her eyes with concern. "I'm sorry, I think I pushed this a little too far and-"

She cut him off, pressing her forehead against his. "Don't apologize. That was the best kiss I've ever had." *You make me feel things I've never felt before.* She blushed at her unsaid words.

He smirked and gently caressed her cheek with his fingertips. "I'm glad you enjoyed it."

Trust me, 'enjoyed it' would be an understatement.

He then cleared his throat and wore a serious expression on. "Let's go now before I remember what got me mad at you..."

CHAPTER 7

They silently walked side by side as they made their way back. Breaking the reticent silence, Drake suggested, "Let's go to my apartment, and then I'll take you back home on my motorcycle, okay?"

Lucy twirled her loose hair strands around her finger, avoiding his gaze. "I don't know...my folks would be worried and-"

He immediately interrupted her to say, "Well, give them a logical excuse. Um...tell them you helped me with that stupid assignment or something..."

She stared into his beautiful dark, blue orbs that held so much warmth. She still couldn't believe that those innocent-looking eyes of his could be so cold and unwelcoming sometimes. Her thoughts were suddenly cut off once he suddenly waved his hand in front of her face, bringing her back to reality.

"Hello! You still there? You just zoned out..." He puckered his brow at her. A smirk made its way to his lips as he said, "I know you can't help it when I'm around. I'm just too damn sexy, aren't I?"

She rolled her eyes and playfully slapped his arm. "Aren't you tired of your lame lines? I mean, come on."

He innocently shrugged his shoulders. "Well, I'm just saying the truth. What's so lame about the truth, huh?"

She couldn't help but giggle at his silly humor. She gave him a warm smile and nervously spoke. "Drake..."

He looked at her, taking in her angelic features. "Yep, that's my name."

She sighed deeply, biting her inner cheek. "When are you going to tell me about yourself? I mean, I barely even know you if you come to think about it."

Drake shoved his hands in his pockets, breaking eye contact with her. He now had a blank expression on. "There's nothing important to know. I'm um...simply a boring person."

She narrowed her eyes and moved closer to him, ignoring his obvious lie. "I highly doubt that." She paused and then added as she placed her hands on her hips. "I mean, I don't know anything about your life, your parents, your favorite color, music, hobbies, and um…food!" Her voice trailed away.

He stopped walking and turned to face her. His jaw tensed as he mumbled out. "It's better if you don't get too attached to me, so not knowing anything about me would be better." He ran a hand through his hair and breathed out, "I think the kiss wasn't supposed to happen, I should have known-"

She cut him off, forcing back the tears that were threatening to roll down her cheeks any second now, "Please don't say this." She felt so vulnerable.

He rubbed his temple and softly lifted her face up to meet his gaze. "Look, I'm sorry, but I need you to understand that I'm not the kind of person you should be hanging out with and getting to know. I know I'm even making it more difficult for you since I'm always around somehow, but-"

She cut him off again, balling her hands into fists at her side, "I don't care how 'dangerous' you are or whatever you claim to be. It's my decision, and I choose to know you better. You're not going to shut me out that easily. I'm not a kid."

He puckered his brow whilst firmly crossing his arms. "Well, this decision of yours is stupid, because if you think you can convince me in telling you about my life well, guess again. I never did and I never will."

She felt her heart ache a little. *Did I really expect him to trust me enough to tell me? Or at least give me a glimpse of his life...I guess I was wrong. So wrong.* She simply stood there and thought of something to say. She wasn't going to let this go and get affected. *Nope, not this time.* "Why Drake? I promise I won't judge you. I would never."

He stared at her intently. "Words are easy to say. Trust me, you won't take it well. At all."

She drew closer to him. "I, um…I-"

Suddenly, he blew up, teeth gritted and fists clenched in anger. "Fine! I'll tell you a little about my fucking life! It's a living hell, Lucy. I hate it, and I hate everybody in it. My parents are long gone; they didn't even give a damn about me from the start anyways. And do you want to know something? I'm so glad they're rotting in hell now, because that's where they belong. My favorite color is black, my favorite thing about life is death itself, don't you think? Oh, and last but not least, one of my favorite hobbies would be, of course, to torture every single soul."

Lucy's mouth was agape as she froze in her position. Her eyes were practically bulging out of their sockets. She tried to take in all those cruel words that he had said. She was horrified. Why did he hate life this much? She didn't know, but hoped she would someday when he actually opens up to her. What she did next startled him, for she didn't run away like he expected her to, but she drew even closer to him and reached out to touch his cold yet soft face. She stared at his shocked expression and whispered nervously, "But you don't hate me." It was more of a question than a statement.

He furrowed his brows in confusion. "Out of all the repulsive things I said, you managed to pick out the part where I don't actually hate everybody?"

Her face lit up. "You surely exaggerated with all this, Drake. I know you're not as cruel as you say you are. Some people misjudge you and um...your parents made a huge mistake, that I'm sure. They should have given you the care you deserved, Drake."

He simply stood there and stared at her in awe. "Are you my fairy Godmother or something?"

Once she gave him a death glare, he chuckled. "I repeat, you're just too innocent Lucy...I still am trying to figure out how a girl like you is hanging out with a guy like me."

She began to walk again as her face lit up like a Christmas tree. "I have a feeling you'll be as innocent too, one day."

He stole another warm glance at her, realizing at this moment just how much she actually cared about him, and that to him was something that is rather new and wonderful.

She had entered his room before, hell, she even slept in his bed, but she hadn't actually focused on it. As she stood there eying his room, she had noticed that the greyish, black walls were covered with shabby posters of a couple of metal groups. An electric guitar laid in the corner of the room, *I didn't know he played guitar. I guess there's a whole lot of things I still don't know about this guy.* The cover of his medium-sized bed was black as well as the pillows that were scattered on it. On the nightstand near his bed, was a small, wooden box. Once she reached out to grab it, a clearing of someone's throat interrupted her from doing so.

"Don't ever think of touching that." Drake spat out as he leaned on his bedroom door.

Lucy swiftly retracted her hand and nervously gulped, "I'm sorry." she fidgeted with her fingers and thought of a way to break the awkward tension, "I didn't know you played guitar."

He looked away from her gaze, "I rarely do anymore..."

She crossed her arms, "Well, how about you play now? I'm sure you're good at it."

He puckered his brow as he blew a hair strand off his face, "Maybe some other time."

She pouted and batted her eyelashes at him, "Pretty please, for me."

He rolled his eyes, "I said later. Now, come on let's get something to eat."

She followed him to the kitchen and took a seat at the round, marble table. She watched him open the fridge to get ham and cheese. This was somehow all too familiar, déjà vu, to be more precise. Except that this time, she didn't run away and ended up being here, it was simply a mere visit. She picked out her phone from her pocket and texted Chad.

"To: Bro

Hi I'm going to be a little late cause I'm helping my friend out with homework, so see you later x"

Do I know how to lie or what?

Suddenly her cell was snatched away from her, she gasped as Drake ran through her messages. "Wise thing to do," he said while reading the message that was sent.

"Hey! Give that back to me!" Lucy squealed and playfully punched his arm.

He then furrowed his brows in confusion, "Who the hell is 'poop'?"

She bit her inner cheek, trying to suppress the laughter. She almost forgot that she had changed his contact name. His eyes widened, "Seriously? Why would you name me 'poop'?" *Oh, great he saw his number.*

She couldn't help but burst out laughing as she clutched her stomach tightly, "Oh, come on. Do you not think it suits you?"

He shot daggers at her and firmly crossed his arms, "I'm actually surprised you didn't name me 'sexy' or 'hottie' or 'hunk' or 'lady killer' or simply 'drop dead gorgeous' or-"

She cut him off as she lightly slapped her hand on his mouth, shushing him, "Okay, okay. You're so conceited. The name that entirely suits you would actually be 'pig-headed'."

He rolled his eyes and stood behind her. He gently brushed her hair back and she felt his cold lips press against her neck. She took several nervous gulps as he trailed wet kisses up and down the back of her neck, "Stop denying it, you can't wait to name me 'my boo'."

She shuddered at the sound of his low, seductive voice. Breathing in, she managed to say, "You wish." She then swiftly turned around to face him. His face was mere inches away from hers, and she could feel his warm, minty breath against her cheek. She gave him a mischievous grin, "For someone who wants me to maintain my distance or whatever, you sure can't keep your hands to yourself, can you?"

He was expressionless and took a few steps backwards. He was somehow stiff and nervous as he pushed his long hair back. Drake was nervous. Lucy couldn't help but feel victorious. She pressed her lips together and tried hard not to laugh, "If I were you, I wouldn't be able to help it either."

He whipped his head round to look at her as he smirked widely, "Who's conceited now?"

She blushed and lowered her head, "Well, I guess it's contagious."

He smirked, placing her ham and cheese sandwich in front of her. Then he sat down across her. He licked his lips and took a massive bite out of his sandwich, obviously hungry. She smiled at how cute he was with his mouth full. She softly whispered, "Thank you, Drake."

He winked at her and shook his head whilst chewing. "You know what I'd want to call you?" he paused as he contemplated, then added, "Candy bar."

She was about to choke on her sandwich, "What? Why?"

He laughed and his eyes glistened, causing the blue in them to glow. "Cause you're just like a candy bar, half sweet and half nuts." and then he cracked up with laughter as if what he just said was the funniest thing ever.

Lucy's mouth fell open, but still she couldn't hide the giggle that was threatening to come out, "That was the lamest 'pick-up' line ever! Where the hell do you get those from?"

He ran a hand through his hair. "I'm a funny guy, it all comes from up here." he pointed to his head; even though he knew that he had actually read it online or something.

She deeply sighed. "I highly doubt you have a brain."

He rolled his eyes. "Well, I highly doubt you have a sense of humor."

She tightened her grip on her sandwich, "What are we four? You're really moody, you know." she paused then added as she jutted her lower lip out in a pout, "I'm scared of moody people."

He stared at her bottom lip and breathed out, "If you're trying to make me want to kiss you, it's not working."

Her mouth was agape now, "What? Of course not. I um…I would never-"

He cut her off, giving her a lopsided smirk, "Save it princess."

She then ignored him and picked out a folded paper from her pocket. "Can you please give me a pencil?"

He scratched the back of his head, "What for?"

She deeply sighed. "For my English assignment, duh."

"You're going to do it now? Am I that boring?" he eyed her, handing her a pencil from the drawer.

She gave him a warm smile, "No silly. I just want to start with it, since I'm sure that I wouldn't have the time to do it at home." She patted the seat beside her, "And you're going to do it too, so come on, it's studying time!"

He rolled his eyes, crossed his arms, and took his seat, "More like horror time." he paused then added as he rested his chin on his palm, "I can't believe I'm doing this."

She glared. "Shut up, I'm trying to focus here." she cleared her throat and read aloud, "Write a 1500 word essay concerning the social problem we are facing today which is suicide..."

Drake suddenly winced and she felt his whole body stiffen. She had a worried expression as she tenderly touched his shoulder. "Are you all right?"

He immediately pulled away from her touch. "Fuck being all right." She hated when Drake was cold and distant. *Doesn't he know that I'll never hurt him?* She nervously stuttered, "Yo-you can tell m-me."

He looked away as he clenched his fists and rushed out of the room swiftly. Lucy was left alone in the silence. She thought of the reasons why 'suicide' was such a sensitive topic to him.

She quietly made her way to his room, knowing that he'll surely be there. She leaned against his bedroom door and her eyes immediately landed on his seated figure. He was sitting on the floor with his back against his bed, he was hugging his knees tightly to his chest as he looked ahead. She nervously bit her lip and approached him. She crouched down beside him and glanced at his angelic face. He didn't acknowledge her because he was deep in thought. He was zoned out as he stared through the window in front of him. His eyes were somehow watery and glazed, they were glittering against the light that made its way through the open window. He looked beautiful. All she wanted to do was hug him so tight and tell him that everything will be okay. He seemed so vulnerable and it was the first time that Lucy had ever seen him in such a hopeless state.

She took a deep breath and softly whispered, "Drake..."

He kept looking ahead as if he was watching something, but it was only an open window that showed the vast, bright, blue sky, nothing special. She dug her nails into her palms and thought of a way to make him feel better, but what could she possibly do? And just when she was about to speak again, her lips parted in shock at the sight. Tears were now trickling down his smooth cheeks as his eyes glinted with sorrow. He didn't even bother wiping them away, he simply sat there motionless.

Lucy was about to panic, she felt the need to cry herself. Drake looked like a lost, little kid and she really wanted to soothe him and take away his pain. She then lifted her hands and gently caressed his wet cheeks as she wiped his salty, bitter tears away with her thumbs. He flinched at first but then he leaned into her touch and closed his eyes shut. She drew nearer to his face and planted a soft yet passionate kiss on his cheek, her lips lingering there. She slightly pulled back once his eyes fluttered open. His eyes were glued to hers and she felt his warm breath tickle her face. She nervously yet confidently spoke, "You can tell me anything Drake, I promise I'll try and make you feel better."

He furrowed his brows and then buried his face in the crook of her neck. Her eyes widened at his action but immediately wrapped her arms around him, molding into his form. He wildly ran his fingers through her hair and clutched her tightly as if she were going to disappear any minute now. He murmured against her hair, "I deserve all the misery. I've been really bad, Lucy."

She ran her fingers up and down his back and pushed away his loose hair strands that were in the way. "Don't say that. No one deserves misery."

He pulled back from her embrace to look at her sharply. Fire danced in his eyes and his blood boiled. Lucy gulped at his sudden mood change. He was filled with anger as his knuckles turned white. He gritted his teeth. "Nobody cared about me, I used to feel like shit, Lucy."

She hesitantly traced her finger against his jawline and nervously mumbled out, "I care about you..."

He mockingly smirked, "That's because you have no idea who I am. If you did have a slight idea, you'd never want to see me again or have anything to do with me."

She clenched her fists, huffing. "That's not true, I would never do that. I'm not that kind of person." She paused and then continued, "Instead, I'll do my best to help you."

He ran his hand through his hair and pulled at its ends, "Help me? It's too late for that."

She breathed in, wondering. "Why'd you leave the room when I read the topic out loud?"

His jaw tensed as he pressed his lips together in a tight line. "That's none of your business."

She glared at him, annoyed at getting the same answer every time. "Stop pushing me away. I want to know. If you speak about it, you'll feel better. Trust me."

He stared intently into her warm gaze. "Fine."

Her eyes brightened up as she waited for him to say what he has to say. He rubbed the back of his neck, his eyes darkening. He spat out. "My mom committed suicide and then my dad left me. I was on my own ever since I was twelve."

Lucy's mouth parted as she stared at him with astonishment, it was worse than she thought. She gave him a weak smile, urging him to further explain. He bit his lip harshly and tried to stay put. "She didn't want me as her son, she thought I was a mistake. My dad was always out and about and she had to raise me all on her own, but I wouldn't call that raising at all. She wasn't there when I had nightmares, she wasn't there when kids bullied me, she wasn't there to celebrate my birthday, she wasn't there to play games with me, she simply was never there when I needed her the most. As for my dad, well, I would say he was more of a visitor than a dad. He came to see us once in every two to three months. It was really sad that your own dad did not know how old you were. That's short for saying he really did not give a damn."

Drake bit down harder on his bottom lip, causing blood to well up. "Mom got sick of everything and got sick of me. And one day, she decided she no longer wanted to live and be a part of my world. I remember the way she looked at me when she slammed her bedroom door in my face, I was so scared and hopeless. When I later opened it, I saw her lying lifeless on the floor, her fingers were wrapped around an empty bottle of pills. It was a horrific scene that I will never forget."

He stopped to take a breath as he licked the blood off his lips, Lucy felt so sorry for him; words wouldn't express the way she was feeling. Her heart hammered against her chest and she felt the need to bury all his sorrow away. She wished she could make his problems disappear.

He interrupted her thoughts as he spoke again, his voice cracked with emotion. "When my dad knew about her death, he didn't even come to stay with me or help me through it all. He just gave me a call on the phone, saying it was all too much for him and I was a big responsibility. The last words I had heard from him were that he was sorry. I ended up at an orphanage that I later ran away from, and that is a whole new story that I'm not willing to share with you yet."

Lucy's eyes were filled with mixed emotions, if that was part of his miserable past, she wondered what else there was that he did not want to talk about. She immediately hugged him tightly, wrapping her arms around his neck. He whispered against her ear, causing her to shudder against his chest, "I don't want you to pity me."

She slightly pulled back to meet his cold gaze. "I just think your parents weren't fair at all, I'm sure you were a wonderful kid. I wish I had known you before Drake. I would have never left your side, I wouldn't have let you do the bad things you said you did."

He softly cupped her face in his hands as he pressed his forehead against hers, "Thank you."

She stared at his eyes, then at his lips that looked so tempting. "For what?"

"For listening," he said and pressed his lips to her forehead in a light kiss.

She gave him a wide, warm smile, showing her pearly teeth. Someday, she would know more about his past. *I really want to know why you're truly this messed up.*

"Hold on tight," he stated as he woke his motorcycle to life. She clutched him tightly and buried her face in his back, breathing him in. His scent was her medicine.

"Lucy, dear, I said hold on tight, not squeeze the life out of me." He joked, smirking widely at her through the rear view mirror. She blushed, ignoring him. She rested her head against his back, closed her eyes, and enjoyed the wind that flapped her hair and whipped it in all directions.

CHAPTER 8

She stood on her doorstep, waiting for someone to bother getting up and opening the door for her. She practiced the lie she was going to say in her head over and over. She made sure Drake stopped a few blocks away from her place. She was in no mood for answering questions, mainly because according to her folks, Drake is a girl. No way was she going to tell them about him right now, especially since he was no prince charming, he was a parent's worst nightmare. She was just going to ignore any subject related to 'Drake' for now.

Chad finally opened the door and greeted her with a frown, "So nice of you to finally drop by."

"Oh come on, we were doing homework. It's not like I was at a party getting wasted or anything. So chill." She rolled her eyes and went inside.

Her mom was slumped back into the softness of the couch, and her lame excuse of a father had his eyes glued to the TV. She cleared her throat, grabbing her mother's attention who immediately looked up at her. "Baby girl, you're home. How was everything?"

"It was good..." She paused and then asked whilst sitting next to her, "What are you guys watching?"

"The news...oh look! Look, they're going to talk about it right now!" Her mom narrowed her eyes as she waited for the reporter on the TV to speak.

Lucy had a puzzled expression on, *what are they talking about?* She stared at the TV and read the news banner at the bottom,

'Killer on the loose..." *Wait, what? A killer?* She bit her lip and focused on the words that were now spilling from the reporter's mouth. The reporter had a stern look on her face as she stared ahead, obviously reading from a teleprompter. "Three bodies have been found this week. All of them were in the exact same condition, no clues whatsoever as to what or who murdered them. An autopsy was even done on one of them, and the doctors unfortunately weren't able to detect the real reason behind the person's death. 'They have never been aware of such conditions' was what they told us. However, the police are in constant search of this murderer who seems to have his or her own unusual ways of killing. We will always keep you updated. As for now, be very careful and keep yourselves safe. This is Anne Martin, reporting for ADC news." She pressed her lips together as she nodded slightly.

Lucy's mouth was agape the whole time, she was practically freaking out. *Three bodies? I only knew of two! Poor Chase, I'm guessing the autopsy wasn't helpful at all. Could it really be Drake? But today he seemed so innocent and fragile, no way was he capable of doing such a thing.* Lucy began biting her nails in a harsh manner as she reasoned with herself. *How can anyone be so cruel?* She intertwined her fingers together and shut her eyes tight, murmuring to herself, "Please don't let it be Drake."

"Lucy, you heard the news, you're going to stay at home until it gets safe again..." Her mother shook her head and placed her hand on her daughter's shoulder.

Lucy furrowed her brows. "What? Are you serious? What if they never get to catch the killer, am I supposed to sit and wait for like forever?"

Her mom sighed deeply. "You should understand Lucy…"

She breathed out. "Mom, what's going to happen, will happen. I mean it could be my fate or not, so I'm not going to be scared. The killer could climb up my room for heaven's sake!"

Her father butted in. "Oh shut up, you're such a pain in the ass."

Lucy clenched and unclenched her fists. And just when she was about to say something, Chad spoke out of nowhere, obviously wanting to cut the tension between those two. "I really hope they catch the killer soon."

Lucy eyed Chad and mouthed a 'seriously?' He shrugged his shoulders as he winked at her and made his way out of the living room. She climbed up the steps to her room and then hopped on her bed. She swiftly grabbed her phone. *Should I text him? Never mind, I don't want to be too clingy.* She got up to blast some music on her CD player. She went through all the music albums that she had as she decided on what to listen to. As soon as she picked a song, her phone vibrated against her pocket. She pulled it out and her eyes widened at the screen, poop.

"9:01 pm

I'm going to give u a ride to school tomorrow, since I now know where u live.

-Poop-"

Is he bloody serious? On his motorcycle? What will my parents say? Does he want my mom to have a heart attack or something?

"To: Poop

Thanks but no way. My folks don't know about ur existence."

She tapped her fingers against her cheek and waited for him to reply. She suddenly decided to change his contact name to plain 'Drake' since 'poop' was getting pretty old.

"9:11 pm

I guess they're going to have to meet me ;)

-Drake-"

Isn't he quite the charmer? Does he seriously think they're going to welcome him with open arms?

"To: Drake

Absolutely not! I don't want to have to face them Drake. I will have a lot of explaining to do, maybe some other time."

She added the last part, hoping to change that stubborn mind of his.

"9:19 pm

Mmm u have plenty of time to think of some good excuses for tomorrow, see you babe ;)

-Drake-"

Drake was back to being a jerk again. Just when she was about to put her cell aside, it rang once again. *Is he that bored?*

"9:23 pm

Oh and try not to have wet dreams of me tonight, don't want it to be all awkward in the morning, now do u?

-Drake-"

Her mouth fell open as a blush rose to her cheeks. *He did not just say that.* Her cell vibrated again. *What the hell?*

"9:25 pm

God, I wish I was there to see that priceless expression of urs right now.

-Drake-"

She grinned widely and couldn't help but giggle at his words. She then took out her assignment and placed it in front of her. She never can understand how Drake can switch from being dejected to being serious to being happy and even to being a jerk. All she knows is that he was affecting her a lot. Who knows how long she'll last without accidentally revealing the way she feels about him? She really wants to be a part of his brooding life. She closed her eyes and hoped that everything will work out and that the killer won't be who she thinks he is. *Oh Drake, what are you hiding?*

She shook her head and focused on what to write, pressing the tip of the pen against her lower lip. Her eyes glinted with mixed emotions as she thought of Drake. 'Suicide is indeed a tragic event that affects everybody. People shouldn't get rid of their lives, they shouldn't be so negative and...'

Lucy nervously paced back and forth in her room as she thought of what to say to her parents when Drake miraculously shows up. She narrowed her eyes at the clock beside her bed and rubbed the back of her neck. '6:15 am' *Why am I up this early again? Oh, yeah, it's because of Drake. How nice of him to offer me a ride on his noble steed.* She groaned, *I know, I'll tell them he's mistaken with the address or something. Oh, who am I kidding? I guess I should just go with the flow. I hope Drake thinks of some excuses though.* She lightly banged her head against the wall, *I think I'm going crazy; I'm talking to myself a whole lot.* She took a deep breath then let herself fall back on her bed as she stared at the ceiling above her. She then immediately grabbed her phone.

"To: Drake

My back is killing me today, I don't know why, I don't think I can go on your motorcycle."

She smiled slyly and held her head high, thinking she was indestructible now.

"6:23 am

Are u sure ur up this early cause of ur back? Or cause u can't control ur excitement? Oh and I'll be sure to get u some meds with me, don't want ur poor back to ache, now do we? ;)

-Drake-"

Lucy gritted her teeth as she slammed her phone against the nightstand. It was useless.

She went through her closet and grabbed a pair of shorts and a blouse to go with it. She tied her hair in a ponytail, brushed her teeth, applied red lipstick on her lips, and headed to the kitchen. She was going to fool her mother. She wore the yellow, rubber gloves that rested beside the sink and then began to wash the dirty dishes. She later got some jam out of the fridge, and prepared a bunch of sandwiches. She poured orange juice into four cups and placed them neatly on the table. That should win their hearts.

"Lucy? What are you doing?" Her mom asked, her eyes widening.

A smile was plastered on Lucy's face. "Well, I thought of making you guys some breakfast."

"Are you feeling all right dear?" Her mom drew nearer to her and placed her hand on Lucy's forehead, checking her temperature.

Lucy frowned as she removed her mother's hand. "Mom, I'm fine. I just felt like it."

Her mom puckered her brow, not buying what she had just said.

Lucy rolled her eyes. "Fine! My um…friend is going to come pick me up to school today, and I didn't think you'll approve of him." She paused and then blabbered, "But didn't you always tell me not to judge people? He um…is really lonely and I thought I'd be his friend and show him that life can be really fun. I told him that you would understand since you're a very great person."

Her mom rested her hand on her cheek as she nodded. "I'm so proud of you." *That was easy.*

After a couple of minutes, Chad joined them. He stared at the food on the table and licked his lips. "Yum."

Lucy sat down as she took a big gulp from her cup. Her father later entered the kitchen and stared at the table with disgust. "Who said I wanted to eat jam? I want some real food!"

"Honey, Lucy woke up early and made us breakfast, I think you should be a little grateful," Her mom said whilst taking a bite of her sandwich.

He slammed his fist against the table. "Don't tell me what to do woman."

Lucy's nostrils flared as she clenched her fist underneath the table. He then furrowed his brows with anger. "I said I want food! Are you bloody deaf?"

Lucy couldn't handle this anymore. "Get some yourself!"

He approached her and gritted his teeth. "Repeat what you just said, you little-"

"I guess you're the one who's deaf because what I said was loud and clear," she boldly stated.

He then raced towards her, wanting to teach her a lesson she'll never forget. Lucy's mouth fell open as she realized that she's about to get beaten. She instantly ran to the door. Her fingers trembled as she fumbled with the lock, *come on, come on*. It finally opened. She hurriedly got out, it was really hard to run since her legs felt like jelly. Just as she was about to make her escape, a rough hand pulled her hair back by her ponytail. She winced with pain and shut her eyes tightly. He violently shoved her to the ground, and stared down at her with no emotion. His cold stare made her flinch.

He spat out bitterly. "You're going to regret those words you said. You should respect me!"

Lucy took several nervous gulps, shivering all over. She felt so weak. Howard smiled wickedly as he kicked her hard in the stomach. She cried out as soon as she felt the intense, piercing pain shoot throughout her body. Her eyes were now watery and tears threatened to fall down her cheeks. She clutched her stomach tightly and harshly bit down on her bottom lip. She knew that it would take more than only one kick. She saw her brother and mother stand outside with worried expressions on. *Aren't they going to help me?* She didn't expect them to. Chad was turning into a pussy after all. Her dad suddenly yelled in her face. "Look at me!"

Lucy looked up at him and breathed in. He kicked her in the stomach again but even harder than the first time. She screamed out and felt the bitter tears rush down her face. She was now whimpering like a lost puppy. Just when he was about to kick her once again, he was violently pushed back by someone. Drake.

Drake clenched his fist very tightly, his knuckles looked like they'd bust through his skin. Fury raced through his body, heating him to his very core. He quickly rammed his fist against her dad's jaw with full force, causing him to fly and hit the hard ground. He then lunged towards him and kicked him hard in the ribs, making him howl in torment. Drake was losing it, he wanted to knock out the air from his lungs. He wanted to end him.

Drake shouted in anger as he pulled him up and slammed him harshly against the wall. "Do you like that? Huh? You fucker! Not so pretty when it's the other way around, don't you think?"

Her dad was about to panic. Fear crept over him like a thousand thorns. His body was shaking in an aggravated manner. His heart was pounding so hard, it might burst out of his chest. Just when he was about to say something, Drake roughly punched him in the nose, causing a loud crack to be heard. He then kneed him in the stomach three times in rapid succession. Blood was now dripping down from his mouth, and his eyes were bloodshot. He looked like a mess. He coughed out and then collapsed to the ground with a loud thud. Drake was breathing heavily as he stared down at the motionless body in front of him. His eyes showed no remorse whatsoever for what he had just did.

Her mom let out a loud and high-pitched cry as she ran towards her husband. As for her brother, he simply stood there with his mouth hung open. It was one hell of a scene.

Drake made his way to Lucy and crouched beside her. His eyes were deep, black pools; they were so intense. He licked his lips and stared intently into her wide eyes that were filled with mixed emotions. Slipping his strong arms beneath her, he carefully picked her fragile body up. She wrapped her arms around his neck and closed her eyes shut, ignoring the smell of blood that lingered on his clothes. She just wanted to feel his warmth. Drake had saved her. Even though he almost killed her father, he had actually saved her, and that's all that matters now.

Natasha's eyes widened when she realized that Drake was heading towards his motorcycle with her daughter held in his arms. "Where a-are you taking her?"

Drake gritted his teeth as he slightly turned around to shoot daggers at her. "She's coming with me."

Lucy looked up at him, staring at his tense features. She didn't care where he took her, she just really wanted to get away from here. She couldn't handle facing her family right now.

"You're not taking her anywhere! I'm her mother-" her mom was cut off by Drake.

"When you learn how to play your part as a mother, then and only then will you actually have a say in this," He hissed. He then gently placed Lucy on the ground, steadying her with a possessive hand on her hip. She leaned into him, avoiding her mother's intense gaze.

Her mom gasped in shock. "I'll call the police! Look what you did to my husband!" she cried out, pointing at his body that was in such a terrible condition. He most certainly should be taken to the nearest hospital.

Drake's eyes darkened and he drew nearer to Natasha. He gave her a sinister smile. "I dare you." He paused as he stared at her husband who was breathing heavily, not daring to utter a single word. "But then again, I could always tell them about what your husband did...and that I was simply defending a poor girl in need of help..."

Her mom opened and closed her mouth without saying anything, looking remarkably like a fish. Fear radiated off her body as her fingers trembled.

Drake's lips lifted up in a smirk as he stole a glance at Lucy who was watching him intently this whole time. He grabbed her hand in his, intertwining his strong, warm fingers with hers. Lucy's eyes widened at his action, he had never done this before. It felt good, real good. A rosy, scarlet color spread over her cheeks and she bit down on her lip.

"Are you all right? Should I take you to the hospital or something?" Drake suddenly asked Lucy with a worried expression on, his eyes searching her body for any visible bruises.

"I'm okay...well, I'm used to it." Lucy sighed deeply and gave him a reassuring smile, wanting to wipe that dark frown off his face. He clenched his jaw and knitted his brows in anger, not liking the fact that she was used to this.

Her brother butted in out of nowhere, grabbing their attention. "Please take care of my sister."

Her mom furrowed her brows at him. She gulped nervously and murmured in a very low tone, "You say that as if she's never returning home again...she's ju-just going to school with him on that thi-thing." She scrunched her nose, staring at the parked motorcycle.

Drake breathed out, irritated. He's surely not going to let her come live with those idiots afterwards. So, he simply ignored her mother's response, not wanting to face anymore drama. He then looked at Chad, who was obviously struggling with himself. "Save it, you pussy," Drake spat out.

Chad didn't defend himself for he knew he deserved that. He wasn't such a good, big brother, especially when she had needed him the most. Lucy gently tugged at Drake's arm, causing him to turn and look at her. She mumbled out in a low tone, "We have to go to school now, we're already running late."

He nodded solemnly as he climbed up his Harley, turned a small key in the ignition, and twisted his right handlebar. He handed Lucy his helmet, motioning for her to put it on. She gazed into his warm, mesmerizing eyes; they were so enticing, she could stare at them all day. She simply wanted to drown in those majestic eyes of his. "What about you?" She asked with a worried expression on.

He gave her that sexy lopsided smirk that sent her pulse into overdrive. "Don't worry about me, I'll be fine."

He stretched out his hand and pulled her up behind him. She then placed the helmet on, buckling the strap around her neck. She pressed her body against his and wrapped her arms firmly around his waist. She was so close to him, she was able to feel the heat radiating off his body. She was glad she was on his motorcycle, so that she can hold him. Even though she wasn't in a good condition to ride a motorcycle, she didn't care, she just wanted to get away from here with Drake. She glanced one last time at her mother and brother who were simply standing there and staring at them in complete shock as they finally left off. She hoped her mother would let this go for now.

Drake wasn't driving too fast, which was a relief to her since she really didn't feel like dying today. Her thighs bracketed his in an incredibly intimate position, she had no idea how she hadn't noticed that before. But she really didn't mind and that caused her cheeks to flush red. She began to softly stroke his hair from behind, causing him to stiffen at her gentle touch. One hand was holding him tight, and the other was twirling each and every strand of his around her finger. She then began to rub his strong, muscular back. She slowly ran her hand up and down his spine, loving the way his muscles tensed. He tightened his grip on the handlebars as he looked at her in the rear view mirror. His eyes were dark with lust. "Lucy...don't make me want to have to stop right here and take you, hard." He threatened as he slowly licked his lips, his tongue sweeping over his bottom lip.

Lucy's breath got caught in her throat and heat rushed into her cheeks. Hot tingles erupted all over her body. She bit her inner cheek in embarrassment and readjusted her arms around his waist. He smirked wickedly at her reaction as he revved up his motorcycle, causing her to clutch him even tighter.

As soon as Drake parked his Harley in front of the school, every single student stopped doing whatever they were doing and stared right at the two. Lucy ignored their stares and whispers. She watched Drake glare at them as he got off his baby. He puckered his brow. "What?"

She ran a hand through her hair, tugging at their ends nervously. "I um...didn't say thank you, so thank you, Drake."

His features softened as he brushed his fingertips lightly over her soft cheek. His eyes suddenly darkened once he lifted her chin with a curled index finger and forced her to meet his piercing gaze. "You don't have to thank me." He paused and then added, "Your father should thank God I spared his life, because next time, I won't be so gentle." *Gentle? He calls what he did gentle?*

His face then suddenly lit up. "Oh I almost forgot." He rummaged through his bag, searching. Once he found what he was looking for, he handed it to Lucy with a huge smirk plastered on his face. She narrowed her eyes at the bottle of Tylenol. "Um...what's that for?"

His brows rose up, smirking wickedly. "Didn't you say your back hurts? Or was it all just some lie?" He winked at her. He had actually remembered to get her a medication like he promised. This brought a blush to her cheeks and she tried her best to hide it.

Lucy rubbed the back of her neck. "Well, I-I-"

He cut her off and drew nearer to her, his hot breath grazing the sensitive skin of her cheek. "Well, babe, now you most certainly can't avoid me, because you're going to have to live with me."

CHAPTER 9

Lucy and Amy were heading towards the cafeteria, their eyes scanning for two vacant seats. Lucy knew that Amy was going to question her on and on, especially since she came to school with Drake on his motorcycle, looking real comfortable. Lucy bit her lip nervously as she took a seat at a table in the middle. Taking a seat next to her, Amy eyed her friend intently. "Start spilling."

She huffed, she's surely not going to tell her what he did to her dad. Besides, Amy didn't even know that her dad was rather abusive, and Lucy wanted to keep it that way. "Well, we're friends now, duh-"

Amy immediately cut her off as she furrowed her brows. "I know it's none of my business, but it's my job as your friend to tell you to be careful. You promise me you will?"

Lucy breathed out. "Promise." She puckered her brow and further asked, "But I don't understand why you think he's such a dangerous person to hang out with? I mean he didn't do anything to you."

She tapped her fingers against the table. "I just feel it Lucy. Let's say he's not so dangerous, he's surely weird, and you can't deny that. There's something off about him."

Lucy clenched and unclenched her fists, she didn't like it when people judged him. He had been through a lot. Just as she was about to speak, Josh came out of nowhere and stood there beside their table. He smiled widely at both of them. "Hey guys."

Amy's face lit up as she batted her eyelids. "Hi there." she patted the seat next to her, motioning for him to sit down.

Lucy gave him a warm smile and then took a sip from her mango juice. He crossed his arms, staring at the two. "So are you guys free tonight?"

Amy nudged Lucy by her elbow, she clearly liked the guy, a lot. Lucy rolled her eyes when they both said "Yes." at the same time.

He chuckled, his eyes glinting. "Great! So how about we go watch a movie or something?"

Amy giggled and flailed her arms in the air. "Sure! I'm craving popcorn!"

Lucy bit her lip, she couldn't help but wonder if she should tell Drake to tag along. She's staying at his place anyways, so she's bound to tell him. *I'm staying at Drake's place, oh my God.* That little fact wouldn't stop replaying in that head of hers. Speaking of Drake, he wasn't around in the cafeteria. He always seemed to disappear during breaks, but that's really none of her business. He didn't like crowds and she knew it. She took a deep breath, trying to ignore thoughts about him, which was impossible, but she had to try.

"Hello! Earth to Lucy," Amy waved a hand in front of Lucy's face.

She suddenly shook her head. "What?"

"We were deciding on what movie to watch. But you're obviously lost in thought and I know exactly 'who' you're thinking about," Amy wiggled her brows.

Lucy's face flushed bright pink. "Am not."

Josh's face fell as he stared right into Lucy's bright blue eyes. "You like that guy? I forgot his name, um…he's the one with the long red hair…"

Lucy fiddled with her earrings nervously. "I-I"

Amy cut her off for the second time today, but this time it was for her own good. "Oh, come on Josh, who would like a weirdo?"

Lucy glared at her friend and gritted her teeth. "He's not a weirdo! He's a beautiful person, on the outside and on the inside." She suddenly widened her eyes, realizing what she had just admitted.

"Babe, I wouldn't agree on the inside part, but I'm glad you think I'm beautiful." Drake winked at her, surprising everyone by his sudden appearance. He lowered his head to whisper huskily in Lucy's ear. "We're going to have so much fun, tonight." A rush of heat shot through her and pooled at the juncture of her thighs. His deep, hoarse voice was enough to make her go crazy in need. She blushed a deep shade of red and immediately turned her head around. She couldn't possibly get more embarrassed. Amy was staring at the two with wide eyes, while Josh was frowning, obviously irritated by Drake's presence. Drake took a seat right beside Lucy as he placed a possessive arm around her shoulders.

Josh furrowed his brows. "Not trying to be mean but who invited you to sit here?"

Drake rolled his eyes. "I don't need an invitation you fool. This is the 21st century, in case you haven't noticed."

His jaw tensed as he spat out. "Oh, I didn't know that with every century, jerks should increase in number."

Drake growled in annoyance. Lucy butted in, trying to get rid of the tension between those two. "So Drake, do you want to watch a movie with us tonight?"

Both Amy and Josh shot her a dark glare. She ignored them as she stared at Drake, waiting for an answer. He scrunched his nose in disgust. "I'm not going to watch a movie in the same room with this guy." He paused and then added, "And neither are you."

As soon as Josh grinned at his response, Drake suddenly changed his mind. "You know what? I'd love to join you guys. I'm sure Josh would love my company." His eyes darkened and he smirked wickedly.

Lucy gulped nervously, the show that Drake and Josh are going to pull off tonight would be more interesting than the movie itself. *That's exactly what I'm fearing. I just hope Drake controls his anger.*

"I don't like the way he fucking looks at you," Drake sneered as he pulled out a towel from his drawer, wanting to take a bath.

Lucy watched him pace back and forth in his bedroom while she twirled a hair strand around her finger nervously. "What do you mean?"

118

He drew nearer to her, their faces only mere inches away. Her breath got caught in her throat as soon as his soft, wet lips pressed against her neck. He ran his tongue along her neck and nipped it softly with his teeth, teasing her. She shivered all over with desire. Her heart was pounding so wildly, she was finally forced to gasp for air. He slightly pulled back to look at her now flushed face. His eyes bored into hers as he said in a low, dark tone. "I'm the only one who can look at you that way."

Lucy took a long, deep breath, feeling as though she had just ran a marathon. "Why are you acting this way? Josh is just a friend."

He chuckled darkly. "A friend? To you maybe, but to him, he surely wants to be more than just friends."

She had a puzzled expression on. "But he shouldn't want that! Amy really likes him."

He gently tucked back the loose strands of her hair behind her ears, sending warm tingles throughout her entire body. "If he dares touch you, I will rip his fucking throat out."

Lucy took several nervous gulps at the sound of possessiveness in his voice. No matter how cruel he seemed, she couldn't help but feel tempted by him, by all of him.

He then suddenly motioned for her to sit up straight. "Take off your shirt, I want to check if you have wounds or bruises of any sort."

Lucy's cheeks turned red and she immediately wrapped her arms around her chest. "What? No! I'd only be in my bra!"

Drake rolled his eyes as the corners of his lips lifted up in a smirk. "And what's so wrong with that? Don't worry, I won't be bothered at all." He winked.

She narrowed her eyes at him, not liking his sarcasm right now. He then ran a hand through his long locks and clenched his jaw. "Just take the damn shirt off."

She bit down on her bottom lip and hesitantly took off her shirt. She was glad she was wearing a black lace bra and not something embarrassing. His eyes widened as soon as they landed on her chest. "Black. I love black." He slowly licked his lips, his dark eyes glinting with desire.

She cleared her throat and crossed her arms over her chest. He then immediately shook his head and examined her bare tummy. Two minor cuts were visible just below her rib cage. He huffed as he got up to get the first aid kit. He later returned and got out alcohol, an antibiotic cream, a cloth, and bandages. He wetted a cloth with alcohol and slightly wiped both of her cuts with it. "This may sting a little," He breathed out. Once he applied a thin layer of antibiotic cream on both of her cuts, he covered them with the bandages. Lucy was watching him with wide, warm eyes the whole time. She was simply mesmerized by his actions. From the way he flexed his arms to clean her cuts, to the way he blew gently at them to relieve her from the stinging sensation. She couldn't help but get up and wrap her arms tightly around him. She didn't care that she was in her bra, she just wanted to hold him.

He didn't hug her back at first since he was taken aback by her sudden actions. He then slowly wrapped his arms around her bare waist and rested his head on her shoulder, breathing in the fragrance of her shampoo. She felt so good in his arms, he just wanted to hold her like this the whole night. Heat radiated off him and enfolded her. Her cheeks flushed light pink at the dirty thoughts she was having. She wanted to feel him, all of him. Her thoughts were suddenly interrupted as soon as she felt his gentle fingers tangle in her hair. He twirled her strands around his fingers very tenderly, watching them fall softly against her back. She automatically shut her eyes, loving the tingling sensation that warmed her heart. A simple action like playing with her hair caused her to feel such emotions, what if he actually touched her? Her body shivered with desire at the thought as she leaned into him. He tightened his grip around her waist, his chest pressed against her bra. He was holding her as if it was the last hug he'll ever get. She was somehow worried, but immediately shrugged off the thought.

He slightly pulled back to look at her. His eyes were filled with so many mixed emotions. It was hard for her to know what he was thinking, but she was a hundred percent sure that lust swirled in those dark eyes of his. He leaned in, their noses touching. She sucked in a breath, *is he going to kiss me?* And her question was immediately answered when he unfortunately brushed his lips against her cheek, his warm lips lingering there. His hand trailed up from her waist to her bare stomach, then to her neck, gently tugging her closer. Goosebumps formed wherever he touched, warm tingles running up and down her entire body. Just when she was about to hold him even closer, even tighter, he pulled away. She suddenly felt empty and cold, she wanted his warmth so badly.

She suddenly felt so exposed in just only her bra. She blushed uncontrollably and reached out for her shirt, wanting to cover herself up. Drake eyed her, the corners of his mouth curling up into a sexy smirk. "Don't hide yourself from me. Ever."

She gulped, her cheeks burning red. "I-I-"

He cut her off as he approached her. He whispered huskily, brushing his lips along the curve of her jaw. "Like I said, don't hide yourself from me. I will soon see you fully naked babe, so don't bother."

Lucy's mouth fell open, *how can he be so open about this?* "In your dreams," she said whilst putting on her shirt.

He chuckled and it was the best sound that she has ever heard. "Nah, I'll leave the fantasizing to you, you're really good at it." He winked, earning a dark glare from her.

She furrowed her brows. "I do not fantasize about you!"

He smirked wickedly as he took off his shirt and threw it on the floor, then he unbuckled his blue jeans and pulled them off. "I'm going to take a shower. If you want, you can join me and your fantasizing will come true. Well, that is if you picture me having-"

She immediately cut him off and let out a squeal, her eyes widening at his well-built body. Not like she hasn't seen him with boxers only before, but still she couldn't quite get used to it. He was such a breathtaking sight. She hadn't realized that she was holding her breath, she let it out as she stared at the drool-worthy planes of his six-pack. His body was a work of art. She swallowed hard when her eyes landed on his tight, black boxers. She felt herself tremble and forced her eyes to look up. He was staring at her the whole time, amusement filled in his eyes. "So you're thinking about joining me, huh?"

She looked away and flipped her hair back. "No. I'm not easy you know."

He drew nearer to her, his warm fingertips lifted her chin until she met his soft eyes. "I know. That's why you're still a virgin." He paused and gently cupped her face in his hands, then added, "And that little innocent fact is making it so hard for me to control myself around you."

Lucy was simply shocked. Sparks were now exploding inside of her. He had such an abnormal effect on her. She had never felt this way before. Yes, she was a virgin and she was so proud of it. It was really valuable to her, *but how did he know? Am I that inexperienced or something?* He then broke the tension. "I'm going to take my bath now, so just wait here."

As soon as he shut the bathroom door, she plopped herself down onto his bed. Her eyes searched his room until they landed on a familiar small, wooden box on his nightstand. She bit her lip, *should I open it?* She sat up straight and examined the box. She knew that it was wrong to invade his privacy and that he wouldn't want her to open it but she desperately wanted to know what was hidden in there. She took a deep breath and slowly yet hesitantly opened it. Knowing she would later feel guilty about it, she looked inside anyways. A thin, bright, blue bracelet with a writing on it rested inside the box. 'God is good' was written in black on it. A folded note was inside as well. She unfolded it and read it, 'from Annie and Scott, we love you'. The note was covered in dust, obviously given a few years ago. *Who are Annie and Scott? Could they be his parents? I'm sure they're not. He hated them...*She wondered as she placed the bracelet and the note back in the box and put it aside. She will have to keep this new info for herself right now. She'll ask him about it later, when the time is right.

"Let's just watch a movie without him, he's not coming," Drake spat out, tapping his foot against the ground as they all waited for Josh to show up.

Amy glared at him, crossing her arms. "He'll come."

Lucy couldn't stop thinking of who exactly could Annie and Scott be. Drake has been through a lot in his life, no wonder why he's the way he is. All she knows is that she won't give up on him like everyone did. She'll be there, always.

Josh finally showed up. "Hey guys, sorry I took long, had a couple of important things to do."

Drake rolled his eyes as he snaked his arm around Lucy's waist, pulling her to him. "Whatever. Now let's go choose a fuckin movie."

Lucy nudged Drake with her elbow, muttering. "Stop swearing."

Drake smirked, clearing his throat. "Oh yeah, I almost forgot I have a saint standing right by my side." He chuckled as he mocked her. "Can you ever forgive my terrible sins?"

She ignored his silly comment as she trudged beside him. "So guys what do you want to watch?" Josh asked.

"Let's watch Annabelle 2," Drake grinned, wiggling his brows.

Lucy and Amy both yelled at the same time with terror, "No!"

Josh drew nearer to Lucy. "Would you like to watch a romantic movie?" He winked at her, a huge smile plastered on his face.

Drake butted in, his eyes were now dark, black pools. "Would you like to taste one of my punches?" He mocked him cruelly.

Amy huffed as she jutted her lower lip out in a pout. "I'm still here if somebody wants my opinion!"

Josh clenched his fists, ignoring Amy's comment. "I was talking to Lucy. Mind your own business Drake."

Drake gritted his teeth. "Lucy's mine, so fuck off." He looked him straight in the eyes with so much hate. Josh took a few steps backwards, gulping nervously. His hands were slightly trembling at his sides.

Lucy cleared her throat. "I'm no one's." She looped her arm through Amy's and said, "Come on." Even though she really was in no mood for such acts, she couldn't help but smile to herself at what he just said.

"Hey, wait up! I won't kill the bastard just yet!" Drake shouted. Lucy and Amy glanced at each other and then nodded their heads. The two guys followed, both of them shooting daggers at each other. This is going to be one long, long night.

How did they end up watching Annabelle 2? They all had no single clue. Josh was seated next to Amy, and Drake was of course seated right next to Lucy. He made sure Lucy was seated at the end of the row so that nobody would sit next to her, except him. Josh wasn't that close and that was a huge relief for Drake. He knew he was being somewhat domineering, but he just couldn't help it.

"Drake, I really don't want to watch this scary movie," Lucy whispered in his ear. She wrapped her arms around herself as she avoided looking at the wide screen in front of her. It was really dark and the movie was loud and horrifying.

He huffed, exhaling loudly. "Lucy, it's just a movie. Besides, you somehow witnessed two deaths. You couldn't possibly be scared of that." He pointed his finger to the screen that was now displaying a weird, creepy looking doll.

He did not just bring that up. How can he talk about such sensitive topics so easily? He didn't even show any emotion. Lucy's eyes widened, she really wanted to know if Drake truly had something to do with the death of those poor people. She kept ignoring such thoughts for a while now, but she just had to know the truth soon. She gulped nervously, what could she possibly do if it were him anyways? Well, she'll surely freak the hell out and God knows what else.

Drake suddenly tugged her by her arm, a concerned look plastered on his face. "Why are you crying?"

Lucy whipped her head round to face him, she hadn't noticed that she was actually crying. She hastily wiped away her tears and batted her eyelids, trying to push back the other tears that were threatening to fall down her face. "It's nothing."

He furrowed his brows as he cupped her face gently in his rough yet tender hand and lifted her face up. Her red, watery eyes met his. She felt so vulnerable, she wasn't able to face him and she didn't even know why. He leaned in and whispered softly, his warm, sweet breath fanning her lips, "Don't you ever cry. I always want to see that beautiful, sparkly smile of yours. You hear?"

126

Did Drake just compliment me? She didn't know if she should squeal with joy or simply check his temperature, because Drake somehow never complimented her. A warm, small smile crept over her lips and her eyes glistened. Drake grabbed her hand in his and squeezed a little, trying to reassure her that he's here.

A sudden wild, ear-piercing scream made Lucy jump in her seat and involuntarily place her hands firmly against her ears. The popcorn flew everywhere and was now scattered all over the floor. Another scream followed, and then another, Lucy now had her eyes shut so tight. When the screaming finally stopped, she slowly opened her eyes and let out her breath in a long sigh of relief. She noticed that she was not in her seat. She was in Drake's lap. *Uh-oh*, she began to squirm away as her face blushed tomato red. Drake wrapped his arm tightly around her waist, not wanting her to move. His other hand rested on her thigh and he leaned in to whisper in her ear, "All our popcorn is on the floor," He paused, easing his hand up her inner thigh. "And now you owe me by remaining in your current seat." He patted his leg as he smirked.

Tingles of pleasure erupted all over her body as soon as his warm hand made contact with her cold skin. Her heart was hammering in her chest as she sucked in a deep breath. She wasn't able to think right at all. When his fingers rose higher, she immediately stood up. She was breathing heavily while she smoothed out the creases on her dress. "I'm going to go to the um…restroom."

Drake's eyes darkened and he slowly nodded his head. "Be quick, babe."

Lucy rolled her eyes and sprinted out of the cinema hall. As she made her way towards the restroom, she noticed that there was no sign of anyone. They were all obviously inside, watching a certain movie of their choice. Whew, I'm so glad I'm out of there. She really didn't want to watch this movie and Drake was being very intense somehow. She entered through the door and immediately looked in the mirror. She fixed her hair with her fingers and tried to comb out the knots. She suddenly heard footsteps of someone coming her way. She shrugged, it could be anyone.

Taking out her pink lipstick from her purse, she abruptly felt someone's presence behind her. Just as she was about to move away, she was pinned against the wall and a rough hand was now placed over her mouth. Her eyes widened as she squirmed in his grasp. It was a man, an old man. He seemed to be in his early fifties. He had grey hair and a long beard. She tried to wrench free from his grip as she twisted and turned, but it was no use, he was too strong for her. She let out a muffled scream and kneed him in the groin. The only reaction she got was a smirk. *What the hell?*

He clenched his jaw and looked her in the eyes. "You're going to have to do better than that." He paused and then added, "Besides, I don't want to hurt you. I just want to enlighten you about something, well, about someone."

Lucy's chest rose and fell, trying to control her rapid breathing. *What did this man want?*

He huffed. "What I want? Nothing." *Whoa! Did he just read my mind or something? Nah, it's probably written all over my face. Yes, I'm positive.*

He continued as he tightened his grip on her. "If I were you Lucy, I'd be more careful with whom I hang out with. You sure are clueless, that's why I bothered showing up to warn you before you get yourself further involved."

She furrowed her brows in confusion. *What the hell is he talking about? And how does he know my name?*

He then winked at her. "You didn't notice who I am yet? Oh yeah, you were too busy ogling your boyfriend."

Her heart was pounding wildly. *Oh shit! It's that guy from the woods! He was the one talking to Drake! Wait, what about Drake?*

The man sighed deeply. "Don't be afraid please. I'm not the one you should fear. It's the one you're waiting for to come get you right now. That's the person you should fear."

CHAPTER 10

I should fear Drake? What? Why? What does he mean?

Lucy let out another muffled scream, she couldn't take this any longer. She wanted to get away from that nutty man, but first of all she wanted to ask him all the questions that were now playing in her head. She wanted real answers. Whoever this man was, he surely was keeping something from her. She whipped her head from side to side, hoping he'd understand to let her go or at least to let her speak.

He eyed her intently. "Promise me you won't scream."

Lucy immediately nodded her head. He then slowly lifted his hand from her mouth. She let out a long, deep breath as she touched her trembling lips with her fingertips. He still had his grip on her but at least she could speak now. She wanted to cry out so badly but she knew that it wouldn't be such a smart thing to do, so she remained quiet.

He gritted his teeth and tapped his foot against the floor. "I'm going to leave now before Drake comes. I advise you not to tell him about our little encounter, it's for the best. Be wise. Good bye, Lucy."

Lucy furrowed her brows, *who the hell does he think he is? I'm going to tell Drake for sure. I don't trust him.* "Wait. Who are you?"

He let go of her as he took a few steps backwards. "You won't believe me if I told you, so knowing my name would be quite enough. The name's Bernard." With that, he waved bye and headed out the door.

She got out of the restroom as well, searching for him. There was no sign of that strange man. That's odd. She really had so much to ask and he just disappeared like that. Heading back to the cinema, she noticed someone coming towards her, Drake, a fuming Drake.

"Where the fuck have you been? I was so damn worried!" Drake yelled and clenched his fists at his sides.

Lucy fiddled with the hem of her dress as she had an inner battle with herself. *Should I tell him? Oh, what the hell.* "A man...he um...wouldn't let me go until he-"

Drake cut her off as his eyes widened in horror. He bit his bottom lip harshly and cracked his knuckles. "What man? Come on, speak!"

She stared into his dark, steamy eyes. He was infuriated. She gulped nervously. "He told me to ge-get away from you."

Drake's furious look turned into a pained one. His face fell as he clenched his jaw, irritated. "Fuck."

Lucy bit her inner cheek, thinking of a way to calm him down. *Why was he so mad anyways? Shouldn't he be relieved that I was okay or something?*

He then rubbed his face with both of his hands and drew closer to her, his eyes glistening with sorrow. "Go ahead, leave me. I'm not stopping you."

He looked away, his face contorted with bitterness. Lucy lifted her hand and softly caressed his warm cheek, causing him to turn and meet her deep gaze. She drew even nearer, their chests touching. "I'm not going anywhere."

As soon as those words left her lips, she felt him relax against her. She wrapped her arms around his waist tightly and buried her face against his strong chest, breathing him in. He gladly returned her hug, smiling to himself. He smoothed her hair and then rested his chin on the top of her head. He began to gently sway from side to side, tightening his grip on her. "Oh, Lucy."

She gradually looked up, staring into his intense dark, blue eyes that she loved so much. "I don't believe the bad things they say about you, Drake."

He licked his lips, his eyes glinting mischievously. "You should."

Lucy's eyes widened. *What has he done in order to think so lowly about himself?* "What do you mean?"

He chuckled darkly, swallowing hard. "I wouldn't want you to run away, now would I? So you don't have to know, for now."

Lucy cocked her head as she crossed her arms nervously. "Are you a murderer?"

Drake's mouth fell open at her straightforward question. His eyes dangerously darkened and his breathing was fast. "I wouldn't ask such a question if I were you."

Just as she was about to speak again, he interrupted her. "That man, did you know his name?"

Lucy nodded, wishing her question could be answered, *couldn't he just say no and make me feel better?* "Yes, it's Bernard."

Drake's nostrils flared as his blood boiled with rage. "That little piece of shit. I'll show him." He paused and then added, irritated. "Next time, don't interfere! I repeat. Do. Not. Interfere. Am I clear enough?" He was obviously referring to the time she followed him and eavesdropped. She'll make sure not to do something like that ever again. She was actually scared of the truth. *I'm scared of what he might be hiding from me, it is better not to know, right?* She asked herself, unsure about that notion of hers.

Drake broke her train of thought with his booming voice. "Come on, let's go back inside before your friends start getting suspicious."

Lucy didn't move, she was not going to let this go just yet. "I want to know who that man is! Aren't you going to tell me?"

Drake sighed deeply. "No. Now let's go back inside." *Ugh, he's so difficult!*

"That movie was awesome! So wicked! Too bad you missed half of it," Josh said to Lucy and Drake as he shrugged his shoulders.

Drake smiled mockingly. "Oh, really now? I thought 'romantic movies' were your thing."

Josh glared at him. Amy crossed her arms. "I didn't like it one bit. I'm just glad that Josh was in there with me." She batted her eyelids at him.

Lucy placed her hands on her hips as she looked at Amy. "I was in there too, you know."

Amy rolled her eyes and then gently tapped Josh's shoulder. "Um...shouldn't we get going now?"

Josh quickly nodded his head. "Yeah, I guess." He drew nearer to Lucy and hugged her tightly, earning a dark, cold death glare from Drake which made him let go. "See you guys. We'll make sure to hang out some other time."

"If you make it out alive," Drake murmured in a very low voice. Lucy nudged him by her elbow and scowled at him defiantly.

Amy waved bye to both of them. "I'll text you tonight," She yelled out to Lucy as she trudged by Josh's side.

I was left with Drake.

Lucy's phone suddenly began ringing. She looked at the screen, "Mom". *Oh, great.*

"Hello," Lucy pressed her phone against her ear.

"Baby! You're okay, right? Everything's fine? Aren't you going to come home-" Her mom sobbed.

Lucy cut her off. "I'm fine, mom. Well, no, I'm staying over at Drake's for a little while..."

"No! He's dark and violent-"

Lucy interrupted her again, irritated. "Violent? Dad's the one who's dark and violent. At least Drake cares about me, at least he helped me!" Lucy hadn't realized that she was yelling now.

"I'm sorry, I'm so sorry," Her mom continued sobbing over the line.

"It's okay, mom. Just please give me some time. I'll come back when I can face that animal," Lucy sighed deeply.

"But Lucy dear, your father is in the hospital now, so you can come home..."

"I hope you understand but I need time away. I promise I'll be back soon though. Take care, bye," Lucy held back the bitter tears, she won't cry, no, she'll try and be strong.

"Call me soon. I love you," Her mom whispered, her voice cracking a little.

"Love you too," With that, she hung up. She took a deep breath, and turned around to face Drake who was watching her intently the whole time.

Drake shoved his hands in his pockets as he swayed slightly on his feet. "Is everything okay?"

He looked adorable with his long hair in his face, oh, how she wanted to run her hands through them. She shook her head, bringing herself back to reality. "Yeah."

"Good. Now, come," He stretched out his hand for her to take as he pulled her to his side.

Lucy yawned and sat down on Drake's bed. She surely wasn't going to sleep so soon. *Nope. I want to spend some time with him.* He came out of the bathroom and sat down beside her. He cleared his throat as he tapped his fingers against the mattress. *Is he nervous? Oh my God. Drake's nervous. I should be happy, right?* She bit her lip in thought.

"Lucy," Drake whispered huskily. *He sounded so sexy.* She gulped and felt her knees go weak.

"Yes?" She stared at his strong yet tense features.

He ran a hand through his long red hair, tugging gently at its ends. "When Bernard said that you should fear me, did leaving ever cross your mind? I mean did you want to run away from me or something?"

Lucy's eyes widened while she stared at him. He looked like a lost, little kid. *Did everyone misjudge him? Did they all want nothing to do with him?* She felt sorry for him. She wanted to take away his pain. Even though he looked weak, she couldn't help but smile, he truly cared about her opinion of him. She gave him a reassuring smile. "Nope."

His face brightened up as he rubbed the back of his neck. "Thank you."

"For what?" She puckered her brow.

He drew nearer to her, his thigh slightly touching hers, and that itself made her shudder all over. He stroked her face gently with his long fingers. "For not running away."

Lucy then suddenly threw herself at him and wrapped her arms around his neck, knocking him over backward. This took him by surprise. Lucy's cheeks reddened as soon as she realized that she was on top of him. She began to move but was stopped when Drake instantly flipped them over and pinned her down, underneath him. He was leaning on his left hand to support his weight, the other was softly brushing Lucy's hair off her face. A full-body shiver raced over her from head to toe as she felt her heart beat accelerate. He knitted his brows in concentration and stared at her, his eyes filled with mixed emotions. Lucy didn't dare utter a single word, she was simply mesmerized by him, wondering what he'll do next.

He slowly bent his head, his warm lips planting delicate, wet kisses up and down her neck. She sucked in a breath and shut her eyes, enjoying the pleasurable feeling. He then slightly pulled back and looked at her parted lips. His hot breath fanning across her lips as he drew nearer and nearer. His warm mouth suddenly closed over hers. They both felt the shock wave as soon as their lips met. Bolts of electricity shot through her entire body as their lips moved in perfect sync. The kiss was hot and demanding. She moaned softly and he deepened the kiss, sliding his tongue inside her mouth. Her fingers curled in his hair as they turned and twisted their tongues around. He pulled her firmly against his hard body, feeling the heat that radiated off her.

She was breathing heavily, in and out, and her body was on fire. Her legs were wobbly, she literally couldn't move. He licked and sucked her lower lip softly, growling against her mouth. Her eyes widened as a rush of heat ran north and south through her body. She wrapped her arms tighter around him, never wanting him to let go, ever.

Just like that, he suddenly broke the kiss and got off her. He buried his face in his hands. "Fuck."

Lucy gulped, *what was wrong?* Her cheeks flushed tomato red. He looked up at her, his face contorted with pain. "I'm sorry. I-"

She cut him off, standing up and placing her hands on her hips. "Stop." She paused and then added, "Is kissing me that awful?" She swallowed hard.

He rubbed his temple. "No! I just-"

She cut him off again. "Save it." Tears trickled down her cheeks as she stormed into the bathroom and shut the door behind her with a loud slam.

He gritted his teeth as he swore under his breath. He stood against the door, knocking softly. "Please open the door. Let me explain."

"Go away," She mumbled as she sniffed loudly.

He then opened the door and got in. "You do know it's open, right?"

She glared at him and huffed. He cracked his knuckles nervously. "Lucy, I..."

She eyed him curiously from head to toe, waiting for him to say something. When he didn't, she immediately looked away.

He sighed deeply and shut his eyes tight. "I don't want to grow attached to yo-you..."

Lucy whipped her head round, her eyes widening in surprise. "What?"

He clenched his jaw and she realized how serious he was. "Nobody stays Lucy. That's why I don't hang out with people, nobody really cares...I don't know how I'll take it when you realize who you're actually spending time with and leave."

So this is what it was all about? He was afraid that I'll leave one day. She approached him and crossed her arms firmly against her chest. "How many times am I going to have to tell you that I'm not going anywhere? I promise, Drake."

He forced out a smile. "I wish I can believe that."

Her face fell. "Well, believe it Mr. Negative."

He smirked. "Another nickname?"

A wide, warm grin spread across her face. "Yes. Now, come on, I want to talk to you a little before we sleep."

His brows rose. "Talk? Aren't we talking now?"

She rolled her eyes as she grabbed his arm and pulled him out. She sat down on his bed and patted the space next to her. "I want to get to know you better."

"Oh boy," He groaned.

"So, what do you usually do every day?" Lucy asked as she rested her chin in the palm of her hand and stared at him with warm, wide eyes.

He crossed his arms, raising his eyebrows. "Seriously? What kind of question is that?"

She rolled her eyes at him. "Oh, would you just answer it?"

He shrugged his shoulders. "Nope. How about I ask?"

Lucy eyed him curiously. Drake never asked her any questions, well, any random questions.

"What do you like about me the most?" Drake whispered softly. Lucy's eyes shot open, *did he ask what I think he just asked?*

She fiddled with her fingers nervously, avoiding his intense gaze. "Um..."

Drake cleared his throat. "Well?"

She narrowed her eyes at him as she bit her inner cheek. She didn't know what to say at all. To her, that was a really tough question. She accidentally blurted out, "Your eyes." *And your hair, your nose, your lips, your shoulders, your chest...Okay, that was awkward.*

His mouth twisted into a wry smile. "Why?"

She twirled her dark, blonde strands around her finger. "Sometimes I think they're magical."

Drake's eyes widened in shock as his whole body stiffened. "They're not. Not one bit."

"But they always change color somehow! I mean sometimes they're blue, sometimes they're this dark shade of blue, and other times they get so dark, I think they turn black. They're bea-beautiful," Lucy blabbered as she flailed her arms in the air, trying to make sense. She then murmured in a very, low tone, only for her to hear. "You're beautiful." She slapped her hands over her mouth after realizing what she had just admitted.

His eyes looked broken and empty. "Oh, Lucy. I'm not beautiful, I'm a monster." He buried his face in the crook of her neck, breathing her in.

She softly ran her fingers through his thick hair, trying to comfort him. "You may think you are. I don't know what the hell you did Drake, but you're no monster to me."

He nuzzled his nose up against the back of her neck, slightly tickling her. He lifted his head and gently kissed the soft spot just below her ear, making her shudder against him. His lips then trailed kisses down her throat and along her collarbone, his tongue flicking against a sensitive spot there. Lucy couldn't help herself as she let her head fall back, giving him better access. His lips, his touch, his everything was her undoing.

"You're the one who's beautiful, Lucy. Do you want to know what I do every day? I sit and think, how the hell did I get so damn lucky to have you around?" He whispered against her ear, causing warm tingles to burst through her body.

She giggled, blushing bright red. "You're such a romantic."

He ran a hand through his hair, disheveling it. "See? I can be a sweetheart sometimes." He paused then added as he tapped his finger against his lips. "I think I deserve a new nickname now."

She rolled her eyes playfully. "How about hopeless romantic?" she winked.

He furrowed his brows, crossing his arms firmly against his chest. "How about no."

She laughed out loud as she clutched her stomach tightly.

"What's so funny?" He puckered his brow.

Her lips spread into a wide smile. "You're so cute!"

He placed his hand on his heart as he feigned a pained expression. "Cute? Really? You're kidding, right? Because that's pretty offensive if you ask me."

Lucy let herself fall back on the bed, giggling her heart out.

He smirked, standing in front of her. "I'll show you cute." With that, he bent down and began to tickle her and she swirled, protecting her sides with her arms.

"No-o-o! Sto-o-o-p!" She giggled uncontrollably. She tried pushing him away, but it was no use. She yelled out. "Please!"

"Nope. Not until you take it back," He smirked mischievously.

She squealed as he attacked the side of her neck with his fingers. "Fine! I take it back!" She breathed out.

He gave her a lopsided smile and stopped, watching her chest rise and fall due to her rapid breathing.

"You're a jerk," She flipped her hair back, pretending to be affected.

He licked his lips. "Now that's more like it."

A yawn forced itself out of Lucy's lips. She batted her eyelids as she stared at Drake, who now had a blank expression on. His eyes glinted. "Come on, you better get some sleep."

She suddenly sat straight up, her eyes widening. "Oh, no! I didn't pack my things...I need to get some of my clothes and my books! Ugh! I should have thought about this earlier."

He chuckled at her. "Don't worry, we'll sneak out at about three in the morning. Everyone would be asleep then."

Lucy had a puzzled expression on. "At three?"

He let out a deep breath. "Yes. Now, go to sleep. I'll wake you up..."

"What about you?" She cocked her head to the side.

He lifted the covers, motioning for her to get under them. "I don't want to sleep now."

She nodded her head, tired of trying to argue with him. She slowly closed her eyes, Drake's sexy figure lingering in her thoughts as she drifted off.

"Wake up babe," Drake gently nudged Lucy by her shoulder.

She twisted and turned in her sleep. "Wh-what?"

He sighed deeply. "Come on, get up. It's three."

She knitted her brows in confusion as she slowly rubbed her eyes. "What's free?"

He lightly slapped his hand against his forehead. "Oh, boy." He scooped her up and put her on his shoulder, causing her to squeal.

She let her arms fall against his back. "Oh, three!" She sighed. "I'm awake! I'm awake!"

Once they got out, she stood beside him and watched him bring his motorcycle to life. She really didn't feel like riding a motorcycle right now, it's three a.m. But she somehow didn't mind, because she was going with Drake. The ride won't be bad, no, not at all.

Lucy got in her room through the open window with the help of Drake who had lifted her up. Her mom always seemed to leave her window open when she wasn't home. She made sure not to make a sound as she grabbed the biggest bag she owned and began packing. While she was heading to her closet, she accidentally tripped over a pair of shoes that were scattered on her carpet. She landed on the floor with a thud. *Next time, I'm so going to clean this room.*

Her brother suddenly appeared at her bedroom door, his eyes filled with concern. "Lucy?" Saying that, he immediately approached her and pulled her close in an embrace.

CHAPTER 11

"I'm sorry," Chad murmured against Lucy's hair as he shut his eyes tight.

She took a deep breath, pulling away from his arms. "It's okay-"

He immediately cut her off. "No! It's not okay!" He pressed his lips together. "I should have done something! But instead I stood there like an idiot!"

She sighed deeply. "I know but you had your own reasons..."

He rubbed his temple, frustrated. "That's not an excuse for me anymore. I'm twenty years old! I should get over it. I should just face that bastard." He paused and then added, "To be honest, I'm really glad Drake had beaten him up." Shoving his hands in his pockets, he looked up at Lucy with a cold, intense gaze.

She pecked him on the cheek. "It's okay, really. Stop pressuring yourself." Giving him a faint smile, she said, "I have to go now. Drake is waiting for me."

He shook his head as he looked away. "When are you coming back?"

"Soon, I guess. I need a little time away; mom understands," With that, she hurriedly packed the rest of what she needed, and made her way to her window.

She glanced at Chad once again and waved bye to him, smiling.

"Hold on tight, Lucy. How many times should I tell you?" Drake sneered. She could clearly see his annoyed expression in the rear view mirror.

Lucy rolled her eyes as she clutched him even tighter, her arms wrapped firmly around his well-built torso. She felt him tense against her then relax as he puckered his brow at her and revved up his motorcycle. She pressed her legs against him and rested her face on his back, smiling to herself.

"Can't get comfy enough?" He smirked, wiggling his brows at her.

She ignored him and Drake chuckled. "We're almost there."

As soon as they arrived, Lucy changed into her pajamas and immediately jumped into bed. She was utterly tired. Just as she was about to close her eyes and drift off, the iron frame of the bed squeaked softly as Drake slightly lifted up the covers and crawled in next to her. Her eyes widened and she curled into a fetal position.

He snaked his arms around her waist from behind, pressing his warm body against hers. He brushed his lips below her earlobe, causing a shiver to ripple through her. "Let me hold you while you sleep."

His words instantly warmed her heart as a smile crept over her lips. When she didn't answer, he tightened his hold on her and pulled her even closer to him. Her cheeks flushed light pink. She wrapped her hands around his and cuddled into him. Burying his face in her tousled hair, he inhaled deeply. "I need you, Lucy."

Goosebumps erupted all over her body, she really needed him too. He nuzzled his nose against her hair, murmuring softly. "Goodnight, love." With that, she drifted off in a long, comfortable sleep like never before.

Lucy woke up feeling cold and empty. She furrowed her brows as she spread her arms against Drake's bed. Her eyes shot open as soon as she realized that he was not in it with her. *Has he woken up already?* She sat up straight and looked around the room. There was no sign of him. Her eyes then landed on a tiny piece of paper that rested on the nightstand. She got up and slowly opened it, hoping it wasn't what she thought it would be.

"I have some important things to do. Will be back soon x

P.S. There's ham and cheese in the fridge. Eat."

Important things to do? She bit her bottom lip hard. There's something fishy about this. She'll ask Drake about this later. She rubbed the back of her neck, then picked out a cute turquoise dress from her bag. She put it on and went to the kitchen. She opened the fridge, and for the first time, she actually noticed that Drake only has ham, cheese, water, and peanut butter in his fridge. *Jeez, that's all he eats?* She shrugged and took out a bottle of water.

Lucy looked at the time on her cell, it's been an hour already and he hasn't come back yet. *Where is he?* She pouted and crossed her arms like a child. She'll have to wait. This is turning out to be one boring Saturday. Her cell suddenly began to ring. She narrowed her eyes at the screen, "Amy."

"Hey," Lucy answered her call.

"Turn on the news now!" Amy squealed over the phone.

She furrowed her brows. "Why?"

"They have found another body! Oh Lucy, this is horrible!" Amy's voice was trembling.

"What? Oh my God! How many have they found up till now? Four?" Her stomach turned to liquid as she waited for Amy to answer.

"Yeah! I'm scared, I'm really scared. What if this murderer comes at us next?" Amy was panicking now, she was literally worried to death.

"Don't worry, I'm sure we're safe," Lucy tried reassuring her, even though she was starting to freak out herself. She tapped her finger against her lips, curious. "What time did they find the body?" Switching the TV on, she waited for an answer.

"I'm not sure, but it was late at night," Amy gulped.

She bit her nail and stared at the screen in front of her. Her eyes were glued to the photo that was being displayed, it was a photo of the body, an old, dead woman. Lucy slapped her hands over her mouth, gasping in horror. *Who'd have the heart to kill such innocent people?* She breathed heavily, all she knew was that this person surely knows how to avoid getting caught by the police. She switched her attention back to Amy. "What did you say? Sorry, I-I just saw the b-body and-"

Amy cut her off. "I know, I know." She paused and then added, "Look, just stay with Drake and you'll be fine. As for me, I'm so not going anywhere today. I'm staying with my folks." With that, she instantly hung up the phone.

"Wait!" *Drake's not here.* Her face fell, hoping he was okay and that he'll come back soon. She hugged her knees to her chest and rested her cheek on one knee. She really wanted Drake by her side right now. She just couldn't help it, her feelings towards him were intense and uncontrollable. They grew stronger and stronger every time. *Oh Drake, what are you doing to me?*

Droplets of rain splattered against the window; it was raining heavily now. Lucy wrapped her arms around herself, trying to keep her flesh warm. She simply sat there and watched the rain trail down the glass window as the pitter-patter noise engulfed her. She was starting to feel apprehensive; she had called Drake over and over for the past twenty minutes, but there was no reply from him whatsoever. She bit her bottom lip hard out of irritation, *how could he leave me like this? Where could he be?* And just like that, the door clicked open. Lucy's eyes widened while she took in Drake's appearance. He was soaking wet, water dripped from the hem of his coat onto the floor as he stood there with a dark, cold expression. His eyes were so dark, Lucy couldn't help but gasp out loud. She had never seen them this dark before, they were literally two black pools. She traced her gaze up his face and stopped there, at his forehead. A scratch was visible. *Has he been in a fight? What's going on?* Lucy took slow, deep breaths, trying to calm the wild beating of her heart.

"Drake..." Her voice trailed away. She had so many questions to ask, she didn't know where to start.

His jaw tensed as his eyes seared right through her, making her vulnerable under his intense gaze. "Don't. I'm not in the mood for an inquiry." With that, he walked right past her and went to the bathroom.

Inquiry? She furrowed her brows, no, she won't keep quiet. She'll ask him what she wants to ask. She deserved some answers. Lucy followed him and stood by the door. He was wetting a cotton ball with alcohol and then dabbing at his small cut. "Why didn't you answer my calls?" Lucy asked nervously.

He threw the cotton ball in the trash can, stood right in front of her, and eyed her intently. "I was busy."

She blinked at his response, *what crawled up his ass and died?* "What's wrong with you?"

"Nothing." He replied coolly, taking off his drenched coat.

Her face fell, she felt as if she'd been torn in two. "I was so worried about you." She slid down the wall to the floor and buried her face in her hands. She'll never understand why he affected her so much, but deep down, she somehow already knew.

Drake's eyes softened and then quickly hardened again. He crouched down to her level and pushed away her loose strands gently. "I'm fine, see?" He pointed his index finger at himself.

She looked up at him, her glistening eyes glued to his. "Where were you?"

He sighed deeply, not wanting to answer her. "I had some important things to do, I already mentioned it. Didn't you read the note?"

She licked her dry lips as she crossed her arms. "Are you going to keep giving me dumb, vague answers?" Leaning in, she reached out and traced her fingers softly along his forehead, careful not to touch his cut. "What happened?" She whispered, worry cracking her voice.

He took her hand in his and lowered it to her side. "It's just a scratch Lucy. I'm not a kid."

"You didn't answer my question. Why won't you tell me anything? I have told you several times that I won't judge you! You can trust me, Drake. What should I do to prove it to you?" Lucy was now breathing heavily, her chest rising and falling. She wanted him to open up. She wanted to know his deepest, darkest secrets.

He rubbed his temple, his eyes shut tight. "It's not you, Lucy. It's me. I'm not ready to tell you..." He cupped her face in his hands and pressed his forehead against hers. His face was so close to hers, she could see the glint of stubble on his chin, and she could feel his warm breath fanning against her cheek. She stared up at him, his eyes not so dark anymore. They were their welcoming shade of blue, which she adored. Her heart seemed to stop and then soar as his thumb traced her half-open lips. She started to pant, wanted to beg him for his lips, his mouth, and his tongue. She had such a bad day, she wanted his kiss to soothe her. She flicked her tongue across his thumb, causing him to stiffen. His eyes darkened dangerously as he clenched his jaw hard. "Lucy, what are you trying to do?"

"Trying to make yo-you w-want to kiss me," She gulped nervously, his strong gaze burning a trail across her face.

He inched his head closer, his lips pressed together tightly. "Oh Lucy, I always want to kiss you."

"Then why don't you?" She asked, her eyes pleading him. She felt so desperate but she couldn't hide it anymore.

He took a long, deep breath. "I don't want you to get attached to me. Is it so hard to understand? I'm being selfish for simply even staying around you. Trust me, I tried getting away from you, but I couldn't. So kissing you constantly would be a huge mistake-"

She cut him off. "It's my choice, get it through your big, fat head. I want you, I don't think you're bad for me or whatever. I think you're the best thing that's ever happened to me, as cheesy as that sounds."

"You want me?" He smirked wickedly, loving the words that rolled off her tongue.

She nodded, ignoring his attempt to embarrass her. Without warning, he closed the space between them, his warm lips moving over hers sensually. Her eyes fluttered closed as she wrapped her arms around his neck, her fingers twining in his long red hair. When his tongue ran over her lips, she parted them and gave him access. His tongue explored her mouth, conquering, tasting her sweetness. His hands slowly ran up and down her thighs and her sides while he kissed her over and over. Her heart thundered as pleasure and heat coiled low in her stomach. Easing her mouth away from his, she kissed her way down his neck, over his chest and along his abdomen. He groaned with want and desire, stiffening at the softness of her lips against his skin. He tilted her head up gently, their breathing ragged. "Stop, love."

She narrowed her eyes at him, the pain visible on her face. He tucked her hair back behind her ear, his eyes filled with passion. "I don't want to have to take away your innocence." He bit his inner cheek, his eyes darkening once again. "Not just yet."

She gave him a faint smile and stood up. The sound of the heavy rain seemed to cease, she had almost forgotten that it was raining outside. Drake made his way to the kitchen, motioning for her to follow him. "Are you hungry?"

She shook her head hastily. She was famished. "Let's go have a decent meal then," He chuckled.

"Great," She smiled widely.

He ran a hand through his hair. "So, what are you in for?"

"DD's burgers!" She squealed like a toddler.

He rolled his eyes. "Seriously? Anything but that."

"Oh, come on!" She jutted her lower lip out in a pout.

His mouth lifted into an amused smirk. "How about we go somewhere my choice and we'll get to talk. And by talk, I mean, my answers won't be 'dumb' and 'vague'." He quoted her.

Her face lit up like a Christmas tree. "Deal."

Lucy looped her arm through Drake's as they entered through the door. They were going to eat at the restaurant that Drake had chosen, which was called Aaron's corner. She couldn't help but smile to herself, loving the fact that they looked like an actual couple. She wouldn't mind spending every single day with him, then again, she wouldn't mind spending eternity with him. They took a seat at a table that was right next to the window.

"So Lucy, Luce, Lu-lu, Loo, Lucette-" Drake was cut off by Lucy who nudged him hard by her elbow.

She huffed, batting her eyelids. "Enough with the ugly nicknames."

His lips twisted into a smirk. "As I was saying, what would you like to eat, Lucy Loo?"

She rolled her eyes, ignoring his childishness. "Mmm." She tapped her fingers against her lips as she eyed the menu.

Drake rested his chin in the palm of his hand, waiting for her to pick something. When she didn't, he crossed his arms and narrowed his eyes at her. "Oh come on, you wanted to eat burgers, so go ahead and make up your mind."

She glared. "Correction. I wanted DD's burgers."

"Seriously?" He let out a deep breath. She pouted, leaning in towards him. Drake's eyes glinted with amusement. "Trust me, you're going to love it here just as much."

He stood up and went to order food for the two of them. Lucy bit her lip anxiously, *should I ask him about Annie and Scott?* She shook her head, maybe she shouldn't. She didn't want to ruin that happy mood of his. She'd give anything to see that warm, beautiful smile on his face. She sighed deeply, no matter how much she wanted him to be blissful, she'll have to face him and get an answer, well, answers. Just as she was about to further argue with herself about whether or not she should ask him, Drake came back holding two trays.

"There you go," He said as he placed her tray in front of her, winking flirtatiously.

She smiled, her heart melting at his small gestures. "Thank you." She stared down at the sandwich which was so mouthwatering and scrumptious, and then up to his face. "What's it called? I have um...never eaten here before."

He shook his head. "I know. I noticed. Yours is obviously a grilled chicken sandwich. I thought I'd order this for you since grilled chicken is healthier..." His voice trailed away, and he ran a hand through his hair.

Lucy blushed as she twirled her loose strands around her fingers. He cleared his throat and continued. "And mine is a spicy, chicken grand sandwich."

Her eyes widened, taking in the size of it. "You sure are hungry."

"Yep," He said and took one huge bite off his sandwich.

She sipped her orange juice. "So, are you going to tell me the important things that you had to do?"

His eyes darkened and his chewing became very slow. "To be honest, no."

Her mouth fell open. "But I thought-"

He cut her off. "I lied. I just wanted you to tag along and to actually feed you."

She felt her throat constrict. "Please."

Wanting to wipe out that frown off her face, he spoke, "I left late at night when I made sure you were warm and asleep."

She furrowed her brows. "Why? I-I thought you left in the morning."

"No, I didn't," He bit his bottom lip hard.

Lucy had a lot of thoughts racing in her head, *why won't he just spit it out?* "You're not going to tell me, are you?"

"I had to satisfy my needs..." He stated casually as he took another bite off his half-eaten sandwich.

What needs? She felt confused as ever. She took in his features carefully, his jaw was tensed and his eyes were getting darker by the minute. He was obviously trying to control himself. From the way he was digging his fingers into his poor sandwich and the way he was breathing.

She reached out and touched his cheek lightly, her fingertips grazing his soft skin. A muscle in his cheek clenched as she traced her fingers over his cheekbones. She then let her fingers move down and trace the line of his strong jaw. His eyes were open wide, watching her every move. He sucked in a sharp breath. "I don't deserve you."

She stopped and let her hand fall to her side. "Stop it. I'm not a saint, you know."

He rubbed his temple, avoiding her gaze. "What do you think I did late at night, Lucy? It's not a pleasant thing at all. Be sure to know that."

"I do-don't know," She stammered.

He breathed out as he picked up a French fry from his tray and held it to Lucy's lips. When she opened wide, he popped it into her mouth. "Did you know that another body was found? You weren't here and I was so scared." She blurted out, fiddling with her fingers.

He gritted his teeth. "You were scared because I wasn't there? Trust me love, you shouldn't be."

"But I was really concerned-"

He cut her off. "Don't ever be. I'm the last person you should be concerned about it."

She gulped nervously. "What do you think about the killer? Those poor people that he had killed, I feel so sorry for them..."

He clamped his eyes shut then quickly snapped them open, wanting to drink her in. "Do you want to know a sick fact? I don't pity them one bit."

Lucy's breath got caught in her throat as unpleasant shivers ran down her spine. "You don't mean that."

He smirked darkly. "Yes, love." Swallowing hard, he spat out. "I do."

Lucy shook her head, wanting to desperately know why he was so tormented. "Then at least tell me why. Why do you think so?"

He dipped his head back. "Because life is a tough test that isn't fair at all. Some had it easy and still were foolish...they deserve it, I just know."

She took a long, deep breath. "I thought you weren't going to give me dumb and vague answers. I already know that you highly dislike life Drake...and by 'why', I mean I want to know the real deal. The whole truth."

He suddenly smashed his fist against the table, his blood was boiling as he spat out. "You don't know when to stop, don't you? I fuckin said I'm not ready to tell you!"

Lucy slumped back in her seat, shocked at his sudden outburst. "I-I'm sorry."

He buried his face in his hands. "Don't apologize."

She nodded, not knowing what to say. He leaned in and cupped her face in his hand gently. Murmuring softly, he skimmed his thumb across her cheek. "I understand how you feel. I always wanted answers. I wanted to know why my parents didn't love me like they should have, wanted to know what the fuck I did to deserve such a horrible, lonely life..." He sighed deeply. "I'll give you answers Lucy, I promised you."

CHAPTER 12

Lucy wanted to comfort him so badly, but what was she supposed to do? *If I could go back in time and change his past, oh, trust me, I would have.* Her eyes glinted with sorrow, staring intently at how painful his expression was. He looked very vulnerable as he twisted and turned in his seat. She somehow could not get used to how broken he actually was. Drake was tough on the outside, but he surely was the exact opposite on the inside. Fragile and insecure, that's what he was.

Just as she was about to speak, Drake muttered, picking up the straw that he hadn't used and began to bend it into shapes. "When I was a kid, at about age six, I remember my mother had this huge obsession with bows. I mean she'd wear sweaters and shirts with bows on them and would always have her long hair tied back in a bow. Weird but true." He nodded as he twisted the straw in his hands. "So one day after school, I grabbed a blank paper and drew bows of different shapes and sizes with very bright colors. I went up to my mother with a wide smile plastered on my face. I thought she'd be happy with my drawing, but you know what she did, Lucy?"

His eyes were glued to Lucy's who was completely enthralled by what he was saying. He sucked in a shaky breath. "She snatched it from my hands, tore it to pieces, threw it in my face, and crouched to my level. Her face was contorted with disgust as she spat out, 'I don't need your pathetic drawings. You did nothing but bring problems to this family. Now, go back to your room, I don't have time for you.' With that, I scurried to my room and buried my face in my pillow, trying to understand what the fuck I did." Drake lowered his head, smiling painfully. "And the ironic thing was that she actually never had time for me."

Lucy bit her bottom lip hard, grieving for the little boy with big, dark, blue eyes and ruffled, red hair who never had the chance to experience a good childhood. She whispered softly. "What did your mother exactly mean by problems?"

"Money, but I'm sure that was not just it," He clenched his jaw, swallowing hard.

She furrowed her brows, eying his strong, intense features. "No matter what the problem was Drake, it was not an excuse for them to treat you the way they did. You didn't have to face that, you were just a kid."

He clamped his eyes shut, his chest rising and falling with every breath he took. "That little event was nothing. I used to deal with a whole lot of worse things."

She wrapped her arms around his neck and buried her face in his chest. He immediately reacted to her sudden hug, holding her close to him. He rested his chin on the top of her head as he squeezed her tightly, afraid she'll let go. Pressing their bodies together, she could feel the erratic beating of his heart against her cheek. He slightly pulled away to plant a soft, warm kiss on her forehead. He smoothed her hair back from her face as she looked up, drinking in his affectionate expression. "It's all okay now," Lucy murmured.

His features suddenly tensed, his eyes darkening dangerously. "I wish."

Her eyes widened, desperately wanting him to tell her what he was hiding. Reading her expression, he blurted out. "We should head home now."

She nodded, sighing deeply. Standing up, she said, "I'm going to go to the bathroom."

He shook his head, his expression as serious as ever. She scurried to the restroom, her boots click-clacking urgently over the ceramic floor tiles. Trying to unbutton her jacket on the way, she bumped into a hard chest. "Oops, I'm sorry," She glanced up at the person in front of her who was a boy her age with short, blonde hair and a buff physique.

The guy smirked widely. "That's okay-" He then immediately frowned, seeming to recognize her. "Wait. Aren't you the girl who hangs out with that heartless asshole?"

Lucy's mouth fell open, the guts of that guy. "Excuse me?"

He clenched his fists at his sides. "We go to the same school, I'm in your chemistry class...Anyways, you know what I mean, so don't act all shocked." *Chemistry class? Drake's in my chemistry class too, no wonder why I haven't paid attention to any of the other guys.*

She crossed her arms, tapping her foot against the floor. "No I don't, do enlighten me." *What a dick.*

"He goes around threatening and scaring the shit out of everybody. I mean who does he think he is?" The guy said, flailing his arms dramatically.

Lucy cocked her head to the side. "If most people are like you, then, I totally understand him."

He rolled his eyes at her. "Whatever."

Moving away from him, he grabbed her by her arm, stopping her. "Wait. If you ever feel left out when you're around him. The name's Sean, I'll be here." He winked at her, earning a glare from Lucy.

"First of all, take your fuckin hand off her. Second, it's good to know that you'll 'be here' so that I'll kick the shit out of you." Drake spat out viciously, suddenly appearing behind Lucy. His eyes were searing right through Sean as he shrunk under Drake's dark, cold gaze.

Sean took several nervous gulps, not expecting Drake to just show up like that. He held his head high, trying to prove how unaffected he was, which was absolutely untrue since he was practically trembling in his position. "Whatever, man," He mumbled, avoiding any eye contact with Drake. The paleness of his face and the way he took quick breaths showed just how much he actually feared Drake's presence. It was Chase's and Drake's encounter all over again. Sean then quickly disappeared as he bolted out of Drake's way, not wanting to piss him off any further. *So much for a buff guy.* She stole a glance at Drake who was still fuming with anger. "Drake-"

He cut her off, taking a few steps forwards. "Do you want me to follow him and strangle the life out of him?"

Her eyes searched his face for any sign of sarcasm, but found none. He was dead serious. She ran a hand through her hair. "It's fine really. I mean, he barely did anything, he's just a dumbass-"

Drake cut her off again, his face was now mere inches away. "Barely did anything? He was going to take you away from me!" He cupped her face with both hands, pressing his forehead against hers. She leaned in, loving the warmth that radiated off him and onto her skin.

"Let him say what he wants. I'm not going anywhere, it's my decision, you know, not his," Lucy tried reassuring him, like she always did. *Oh, Drake, you really are messed up. I'll mend you, I promise.*

As soon as they arrived at Drake's place, a light bulb flickered to life above Lucy's head as realization struck her. She had a great idea as to what she could do for Drake, since he had had a horrible childhood. She'll have to know all the things that he had missed or that he haven't done and do them with him now. She chewed on her bottom lip, thinking of a way that wouldn't be too suspicious. A huge smile crept over her lips and she quickly stood right in front of Drake. He was busy rummaging in his drawer for a shirt as she batted her eyelids. He slowly looked up at her, puckering his brow. "What?"

She rocked back and forth on her feet, flipping her hair back. "Drake...?"

"Yes?" He stood up, crossed his arms, and eyed her curiously.

She fiddled with her fingers. "Can we play a game?"

He narrowed his eyes at her. "What game?" He gave her one of his sexy lopsided smirks as he drew nearer to her, brushing his lips against the soft spot beneath her ear. "Because I know a whole lot of games we can play."

She blushed deep red. "Um...that's not what I meant." She ran a hand through her hair nervously. "Can we play truth or dare?"

He furrowed his brows in confusion. "Why the hell would you want to play truth or dare?"

She put on her best puppy dog face and joined her hands together. "Pretty please."

Sighing deeply, he said, "Fine." He paused and then continued, looking at her with big, dark eyes. "But on one condition; do not exceed your limits with those questions of yours."

She immediately nodded her head, knowing exactly what he was talking about. She then jumped on his bed, crossed her legs, plumped a pillow up behind her, and patted the space next to her. "Come, sit."

He smirked widely and plopped down beside her. He suddenly crawled up and positioned himself on top of her, supporting his weight on his left arm. He leaned in and pressed his lips on her bare neck, planting hot, wet open-mouthed kisses up and down. Lucy froze in her position, her heart hammering wildly in her chest as she instantly forgot how to breathe. He slowly grazed his teeth along her heated skin, nipping and biting. She let out a soft moan and closed her eyes shut; she wasn't able to suppress the warm tingles that ran through her entire body. He slightly pulled away, lust dancing in his eyes. "We can do so much more than just sitting, it is a bed, you know?" His warm breath tickled her now burning cheeks.

Lucy knew she wouldn't be able to resist him, he was certainly her weakness. She simply stared back at him, her eyes warm and wide open. She wasn't able to speak, she just couldn't. His closeness was going to be the end of her. Drake smirked wickedly as he slowly got off her, straightened up, and cleared his throat. "I pick truth."

Taking a deep breath, she tied her hair up in a messy bun. "When's your um...birthday?" *I better start with the easy questions. Besides, I really want to know his date of birth.*

Drake's warm smile disappeared and was immediately replaced by a frown. He clenched his jaw, looking away. "It's in January. I-I don't remember the exact day though."

Lucy's face fell, it was obviously because his parents never have celebrated his birthday. *I hate those parents of his. They're so cruel. How were they able to do this to a child?* She reached out and brushed a loose strand of hair away from his face. Running her hand up and down his arm, she whispered softly. "Well then, let's set an exact date."

He puckered his brow, confused. Not letting him speak, she rested her chin in the palm of her hand and asked, "What's your favorite number?"

He rolled his eyes playfully. "Fourteen."

"Then your birthday will be on January 14," She grinned victoriously.

He chuckled, leaning in closer to her. "Oh, really now?"

She quickly nodded her head, happy with her decision. He ran his tongue against his upper lip. "When's yours?" When she answered with 'June 7', a smirk tugged at his lips. "Now, come on, choose."

"Truth," She blurted out, wondering what he'll ask her.

He lifted her chin with a curled index finger, making her meet his intense gaze. "What have you always wanted?"

Her eyes widened, she didn't expect him to ask her such a question. She thought he'd tease her or something. She wanted to whisper out, to shout out, you, but that would be too awkward. She blushed bright pink, twirling her locks around her fingers as she admitted. "I always wanted to have a killer whale tattoo, but I was never that courageous to go get one..."

Drake was somehow shocked and eyed her skeptically. "Saint Lucy is a fan of tattoos?" When she stuck her tongue out at him, he asked, "So why a 'killer whale' tattoo?"

She sighed deeply, shooting him a wide smile. "They're just amazing; they're really smart and they look majestic."

"Yeah, yeah," He nodded, not seeming to care about them. He rested his hands behind his head. "Truth, again."

Good. She bit her bottom lip nervously. "Drake...wh-what were some of the things you wished you were able to do with your parents?"

He swallowed hard, his eyes glinting with sorrow while he recalled past events. He clamped his eyes shut as he finally murmured, his voice slightly cracking. "I used to spend most of my time in my room, either watching movies or playing puzzle. One day, I got this stupid idea of asking my dad if we could go to the amusement park. I had always wanted to know how fun it actually was, but he as usual turned me down. I got used to it though, I thought it was normal back then, since mom had convinced me that happy families only existed in movies." He let out a long, deep breath. "I wanted a lot of things; I wanted my mom to bake me sweets, read me bedtime stories, play games with me, and comfort me. I wanted my dad to be there, wanted him to be proud of me." A single, bitter tear forced itself to trickle down his cheek. "But most of all, I wanted them to tell me they loved me."

Lucy couldn't bear see Drake in such a heartbreaking state; she just couldn't get used to it at all. Though, she appreciated the fact that he was opening up to her, bit by bit. With the pad of her thumb, she brushed the stray tear off his cheek gently. He buried his face in the crook of her neck, inhaling deeply, as if her scent was what he exactly needed. He tightened his grip on her, pressing his warm body against hers. She curled her fingers in his hair, tugging at his strands. He was breathing heavily as she felt his chest rise and fall. He whispered huskily, nuzzling her hair. "I want..."

Lucy's breath got caught in her throat as his hand slowly trailed up her thigh. His fingers kept moving up and just when he reached her inner thigh, he stopped. He sucked in a breath, taking a look at Lucy who was blushing red and unable to move. "I'm sorry." Not letting her answer, he stated, "It's your turn to choose."

Ignoring what was just about to happen, she answered, "Dare."

His features softened and he smiled warmly at her. "Lie down next to me." He opened his arms wide and she jumped into his embrace, slumping down into the bed. She wrapped her arms around his waist, snuggling against the firmness of his muscular chest.

Blinking, Lucy slowly opened her eyes to realize that she was in Drake's arms. Her head was buried in his chest, his arms were wrapped securely around her waist and his leg was between hers. She blushed as she tried getting out of bed without waking him up. He looked so peaceful and innocent. His lips were slightly parted and his fiery hair was cascaded all over the pillow. She smiled warmly, loving the fact that this time she had woken up with him beside her. *Wait. What time is it anyways?* She glanced at the bedside clock and noticed that it was '5:30 am'. *Oh great.* Instantly, a wicked smile crept over her lips as she thought of exactly what to do. She stole a glimpse at Drake's perfection and then quickly headed to the kitchen.

She tapped her fingers against her lips as her eyes searched the half empty fridge. Her face fell, remembering that most of the ingredients she needed weren't available. *Ugh.* She pouted and leaned on the counter. Arms snaked around Lucy's waist from behind, making her jump. "Why are you up so early?" Drake asked huskily against her neck. She let out a long, shaky breath as her body molded into his. Drake's warmth was engulfing her, drowning her, and she loved it.

"I do-don't know," She stammered. Turning around to face him, she asked, "What about you?"

He gazed at her, drinking her in. "You weren't there. I felt it, so I woke up."

She bit her bottom lip, smiling to herself like an idiot. "I wanted to make you some pancakes, but you don't have anything in that fridge of yours."

He smirked and twirled a strand of her hair around his finger then let it unwind and hit her nose. "Thanks love, but food is for sissies, you know?"

She frowned. "No, I do not know." She placed her hands on her hips. "Next time, I'm going to go buy you some groceries." She swatted him on the belly. "Better stay healthy."

He rolled his eyes. "Whatever."

Lucy cleared her throat. "Aren't you going to ask me why next time, not now?"

Drake scrunched his nose in disgust. "Why the hell would I care about-"

She cut him off, crossing her arms. "Just ask!"

He faked a smile as he mocked. "Oh why dear Lucy do you plan on buying me some lovely groceries next time and not now, on this beautiful, happy day?"

She batted her eyelids in feigned innocence. "Because I have some other plans for today."

He puckered his brow. "Oh really? And what are those plans?"

She began to giggle, her hands over her mouth. "I won't say."

"What kind of-"

She cut him off once again. "First go change, and we'll get going."

Drake sighed deeply and made his way back to his room. Lucy smiled victoriously, rubbing her hands together. *I'm going to make sure you have a great day, Drake. I promise.*

After a couple of minutes, Drake came back wearing a black T-shirt that clung to his body, with dark blue jeans that hung low on his waist. She skipped towards him. "Ready?"

He shrugged then eyed her from top to bottom. He wore a serious expression as his eyes darkened. "You're wearing a dress? Go change. We're going on a damn motorcycle. Do you want everybody to see your-"

She immediately interrupted him, huffing. "Who said we're going on your motorcycle?"

He stared at her blankly. Lucy drew nearer to him, suppressing her smile. "We're going to walk there."

"And by there, you mean?" He asked, trying to get an answer out of her.

Rolling her eyes playfully, she said, "You'll see. Now let's go!"

"I don't know why you're not telling me where we're going. Are you planning on getting my hair cut or something?" Drake asked curiously as he walked beside Lucy, his hands shoved in his pockets.

"What? Hell no!" She blurted out. Pointing her finger at his long, red locks, she admitted. "What possessed you to ask such a thing? Your hair is gorgeous."

Drake's hands flew to his hair, smiling. "That's a relief. A huge relief."

She giggled and her eyes lit up. "Trust me, you have no idea as to where I'm taking you, but I assure you that we'll have loads of fun."

"Loads of fun, you say. Mmm, I wonder," He teased, wiggling his brows.

Ignoring him, she stated, "We're almost there!" She quickened her pace and tugged Drake along by his arm.

Drake's eyes widened as he stood immobile, staring ahead. "The amusement park? Are you kidding me?"

"Tada!" Lucy yelled, outstretching her arms in the air.

He took a few steps towards her and crossed his arms. "Do I look like a nine-year-old to you?"

She rolled her eyes and then pouted. "Oh come on, lighten up! We'll have fun!" Standing on her tiptoes to look him in the eyes, she said, "Besides, how would you know if it's fun or not?"

He clenched his jaw. "You have a point there, Loo."

She smiled widely, her eyes creased. "Why thank you. And do not call me Loo, ever."

Intertwining her fingers with his, they walked in. The smell of popcorn, hot dogs and cotton candy engulfed them, filling their nostrils. Kids were laughing and running around, wanting to try out each and every ride. All the rides were lit up with bright colors and passengers of all ages occupied the seats as they screamed and yelled whenever they were whipped around. Lucy clapped her hands, excitement eating her up. "What ride should we go on first?"

Drake looked around intently until his gaze locked on a certain ride to the left. Lucy noticed and bit her lip. "The roller coaster?"

He nodded slowly and stared at it, fascinated by the way it twisted and coiled like a snake. Drake suddenly scooped Lucy in his arms and rushed his way there. She shrieked and then burst into giggles as she bounced in his arms due to his speed. Putting her down gently, he grinned like a toddler. "Ready?"

Even though roller coasters freaked her out, she'd ride it with him without hesitation, since Drake had never been on one before. When she shook her head in a yes, Drake took a seat at the very front. Sitting right beside him, Lucy sucked in a deep breath. Drake strapped them both in tightly and smirked at her. "Is my Lucy scared?"

"No," She lied.

He leaned in and kissed her cheek softly, his lips lingering there. "Don't be. I'm right here, babe."

Just as she was about to answer, the roller coaster began to move. It ascended to the top of the first pinnacle slowly and Lucy's heart began to hammer as she realized that the scary part was about to begin. Suddenly, all the people screamed their hearts out as the metal wheels rolled down the metal track in a way that they all felt as if they were falling straight down. Lucy had her eyes squeezed tight and screamed so loud, Drake was chuckling hysterically at her. Her hair was wildly flying all over, she was sure it'll all be tangled up. She forced her eyes open to sneak a peek at Drake, who had a huge smile plastered on his face; it was breathtaking. She yearned to see that smile of his more often. He seemed so ecstatic, she couldn't help but smile herself.

CHAPTER 13

Adjusting her hair, Lucy stumbled out of the roller coaster's car. Drake wrapped his arm around her waist, steadying her. She gave him a warm smile as she placed her hand on her racing heart. *I should calm down, the ride is over.* Drake cleared his throat, swaying back and forth on his feet. "That was fun."

She inhaled deeply. "Yep, it was." The best part was watching him grow happier by the minute.

He flashed her a lopsided smirk. "Now, what do you want to do next?"

Lucy bit her lip, slowly looking around. She jumped in her position and pointed her finger ahead. "Let's have ice cream and cotton candy!"

"Both? You're already too hyper. I don't think I'd be able to keep up with you." He grinned mischievously. After seeing how her face immediately fell, he said, "I'm just kidding, love."

Her eyes twinkled. "Good." With that, she ran towards the pink and blue lit shop. Rolling his eyes, Drake followed her.

Lucy licked her lips while she stared at all the ice cream flavors in front of her. She tapped her finger against her lips. "I'll have a strawberry, chocolate almond, and blueberry ice cream, please." She turned around. "What about you Drake?"

Drake had a frown on his face and his jaw was clenched as he looked to the left. She followed his gaze and her eyes landed on a little boy about age five. He was crying and pointing to his ice cream which was now melting on the ground. His parents were somehow busy feeding his baby sister. Drake shook his head, stood beside Lucy, and ordered. "I want an ice cream of any three flavors please."

Drake paid for the ice cream and rushed to the little boy. Lucy watched him with wide eyes as he crouched to the kid's level and said with a smile, "Here you go."

The little boy smiled widely, his adorable tooth gap showing. He took the ice cream from Drake's hands and immediately started licking it, afraid that Drake might take it back. The kid wiped his chocolate covered mouth with the back of his hand. "Thank you, mister."

Drake patted him on the head and stood up. He went back to Lucy who had her head tilted to the side and her hand pressed to her cheek. He puckered his brow at her affectionate expression. "Are you okay?"

"That was so adorable!" Lucy squealed, not able to control herself. She jumped into Drake's arms, taking him by surprise.

Drake faked a cough, wrapping his arms around her. "I just did what any person would do."

She slightly pulled away and gazed at his eyes, which were rarely that bright. "No, because any other person would have ignored that little boy. They wouldn't have cared if he had his ice cream or not."

He sighed deeply, pulling her to him and nestling his face in her neck. "I still don't understand why you're so happy about this."

She closed her eyes tight, savoring his touch. "Because you're not as bad as you think you are."

He smoothed her hair back with shaking fingers. "Whatever you say."

Drake pulled back and took out his wallet from his back pocket. Lucy reached out, stopping him from paying for her ice cream. He shook her hand off, irritated. "Stop it, I'll pay. It's just ice cream, you know."

Lucy crossed her arms, trying her best to hide her blush away. "Fine."

They both walked side by side, loving the happy aura that surrounded the place. Lucy took a lick from the side of the cone all the way up to the top, letting the ice cream melt in her mouth. "So, how come you didn't get one yourself?" She asked curiously.

"Because I hate ice cream," He stated casually.

Her mouth fell open. "Really? Who doesn't like ice cream?" She took another long lick, reducing the ice cream down to the cone.

He clenched his fists at his sides and took a long, deep breath. "Would you stop it with the licking?"

Her eyes widened. "What?" She was literally confused.

He grabbed her by her shoulders and made her meet his dark gaze. Smoothing his thumb over her lips, he whispered huskily. "I can't control myself when you do that."

She gulped, her heart pounding against her ribs. "Then, don't."

His pupils dilated instantly, causing his eyes to become even darker. He pressed his forehead against hers and traced his fingertips along her jaw slowly. "I don't think you want that." He leaned in and kissed her nose, her cheeks, and her jaw. Lucy's legs went limp, she couldn't stand still any longer. He breathed against her lips. "I'm very wild when I lose my control, Lucy. I don't think you're ready to scream out my name in front of all those people, now, are you?"

Lucy blushed uncontrollably. She was positive that her face was tomato red now. Just as she was about to think of something to say, her phone rang. *Whew.* She picked it out of her purse and answered it.

"Hi sweetheart! I missed you so much," Her mom said over the line.

Lucy sighed. "Me too."

"When are you coming back? You said you were going to come back soon," Natasha whined.

Lucy bit her inner cheek hard, she knew that she had to come back home, and sadly, she couldn't deny that. "I will."

"Tomorrow?" Her mom asked.

Lucy felt her heart constrict, being with Drake was the best thing she could ever ask for. She didn't want to have to leave. "Okay." She forced the word out.

"Great! I'll make sure to prepare your favorite sweets and make you feel at home. Oh, and your father won't bother you much honey, because he's supposed to stay in bed for a couple of days..."

Lucy hung up and swallowed hard. Drake curled his index finger under her chin and tilted her head up. "What's wrong, love?"

"I have to go home tomorrow..." She murmured, not able to say those words out loud.

Drake furrowed his brows, his breathing becoming heavy. "What? Why? Please, don't leave. I-I-"

Lucy cut him off, pressing her hand against his cheek. "I have to, Drake. But I'll always be around...After all, no one can stop me from seeing you." She gave him a weak smile.

"Promise?" He asked as he placed his hand on top of hers.

She nodded and flung her arms around his neck. He smirked and pulled her face to him roughly. As his lips slowly inched closer to hers, Lucy's phone rang again. *Ugh.*

"Yes, mom?" Lucy asked, annoyed that her mother ruined the sensual moment.

"You didn't let me finish! I wanted to say that Drake is invited for dinner tomorrow-"

Lucy almost choked. "What? Really?"

"Yes. Now stop interrupting me! As I was saying, your brother and I didn't get to know him like we should have; he had been nice to you and took care of you. We did a lot of thinking and came to the conclusion that yes, your dad actually deserved what Drake had done to him. That's why we didn't tell the police about what had happened, and we didn't tell your father's doctor either...So, I want Drake to come over tomorrow."

Lucy was surprised. She'd happy dance here and wouldn't care if anyone was looking. "What's with the freakishly huge smile on your face?" Drake asked, raising his brow.

"Mom invited you for dinner tomorrow. She wants to get to know you," Lucy giggled like a toddler.

His eyes widened. "Get to know me? That's um...interesting."

"You're going to come, right?" She pouted, practically begging him.

He smirked wickedly. "Of course I will. I want to make sure that dad of yours won't lay a finger on you."

As soon as Drake entered through his house's door, he dropped his keys and leather jacket and clutched Lucy in his arms. Lucy was taken aback by his sudden embrace, but smiled to herself like an idiot and buried her face in his chest. Holding her tight, he whispered against her hair. "Thank you."

"It was nothing. I just thought we could have some fun..." She breathed out, ignoring the way her body reacted to his touch.

He slightly pulled back and furrowed his brows at her. "I did. I had a great time, Lucy."

She giggled. Her big, warm, glinting eyes were enough to show that she had a wonderful time too. He made her really happy. Drake brought out the best in her, and she hoped that she brought out the best in him too.

He suddenly lifted her up and carried her to his room. She immediately wrapped her arms around his neck and bit her bottom lip. "What are you doing?"

"I'm taking you to bed, isn't it obvious?" He puckered his brow teasingly.

Lucy flushed bright pink. "Um...why?"

Rolling his eyes, he put her down gently on his bed. "You should get some rest. It's been a long day."

She protested. "But it's early-"

Drake cut her off, leaning in and cupping her face in his hands. "I'm trying to make an excuse to hold you, love. I can't wait any longer." He had the most innocent look on his face and Lucy couldn't help but gasp. His face suddenly hardened. "I really don't know what I'll do when you go back, but I'll find a way. For sure."

She beamed at his reassurance and lifted the covers, patting the space next to her. Drake smirked and hopped in. He wrapped his arms around her waist and curled his fingers in her hair. "I sleep better...much better, when you're beside me. You do know that, don't you?" He mumbled out.

Lucy grinned, leaned back, and snuggled into his chest. She tucked her arms under his, pressing his forearms up against her chest. "Me too."

He chuckled against her neck, sending warm tingles to her scalp, then all the way down her spine. "Good. Now, sleep." He twirled her dark blonde strands around his fingers, repeatedly, as she shut her eyes and relaxed, letting his fingers do their magic. *I wonder what those fingers of yours can also do.* She let out a long breath, ignoring that silly thought of hers, and succumbing to Drake's body warmth.

Lucy woke up, startled, her phone was ringing on and on. She rubbed her eyes and squinted at her screen. 'Mom'. *What does she want so early in the morning?* She jerked her head up and looked around, Drake wasn't beside her anymore. She pouted, then sighed and answered her call.

"Yes, mother?" Lucy said through gritted teeth.

"Hi! Sorry for waking you up, honey. But I want to start preparing for tonight's dinner and I have no idea what Drake likes to eat. So, care to give me a clue?"

Lucy tapped her fingers against her lips, thinking. "Um...ham and cheese?" She knitted her brows, *I'm not sure of what he likes to eat myself.*

"Ham and cheese? What? That won't do! Go ask him now. I'll wait." Her mom shrieked.

She got up from bed and went to see if Drake was around somewhere. "Drake!" She yelled. *Please tell me you're here.*

"I'm in the kitchen!" Drake yelled back.

Lucy's face lit up as she rushed to the kitchen to see him standing beside the stove, pouring a big spoonful of the pancake batter into the hot pan. He was preparing pancakes for breakfast. Drake looked up and smirked widely at her. He was dressed in a blue T-shirt and black, skinny jeans, looking gorgeous, as usual. He licked his lips, ignoring the way she was staring at him. "I thought I'd go buy a couple of things. You wanted to make pancakes the other day...so I got the ingredients and, well, I'm making us some pancakes."

She wanted to jump and hug the life out of him, but she controlled herself as much as she could. He was being so sweet, she couldn't help but sway from side to side and look down, hiding the huge grin on her face. *Was that the only reason why he got up early?* She shrugged off the thought and took a seat at the table. "Can't wait to taste those pancakes of yours. They're mouth-watering." She batted her eyelids at him.

He placed two plates of pancakes on the table and sat down. He drew closer to her, his hot breath hitting her neck, causing shivers to run up and down her entire body. "Trust me, I'm the one who's mouth-watering." He brushed his lips against her earlobe. "So, if you want a lick or a bite, just ask." Wiggling his brows, he took in her stunned expression.

Lucy's eyes widened as she gulped. The tension between them was making her kind of nervous, so she changed the subject. "Oh, I um...forgot to ask you. My mom wants to know what you'd like to have for dinner."

Amusement danced in his eyes. "I like hot and spicy food."

"Oh...okay." She cleared her throat and pressed her cell to her ear. "Mom? You still there by any chance?"

"Yes, dear. So what is it?" Her mom asked urgently.

Lucy puckered her brow. "Seriously?"

"Yes, I don't have anything to do! Now tell me for God's sake!" Her mom begged.

"He likes hot and spicy food." Her voice trailed away.

"Great! I know exactly what to prepare! Tell Drake that he'll have the most delicious dinner ever!" Her mom said and hung up.

Drake chuckled and dug his fork into his pile of pancakes. "Your mom is as eager as ever. She likes me, right?"

Lucy's eyes twinkled. "Who wouldn't?"

He burst out laughing, almost knocking his plate off the table. "Who wouldn't? I have a long, long, long list of people who not only dislike me, but hate me. People aren't that fond of me, as you can see." He sighed deeply. "And I'm not that fond of them either."

She ran a hand through her hair. "Well, they don't know what they're missing..."

Drake's eyes suddenly darkened, taking her by surprise. "You're right, they don't."

"Are you sure your mother and brother drink wine?" Drake asked as he motioned to the bottle he's carrying.

"Yes, they do." She giggled at how nervous he seemed. *Who would have guessed that this anxious, tense Drake can be frightening and cruel as well?* She sucked in a breath and knocked on her front door.

As soon as Chad opened the door, he pulled Lucy into his arms and hugged her tight. "I missed you, you idiot."

Drake glared at them and cleared his throat. Lucy giggled and pulled away, stepping closer to Drake and looping her arm through his.

Chad outstretched his hand for Drake to shake as he greeted him. "Nice to see you again, Drake."

Drake forced out a smile and shook his hand, not saying anything. Natasha suddenly came, running towards them with her arms flailing in the air. She looked like a loony person. Wrapping her arms around Drake as if he were her long, lost son, she squealed. "Hi sweetie! We didn't get to meet each other properly, but it's never too late, isn't that right?"

Drake's eyes widened at her actions and slowly lifted his arms and returned her hug. He eyed Lucy warily, mouthing the words. "What's going on?"

Lucy bit her lip, suppressing her laugh. She tapped her finger against her mother's shoulder. "Um...mom?"

Natasha whipped her head round and threw herself at Lucy, squeezing her tight. "Oh, I missed you so much! I don't ever want to spend another day without you, you hear me?"

Lucy smiled warmly. "Yes, mom."

"Come on in, already!" Natasha motioned for them to come in and sit on the table that she had prepared in the living room. Lucy sat next to Drake and stole a quick glance at him. He was staring at all the food on the table with wide eyes. There were plates of spicy, Moroccan shrimps, fried chicken, spicy steaks, grilled, pepper salad, and so much more.

186

Drake's mouth fell open as he whispered in Lucy's ear. "Either your mom is trying to poison me or she's trying to stuff me, cook me, and then eat me."

Lucy chuckled. "Or, she really wants to impress you."

He raised his eyebrow at her. "Why? Because I almost killed her husband? Or, is it because I took her daughter away from her?"

She sighed deeply. "Oh, come on! She knows that you're actually a nice person. Besides, um...I'm really picky when it comes to guys. So...mom is curious, I guess."

A huge smirk crept over Drake's lips. "Oh really?" He leaned in and brushed his lips up and down against her ear. "You like boys who tease you, don't you?" He started nipping her earlobe as warm chills trickled through her. Her heart got caught in her throat as soon as he eased his tongue out and licked her earlobe. He rested his hand on her thigh and slowly ran his hand up and down, teasing her. She felt her knees get weak and she gulped nervously. "Drake...s-stop."

He slightly pulled away, his hand still on her thigh. "Why?" He wrapped his fingers around the hem of her skirt, grinning.

Just as she was about to protest again, Natasha and Chad came back holding a bunch of napkins and a bottle of water. Her mom smiled widely. "The water is sure going to come in handy." She laughed. "The food is super spicy." *It was hard not to notice.*

Drake leaned back in his chair with a smug expression on his face. He pressed his lips together. "So, you're a fan of spicy recipes?" He eyed Natasha.

Natasha shook her head with a smile. "Oh, no...I'm not. I got up early and searched most of the recipes online."

The corners of Drake's lips curled up into a warm smile. "Thank you. You must have really worked hard..."

"It's all right, dearie! Now let's dig in." Natasha clapped her hands together.

Lucy nudged Drake. "What do you want to eat first?" She pointed at the various plates of food on the table. "This time no ham and cheese." She shrugged.

"But I love ham and cheese," Drake jutted out his bottom lip in an exaggerated pout. *Oh God, that lip.* Lucy ran a hand through her hair nervously. He rolled his eyes. "By the way, I know how to eat. So, you don't have to-"

Lucy cut him off by pressing her finger against his lips. "I want to."

He sighed deeply. "Fine." Picking up his plate, he stated casually. "Fill it."

Lucy's mouth was open wide. "Jerk."

He chuckled and leaned in. "I advise you to close that mouth of yours." His eyes suddenly darkened with lust.

She snapped her mouth shut. "You're such a pervert." Ignoring the blush that invaded her cheeks, she put some salad and chicken in both of their plates.

Drake dug his fork into a piece of fried chicken and a couple of steamed carrots, and shoved them into his mouth. Chewing, he mumbled. "That's really good."

"I'm so glad you liked it," Natasha smiled so widely, her eyes disappeared. She grabbed the bottle of wine that Drake bought and poured into Drake's cup. "You really didn't have to buy something-"

Drake cut her off with a smile. "It's nothing, really. Besides, you cooked us dinner, it's the least I could do."

After pouring a quarter of his cup, she poured herself a glassful. "I don't want drunk teenagers around. So, that would be enough."

Lucy whined. "But what about me? I'm eighteen! Come on!"

"Drink water or juice instead," Her mom shook her head.

Drake began to laugh at Lucy's desperate expression. She crossed her arms against her chest. "Water or juice? I thought you were going to suggest milk." She glared at her.

Drake took her hand in his and squeezed. He whispered huskily to her. "I'd like some milk, please."

Lucy snatched her hand away, shocked. "You like teasing me, don't you? Well, I'm going to hang out with Josh tomorrow and-"

The look on Drake's face made her close her mouth shut and stop talking. His eyes were literally as black as the olives in his salad. They held no emotion as he stared at her with a fixed expression. His jaw was clenched so tightly, his poor teeth were practically suffering. He was breathing heavily while he clenched his fists at his sides. "Don't ever say something like that again." He drew nearer to her, making her feel vulnerable as ever under his dark gaze.

Lucy fiddled with her fingers. "I was j-just joking, you know?"

He chewed on his bottom lip and buried his face in his hands. Natasha's features tensed. "Is everything okay?"

Lucy nodded. "Yeah." She looked at Drake and then back at her mother. "I'm just going to go show Drake where the bathroom is..."

Drake looked up and narrowed his eyes at her. He got off his chair and went along with her. Lucy leaned back against the bathroom door and stared at Drake who was trying hard not to face her. He sucked in a shaky breath. "I don't want any other boy to hang out with you, flirt with you, or touch you." He squeezed his eyes shut. "I know that's exaggerated. That's why I ignore the need to crack their skulls open and simply wait and see if they'll dare exceed the limits, because if they do-"

Lucy shushed him by wrapping her arms around his neck and resting her head against his firm chest. She sighed as the beating of his heart filled her ears. "I am yours, Drake. Only yours."

As soon as he heard those words, he buried his face in her hair and gripped her by her waist. He began to trail urgent kisses down her neck as shivers exploded all over Lucy's body. She

dug her fingers into his back and let her head fall back. "Dr-
Drake..." Lucy breathed out.

"Yes?" He slightly pulled back and looked her in the eyes, his
lips pink and parted.

She flushed bright red. "Tell me that you are-"

Immediately knowing what she meant, he pressed his warm lips
against her forehead. "I'm yours, Lucy. I was, ever since you
came out of nowhere and introduced yourself to me..."

But you haven't said that you loved me yet. She bit her lip hard,
feeling her throat constrict and finding it hard to breathe.
Drake's features hardened as if sensing her sudden mood
change. He smoothed her hair from her face gently. "What-"

"You're here, aren't you? You son of a bitch," A hoarse voice
came out of the room that was right beside the bathroom. It was
Lucy's dad and he was angry. Real angry.

CHAPTER 14

Drake's eyes widened; they were flashing darkly with intense rage. Lucy felt her heart beat accelerate; if Drake's eyes were a weapon, a lot of grave damage could have been caused. He took a long, deep, agonizing breath as his eyes glued to Lucy's. "Go back. I'll follow you later."

She furrowed her brows, shaking her head. "No. I'm staying."

Drake's jaw stiffened, his breathing becoming heavy and ragged. "Go back to dinner, or I'll drag you there myself."

She pressed her lips together in a tight line. "But-"

"Just go! I don't want you to get involved!" He glared, his nose flaring. He was enraged, he looked like a volcano ready to erupt and his fiery, red hair would be the perfect lava.

Lucy nodded hesitantly, swallowed hard, and made her way back to the living room. Drake then stormed into the room and stood right in front of Howard with his fists clenched tight at his sides. He gritted his teeth. "What the fuck did you call me?"

Howard was lying down on his bed, the way he clutched the white covers firmly in his hands, indicated that he was in pain. A sly smile was plastered on his face as he spoke. "Now, now. You need to calm down. Anger and stress are both bad for you." He sighed. "I have only one thing to say to you." He slowly sat straight, wanting to face Drake properly. "Get away from my daughter, you little fuck."

Drake chuckled darkly, his voice dripping with poison. "You call yourself a father? You're sick. You're truly sick. And you need a long therapy."

Howard adjusted his lumpy pillow behind his back and rested his right hand underneath it, smiling wickedly. "You just want to hang out with Lucy because you pity her, admit it. She's nothing to be proud of. Yet, I still have the need to protect her from you. You are dangerous, I feel it." He shook his head.

Drake drew nearer to him, grabbed the collar of his shirt and pulled him up roughly. "You're asking for a death wish, aren't you?" Drake spat out viciously.

He twisted and turned, trying to get away from Drake's grip. "I knew you wouldn't let this go without a fight." He grinned. "That's why I have a backup plan."

Drake narrowed his eyes at him, he sounded like a mad man. Noticing the confused expression on Drake's face, he cleared his throat. "I don't like the fact that you're going to come and save the day whenever Lucy's in trouble, I don't like the fact that you're her hero. She deserves to be beaten up every once in a while. That's the only way she'll learn to behave." He eyed Drake who was now about to attack him and rip his head off. "I know that a man like me is no match for a guy like you. That's why I have a little surprise for you."

Drake shot him a dark, cold glare. It was so intense, a vein on his forehead protruded as his gaze pierced right through the ruthless man in front of him. He clenched his fists so hard, his nails were digging into his palms and his muscles were bulging under his shirt. Just as he was about to attack him and beat the shit out of him, Lucy's dad took out a gun from under his pillow and pointed it at Drake's chest, aiming it at his heart. "I really am not willing to be beaten up once again. Scratch that, I don't want to be beaten up and later end up like this by you, ever. That is why I'm going to bloody kill you."

Drake froze in his position at the sight of the gun, he hated guns and never wanted to have anything to do with them. He gave him a weak smile. "You're wrong, you're so wrong, because I don't plan on only beating you up. I plan on killing you, first. You're a pathetic excuse of a human being and you belong in hell."

Howard burst out laughing and wrapped his finger around the trigger. "I have planned this all right, the minute I heard that you were coming to dinner tonight. Oh and don't worry, this gun has a suppressor attached to it, no one will be able to save you on time." Noticing the fury in Drake's eyes as he inched closer to him, he spat out. "Don't move. This is not a movie. We're not going to continue chit-chatting until you win." He smiled wickedly. "Say good bye." Saying that, he instantly pulled the trigger and shot Drake.

Meanwhile, Lucy tapped her fingers against the table nervously, pushing the food around on the plate with her fork. *What was taking him so long? I hope everything is okay.* Her mom interrupted her thoughts as she asked, "Are you sure the call he's taking is that important? Can't it wait? The food is starting to get cold."

Lucy sighed deeply. "He said it's important. It means it's important. So, let's just wait. I'm sure he'll be back in a few." *Ugh, I should learn to lie better next time.*

Chad shoved a juicy piece of tomato into his mouth. "Stop whining, mother."

Her mother rolled her eyes at him, then averted her attention to Lucy. "So, are you guys together now?"

Lucy's eyes widened and she blushed uncontrollably. "I-I don't know..." Her voice trailed away.

Natasha narrowed her eyes. "What do you mean you don't know? Can't you see the way he looks at you? He seems so happy when he's around you. I have noticed."

She bit her bottom lip nervously, not being able to stop herself from giggling. "What about me? How do I look at him?"

"You look at him like you're about to eat him with your eyes," Chad chuckled.

Lucy glared at him and Natasha quickly shook her head. "You're not going to sleep together, you hear me? Not until you guys get married."

Lucy's mouth fell open. "Whoa, whoa. Hold your horses. Both of you." *Not that I mind sleeping with him or marrying him.* She smiled to herself like an idiot.

Taking a sip of his glass of wine, Chad said, "I'm just joking."

The smile on her mother's face instantly got replaced by a frown as she looked at Lucy. "If Drake doesn't come back in exactly five minutes, you go check on him. Okay?"

"Yeah," Lucy mumbled out, ignoring the erratic beating of her heart. *What could possibly go wrong?*

As soon as Drake got hit, his arms flew to his chest and his eyes clamped shut. The hysteric laughter of Lucy's dad ringing in his ears made him smile, one wicked smile. Drake took off his jacket and threw it on the floor. He gripped his blood-stained shirt and ripped it off. He dug his fingers inside his chest and pulled the bullet out, smiling from ear to ear. "You need to do way better than that."

Howard began to shiver uncontrollably as fear gripped him, suffocating him. His eyes were practically bulging out of their sockets, not believing what he had just saw. "B-but I-I shot you!" His gun fell out of his shaking hand.

Drake chuckled darkly. "So what? I don't and I won't die easily. Bullets kill sissies like you only." He picked up the gun and clutched it tightly in his hands. Gritting his teeth, he broke the gun in two so easily, as if it were only a mere twig.

He was breathing so heavily, as if the oxygen was going to run out any minute now. "H-how? What are you?" His face was filled with terror and dread.

Drake burst out laughing as he bent down and picked up his jacket. "You have the right to be afraid right now. Hell, I suggest you start panicking. Because I'm going to put you in a long, long sleep."

Howard began squirming in his position, wanting to yell and shout but nothing was coming out. "P-please d-don't k-kill me."

Drake's eyes flashed a menacing glare. "Oh, don't pee your pants just yet. I'm not going to kill you, you're fun to toy with. So I'm going to enjoy my time, and then I'm going to bloody finish you up."

Howard choked on his own breath and froze under Drake's piercing gaze. Drake pressed his fingers hard on the man's chest and narrowed his eyes at him, his eyes as black as night. Lifting his hand a little, Drake let out a long breath as he stared at Lucy's dad who was now literally out. He zipped up his jacket, rolled his ruined shirt into a ball, and stuffed it into the pocket of his jacket. Walking out the door, a body accidentally crashed against his, it was Lucy. "Oh my God! What took you so long? I was worried sick! I wanted to go check on you right away, but then your annoying voice rang in my head telling me not get involved and I-"

"Lucy, shut up. I'm fine," Drake cut her off, rolling his eyes.

Her mouth fell open. "But what happened?" Taking in his tense features, she gasped. "You killed him?"

"No, I did not kill him Lucy. Just forget about it for now, and let's go back to your mom and brother," He sighed deeply and pushed her lightly from behind.

She bit her bottom lip nervously and made her way to the living room. Sitting back in her seat, she forced out a smile. "Um…here he is!" She motioned to Drake who sat down and took a sip of his cup of wine. "I'm sorry, I-"

Lucy immediately cut him off. "Like I said, he had a really important call that he couldn't miss…"

Drake eyed her skeptically. She smacked his leg under the table, wanting him to play along. "Oh, yeah. It was important all right." Drake cleared his throat.

Natasha sighed. "Okay, okay. Now let's finish our lunch already." With that, she dug into her plate.

After placing her bag in her room, Lucy turned around and faced Drake who was swaying back and forth on his feet and looking everywhere but at her. "Drake?"

He shook his head, his gaze locked upon his feet. "What?"

She drew nearer to him and rested her hand on his cheek. "What's with the face?"

He took her hand in his and lowered it to her side. "Please, just don't. Your comfort won't make you come back home with me, now would it?"

Lucy twirled a loose strand around her index finger. "I want to go with you and you know that, but I can't."

He took a long, shaky breath and pulled her into him, wrapping his arms around her. He smoothed her hair back softly and kissed the tip of her nose. Lucy buried her face in his chest and smiled to herself. He hugged her tightly, slightly lifting her off the ground. Giggling, she held onto him for support.

"I'll see you soon, love. Real soon," He flashed her a lopsided smirk and made his way out of her room.

Ignoring the lump that was now forming in her throat, she watched him head to the front door. Just as she was about to speak, her mom embraced Drake and said, "We'll see you soon! I'm glad we got to know you a little bit!"

He gave her a weak smile. "Yeah..."

Lucy rolled her eyes, *seriously? That was the best thing he could come up with to say?* Chad waved good bye as well and then went back to his room. Natasha watched Drake hop on his Harley with wide eyes. "Aren't you ever going to sell this deathtrap and get a nice, decent car instead?"

Pushing his long strands back, he placed his helmet on. "Nah, not ever." He patted his motorcycle gently. "Would you ever sell your baby?"

Natasha cocked her head to the side and Lucy covered her mouth with her hand, suppressing her laugh. "But it will put your life in danger!"

He smiled wickedly, wrapping his hands around the handlebars. "Oh Mrs. Natasha, danger is what I live for."

She raised her brows, not liking what he just said. Not letting her say another word, Drake winked at Lucy, blowing her a kiss. "Bye, babe." With that, he revved up his motorcycle and drove away swiftly.

Smiling to herself like an idiot, Lucy sighed and closed the door. She suddenly felt cold and empty, but a loud, ear-piercing scream immediately caught her attention. Natasha, Chad, and Lucy gasped as they rushed to the room in a hurry.

Lucy's dad was breathing in short, quick breaths. His face was as pale as that of a corpse's and he was sweating profusely, as if he just ran a marathon. He coughed and coughed and flailed his arms in the air, trying to express himself. Natasha had her hand pressed against her cheek while she stared at him with wide eyes. "What's going on? What's wrong with you, Howard?"

Howard locked his tormented eyes with Lucy's. "I w-want to talk to you al-alone."

Lucy gulped nervously, *what did you do Drake?* Just before she could say anything, Chad butted in. "Whatever you want to say to Lucy, you can say it in front of us too."

Howard narrowed his lost, blank eyes at Chad. "It's really important-"

"No!" Chad cut him off, his fists clenched at his sides.

Lucy smiled warmly at Chad who was standing up to her for the first time in a long time ago. "Thanks," She mumbled out to Chad and stood right beside him.

"I swear I won't lay a finger on her! I just really have to talk to her alone!" Howard argued desperately.

Lucy took a deep breath as she whispered to Chad. "It's okay..."

Chad furrowed his brows, staring at his dad. "Fine, but we're going to wait right outside the door."

As soon as Chad and Natasha went out the door and closed it shut, Howard gritted his teeth so hard. "He thinks he can talk to me like I'm some sort of a mad man? I'll show him. That Drake, he's affecting all of you! Not just you!"

Lucy puckered her brow. "Of course he's affecting us. Chad can finally be able to stand up for himself now, and tonight my mother was truly happy. We all were. As for you, you have never made any of us smile. Ever."

"Why you little-"

"No. Just, just tell me what you want and get on with it!" Lucy cut him off, annoyed.

His nose flared, his eyes wide and focused, as if he were recalling certain events. "Drake is not human."

Lucy rolled her eyes at him. "And what is he? A cat?" *You've got to be kidding me.*

Howard rubbed his temple. "I'm fucking serious!"

She crossed her arms against her chest. "Oh really, now?"

He began to shiver, his whole body trembling with fear. "The way he did what he did and the way he said what he said-"

"Wow, you're explaining a lot. Please stop, I can't grasp that much information," Lucy glared at him.

"Would you let me finish you little...Ugh, just let me finish," Her father let out a long, agonizing breath.

She tapped her foot against the ground. "Okay."

"He did things that no human c-can d-do, he's some sort of a demon!" Her dad said in a shaky voice.

Lucy's eyes widened. "If anyone's a demon, it's you." With that, she began to walk towards the door.

"Wait!" Her dad yelled. He dug his nails in his palms. "If I tell you something, promise me you won't say anything to anyone?"

She slightly turned around and looked at him skeptically. "Okay. I um...promise." *Stupid, old man.*

He lowered his head and fiddled with his fingers. "I tried to kill him-"

"You did what?" Lucy was now standing in front of him with her mouth wide open and a horrified look lingering on her face.

"Let me finish! That's not it!" He clenched his jaw and chewed on his bottom lip harshly. "It's the fact that he didn't die! He didn't even flinch!"

"Oh God! If something had happened to him, I don't know what I would have done! I would have bloody murdered you in your sleep for all I care!" Lucy was breathing heavily now, and her eyes were watery and glazed.

"That's not the fucking point! Nothing happened to him! And I don't think he can e-even d-die!" Howard took several nervous gulps.

Lucy buried her face in her hands. "You're such a sick psycho! Either you are lying to me, or you have finally lost it. So, what is it?"

"I'm not lying! And I don't care if you believe me or not anymore, but ju-just stay away from him! He's really dangerous!" Her father breathed out.

Lucy forced out a smile. "And since when do you care about me, huh?" She bit down on her bottom lip. "I will never believe anything you say. Why should I? After all you have put me through..." Her voice trailed away. She shook her head, sighed deeply, and made her way to the door, ignoring his silly pleas.

Chad and Natasha were waiting outside the room, and once they saw her, the bored, gloomy look on their faces instantly vanished. "So? What did that mad man want?" Chad asked, rather enthusiastically.

"Exactly, he's a mad man. What do you expect him to say other than plain ol' nonsense?" Lucy rolled her eyes.

Chad puckered his brow, crossing his arms firmly against his chest. "Come on, what did he say?"

"I really don't want to talk about it. It annoyed the bloody hell out of me," Lucy mumbled out and made her way to her room. Slightly turning her head around, she said, "I'm going to bed. Good night, you guys."

Lucy closed her bedroom door, wore her ocean, blue pajamas, tied her hair in a low bun, and plopped onto her bed. Resting her head on her pillow, she gulped nervously, *what had really happened between Drake and Howard?* She felt sick and it was suddenly hard to breathe. *Please, let my dad be lying. Please.* A sound of click-clacking interrupted her thoughts, and made her jolt upright. Lucy whipped her head round, wanting to know the source of the sound. She stood up, picked her wooden baseball bat, and headed towards her window. Her heart was hammering against her chest as she slowly leaned forwards. It was Drake, and he was tossing rocks at her window. *How romantic.* Opening her window, she rested her hand over her heart. "Seriously Drake? You almost gave me a heart attack! I thought you were a thief or a killer or God knows what!"

"Oh, calm down. It's only me," Drake winked at her, smiling wickedly. He climbed up a small tree that was right beside her window, making Lucy gasp. "Move back, babe. I'm going to jump," Drake grinned, grasping the branches firmly.

"What? Are you crazy?" She shrieked, her mouth slightly agape.

"Just move," He sighed. In a flash, he leapt through the window and stood right in front of Lucy. Her eyes widened. "Are you a monkey or something? Because if you are, I really am not attracted to hairy bodies-"

"Shut up, silly," Drake whispered huskily, drawing nearer to her. He cupped her face in both of his hands and pressed his forehead against hers, making her shiver all over with want. "See, I told you I'll see you soon."

CHAPTER 15

Lucy blushed bright red, feeling all warm and fuzzy inside. Drake gave her one of his sexy lopsided smirks. "I haven't even been away that long, and your body is screaming for me."

She sucked in a breath. "What? No."

He rolled his eyes, wrapping a strong, possessive arm around her waist. "Shhh. Your body craves for my touch, and there's no denying it."

Lucy opened her mouth to speak, to argue, but nothing came out. She just pressed her lips together nervously and stared into his dark, ominous, blue orbs. Drake eyed her from top to bottom, his lustful eyes piercing through her, exposing her. Lucy's cheeks were flaming now as she instinctively crossed her arms over her chest. Drake took a long, deep breath. "You really don't want to know what I'm thinking right now. I'm not having good, polite thoughts, Lucy."

She gulped, twirling a loose strand around her finger. "Wh-what do you mean?"

Brushing his plump lips up and down her neck, he mumbled. "I want you." He slowly ran his warm hand down her side and over her hip, making Lucy stumble into him.

"Fuck," Drake cursed as he shut his eyes tight and took a couple of steps backwards.

Lucy lifted her hand and touched his shoulder, making him flinch. "Drake. I um...w-want you too."

His eyes suddenly widened, darkening into a shade of black that she had grown accustomed to. "I won't though. As much as I fucking want to, I won't."

"But why? I don't understand," Lucy chewed on her bottom lip.

He sighed deeply, rubbing his temple over and over. "Not until you accept the monster that I am. I want it to be the best experience of your entire life. I don't want you to regret it ever."

Lucy furrowed her brows. "You're making no sense at all. You never do."

He reached out and smoothed her hair back gently. "You know exactly what I mean, Lucy. I am a dangerous person and-"

"My dad already told me," Lucy cut him off, feeling as nervous as ever.

"What? What the fuck did he tell you?" Drake clenched his fists, his face filled with rage and worry.

She let out a shaky breath, finding it so hard to breathe. "He said he tried to kill you, and you didn't d-die. Is that true?"

Drake's face fell, pain visible in his tense expression. "Yes."

Lucy felt very confused as she pinched her brows together and ignored the lump that was forming in her throat. "I-I don't get it."

Drake ran a hand through his long hair. "I'm not what you think I am. I thought you would have figured it out by now, Lucy."

She averted her gaze. "Maybe I'm just trying to avoid it."

Drake curled his index finger under her chin, wanting her to look him in the eyes. "You'll have to face the truth, you know."

She ignored the shiver that ran down her spine. "I can face it. J-just tell me. But first I want to ask you something. I want to be honest with you."

He narrowed his eyes at her. "What is it?"

"When you were in the shower the other day, I um...opened that wooden box that you warned me not to open. I got curious." Noticing how his breath got caught in his throat and how his knuckles turned white due to the way he clenched his fists so tight, she breathed out. "W-who are Annie and Scott, Drake?"

As soon as their names left her lips, Drake froze in his position. He did not move a muscle, he simply stood there with a horrified look on his face. Lucy had never seen him in such a tortured state before. She wanted to swallow back what she had just said, because she really wanted that pained look on his face to vanish. Drake let himself fall back on Lucy's bed, his red hair spread out on the white sheets like scattered autumn leaves. "I understand why you opened it, I would have done the exact same thing if I were you." He muttered, ignoring the question that she so desperately wanted the answer for.

Lucy took a few steps forwards. "Drake, I want to hear everything you've got to say."

He rubbed his face hard, feeling as though he was stuck in a room full of mirrors. "Okay," He forced the word out.

Lucy's face lit up like a store window going on for the night. "Thank you."

Drake swallowed hard, trying to get rid of the bitter, unpleasant feeling that was already eating him up. "Remember when I told you that I have ran away from the orphanage that I was put in, at the time when I was twelve?"

Lucy nodded her head, staring at him with wide eyes. He bit down hard on his bottom lip, something he always did when he felt tense. "It was the stupidest mistake of my life. But can you blame me for running away? I was only twelve and I lost everything. I didn't know what to do. I felt stuck, literally stuck." He sucked in a long, breath. "I regret it because if I haven't ran away, I probably wouldn't have become what I am now." Clamping his eyes shut, he continued. "I slept on the streets, and I kept stealing food from people I didn't know or just ate their leftovers. I had to steal, to survive out there. I did lots of bad things, but as weird as that sounds, I never got caught, not once. I guess I'd thank all the hard strategy games that I used to play, they needed a lot of logic." His entire body stiffened. "But one day I wasn't able to get any food, so I sat in a corner and cried my heart out. I always told myself no matter what happens, never befriend or talk to any of the people on the streets. Because who knows what might be lurking in that head of theirs?"

Lucy clenched her jaw tight, picturing him in the terrible state that he was in. She felt her stomach twist in knots as she watched how miserable he looked. He cleared his throat. "So this old man saw me and came up to me. He told me that he would let me stay with him and give me food, but on one condition, I should do whatever he asks me to. So being the idiot that I am, I agreed. Why? Because I was a desperate, hungry kid." Drake's eyes darkened dangerously. "He made me do horrible things. He ruined everything, Lucy."

Lucy gulped nervously as she sat back in her chair, *this is going to be one hell of a story.*

Drake grasped the bed sheets in his fists tightly. "His name was Earl, but people knew him by the name 'bull'. That's because every time he got angry, he used to get so red in the face, and he would immediately kill whoever's in his way without hesitation." Rubbing his temple, trying to remember all the details, he continued. "He made me steal people's belongings and break into their houses in order to get whatever he wanted me to get. If I didn't do as told, he used to beat the shit out of me. He made me watch people who disobeyed him shed tears and cry out as he tortured them. He trained me real hard and taught me how to defend myself. He was so cruel and brutal, I never was so scared of anyone that much before." Drake widened his eyes at Lucy, staring at her intently. "The first person he made me kill was when I turned thirteen."

Lucy gasped in horror as her hands flew to her mouth. She was now breathing heavily, trying to slowly grasp the information that he just told her. "First person? Yo-you mean you have killed mo-more?"

Drake chuckled darkly, his eyes darkening intensely. "Shhh. Let's not talk about this now. Let me continue."

Lucy's mouth hung open. *He did kill more.* A sudden shiver ran through her whole body. She couldn't move at all. She simply sat there, frozen in her chair. Drake's eyes softened a little, a tormented expression lingering on his face. "He threatened me. He said that if I didn't kill the boy, he'd kill us both. That stupid boy, Charlie, stole something from Earl the day before, that's why he wanted him dead. No one must ever challenge him." He sighed deeply, his voice cracking. "I felt so bad and ashamed of what I've done that I began to cry and told him to kill me, to get rid of me, because I didn't want to have to do something like that ever again. He made me shoot him, Lucy. He pointed a gun to my head and told me to shoot him or else."

Lucy's face hardened as she tried reaching out to him. "That's horrible, Drake. I'm really sorry you had to go through this."

Drake moved away from her stretched arm, not wanting her comfort just yet. He didn't want her to feel sorry for him, because he didn't deserve the pity. "I shouldn't have killed him, I should have done something to save him."

Lucy took a deep breath. "It's not your fault. You were thirteen and you were scared. Earl is the one who should take the blame. He should rot in hell."

Drake smiled weakly. "You sound just like me."

She puckered her brows, confused, but he didn't let her speak. Instead, he continued. "When Earl refused to kill me, saying that he was proud of what I did, I ran away. I did not care if he'd shoot me or not. I just ran away, away from him." He grasped the bed sheets even tighter. "Since my eyes were so watery and red because of all the crying, my vision became blurry. So, I didn't realize that I was running towards a highway. My heart was caught in my throat as a black Mercedes, I remember it very well, came my way. I thought that it was the end for me. That I was going to die so soon, without even accomplishing anything. But, this car abruptly stopped on time as the man driving it pulled the brakes."

Lucy's eyes were wide and fixed on Drake, picturing everything in front of her, as if she were there with him. She gulped nervously. "What happened next?"

Drake breathed out. "The man, his wife who was sitting right beside him, and his son who was in the back, all got out of the car and rushed towards me. I was breathing so heavily and my heart was pounding erratically against my chest. I was glued to the ground as I shivered all over, feeling shocked as ever. The man kept apologizing to me, feeling really guilty. He kept asking me questions, if I was okay, about my parents, and where I lived. Realizing that I was the same age as his son and that I actually had nowhere to go, he said, 'I'm Scott.' He pointed his finger to his wife and son. 'And these are Annie and John. Would you like to join our family for a while? I mean our house is big, there's always room.' I remember how happy I was when I heard those words, but I still was hesitant. So, he smiled warmly at me, took my hand in his, and led me to the car. He said he didn't take no for an answer and that it was the least he could do for almost killing me."

Lucy parted her lips, now she finally knew who Scott and Annie were. But she still has to know why he was so emotional at the mention of their names, and what the real secret behind their story was. "So, then you started living with them?"

Drake ripped the hem of the bed sheets that he was digging his fingers through all this time. He literally ripped them. Lucy began fidgeting with her hands, suddenly feeling nervous. Drake clenched his jaw hard. "Lucy, please let this go for now." He squeezed his eyes shut. "It was hard for me already to tell you half of my story. I-I just don't want to continue. I can't."

Lucy blinked, nodding her head slowly. "I'm sorry-"

Drake immediately cut her off, straightening up as he eyed her. "I want to ask you a random question."

"Sure," she said in a low tone.

Drake drew closer to her, staring at her pink lips that he wanted to run his tongue over so badly. "Would you ever forgive a killer? A murderer?"

Lucy furrowed her brows. "I-I don't know. I mean it depends. What's with the question?"

He ran a hand through his hair, messing it up. "Just answer me. Is it a yes or a no?"

She averted her gaze. "No."

Drake's eyes darkened dangerously, his pupils widening in a very eccentric manner. Sighing, he pressed his soft, warm lips on her left shoulder. He slightly lifted her shirt over it, making sure that not one part of her body was showing. He really did not want to lose control tonight. Lucy blushed, ignoring the tingles that ran all over her body in waves. He buried his face in the crook of her neck. "Let's just get some sleep."

Lucy snuggled closer to him, wanting to feel his body against hers. Drake curled his finger under her chin and lifted her face gently. "I want to give you a good night kiss." Not letting her speak or even react, he pressed his lips to hers urgently, and Lucy trembled. She wrapped her arms around his torso and closed her eyes. His lips were moving over hers hungrily as he pulled her tighter to his body. He ran his tongue over her bottom lip and Lucy moaned. "Dr-drake-" He took that as an advantage to slide his tongue fiercely into her mouth, wanting to taste her, to get enough of her.

She couldn't ignore the wild shivers that erupted inside of her as she ran her hands up and down his upper body, tracing every inch of his strong muscles. He pressed his body against hers hard and Lucy couldn't handle the way her body was reacting to his anymore. She certainly had never felt this desperate for anyone's touch in her entire life. She wrapped her legs around his and bit his bottom lip gently, taking Drake by surprise. This is when he dug his fingers into her soft skin and kissed her hard, wet, and open-mouthed. Lucy was literally melting into him, her feelings all over the place. He pulled back and buried his face in her hair, his hands exploring her entire body. Just like that, he pulled away entirely, breathing heavily. "I'm sorry, I-I"

Lucy's chest rose and fell, her face all heated up. "Shhh." She curled her fingers in his hair. "That was one hell of a good night kiss." She giggled out loud.

Drake smirked, whispering huskily. "You like it when I lose control, don't you?"

She gulped nervously. "Maybe."

He chuckled, lifting the covers over them. "Good night, angel." Lucy wanted to ask him why he sounded so gloomy, but she quickly brushed the thought off.

Waking up early because of her stupid alarm, Lucy whipped her head round, looking for Drake. What she hated the most was waking up and not finding him next to her. She sighed and got up to get ready for school. *I'll see him there.* She put on a loose T-shirt and a pair of shorts, took a deep breath, and made her way downstairs. As soon as she closed her bedroom door, her dad yelled out. "Lucy!"

Oh, dear. What does he want now? She rolled her eyes. "What?"

"Come here!" He coughed out.

Lucy entered Howard's room and stood in front of him with crossed arms. He glared. "I know that Drake was here. I could feel it. Those devilish vibes of his-"

Lucy cut him off, annoyed. "Would you stop that already?"

"Why was he here?" He asked in a serious tone.

Lucy sighed deeply. "That's none of your business." With that, she rushed her way out of his room.

He shook his head. "Just open your eyes wide. Real wide."

Lucy fiddled with her fingers as she stepped into the kitchen where Natasha and Chad were. She sat at the table and was lost in her thoughts. *What if it was Earl who was responsible for all those recent deaths? What if Drake was really too harsh on himself? I mean I know he had killed before, he was forced to, but now he was free. He was obviously not controlled by Earl anymore. So, he wouldn't have killed again. He couldn't have.* "Earth to Lucy," Chad waved a hand in front of her face, interrupting her ongoing thoughts.

She faked a smile. "Oh, hi there." Natasha placed a cheese sandwich in front of her, motioning for her to eat before going to school with her brother.

After she ate, she waved good bye to her mom and hopped into Chad's car. Gripping the steering wheel in between his hands and pulling the brakes, Chad grinned. "Say hi to Drake for me." The ride to school was quick, and Lucy was pleased that it was. She wanted to see Drake. Her anticipation to see him was always so strong.

"Will do," She nodded, her eyes gleaming.

Lucy entered through the school's main entrance door, and immediately spotted Amy and Josh. She grinned to herself, happy for Amy that Josh was spending some time with her. Amy saw her and instantly turned around. Lucy frowned and went up to her. "And you're trying to avoid me because?"

Amy crossed her arms. "You didn't contact me at all these couple of days. Did you forget about me?"

Lucy rolled her eyes. "Well, neither did you. Besides, I was kind of busy..."

Amy sighed deeply, then whispered in Lucy's ear. "I have lots of juicy details to tell you about." She signaled to Josh who was standing behind her, oblivious to what they were talking about.

"That's great! I'm really happy for you," Lucy clapped her hands together.

Amy giggled. "Don't jump to conclusions. He just asked me out the other day...I'll tell you about it at lunch. He'll be at his football practice."

Lucy shook her head and looked around for Drake. She couldn't get a glimpse of him at all. *Well, I'll see him in class. He is in my English class anyways.* Josh smirked. "Hey, Lucy. How are you today?" Extending his hand for her to shake, he spoke again. "Where's lover boy?"

Drake? Since when does he care about him? He was probably asking to be relieved, to save himself from getting beaten up or something. Lucy pressed her lips together. "I actually don't know. I'll see him soon though. I'll tell him you asked about him."

Josh ran a hand through his hair nervously. "Um...you really don't have to..."

Lucy laughed at his sudden anxiousness. "I won't. I won't." Lucy didn't find it hard to tell that Josh wasn't that fond of Drake. It was obvious. After all, Drake was not a guy who people usually liked and wanted to hang out with. Except for hormonal girls, that was a whole different case. The bell finally rang, and Lucy rushed to her classroom, probably being the only girl who was that excited for her morning class. Lucy went in through the door and sat in her seat. Drake still didn't show up as she eyed the class intently, waiting for a certain red head to pop in. The class was filled, the teacher began her lecture, and Drake still didn't come. Lucy tried her best to ignore the bitter feeling that was now forming in the pit of her stomach. She let her head fall forward and cursed under her breath. "Shit."

CHAPTER 16

Lucy twirled her pen in her fingers, wondering why Drake did not come. She knew that she shouldn't be so dramatic, but she couldn't help but worry. Lucy sighed, looked at the teacher, and began to write down a bunch of notes, and it suddenly hit her. Today was Drake's birthday. She should surprise him and get him a gift that he will love.

As soon as the bell rang, Lucy rushed out the door and made her way to Amy and Josh. They were standing in front of Amy's class, obviously wasting some time till their second class begins. Lucy chewed on her bottom lip as she flailed her arms in the air. "Guys! Today is Drake's birthday! What should I do? What should I get him?" She slapped her hand to her cheek.

"Would you calm down? You have a lot of time. Lots of boring classes to help you daydream about what you could get him and all," Amy smiled and motioned for Lucy to inhale and exhale.

She clicked her tongue. "Do you guys have any ideas as to what I could get him or something?"

Josh tapped his finger against his lips. "A set of silver knives? He'd enjoy them, I'm sure."

Lucy's mouth fell open. "That's not funny."

Josh chuckled and raised his arms as if surrendering. "I'm sorry."

"Plush toys?" Amy suggested, squinting her eyes.

Lucy puckered her brow. "Does Drake look like the kind of guy who would enjoy these kind of things?"

Amy sighed. "It just popped in my head. My bad."

Lucy bit her nail, thinking hard. An idea went on in her head. "I remember Drake had posters of bands in his room. He also plays the guitar, though I've never heard him play yet. Anyways, I'm thinking of getting him a band tee and a guitar pick and a cake and I'll write him a cute, rhyming poem in class and-"

Amy cut her off, giggling. "I think that would be enough presents. Good thinking."

Lucy beamed. "I was thinking of making him a surprise party or something, but he doesn't like crowded places, if you know what I mean..."

Josh shook his head. "I know exactly what you mean. He doesn't like people."

Lucy glared at him, wanting to wipe that smile off his face. "It's not that..."

Amy nudged Josh, and then glanced at Lucy. "Well, good luck. I hope he'll enjoy his birthday."

She smiled warmly. It was going to be the first time someone celebrated his birthday, since he had mentioned previously that his parents never did.

Lucy stared at the blank, white paper in front of her as she shut her philosophy teacher out and focused on what to write for Drake. She took a deep breath, held her black pen in her hand, and began to write.

"Have I ever mentioned
that you take my breath away
and you always have my attention?

Have I ever mentioned
that you make my heart flutter
and we obviously have a connection?

Have I ever mentioned
that you actually are my angel
and there is no question?

Have I ever mentioned
that you make me feel warm inside
especially when you want my protection
and when you give me all your affection?

But have I ever mentioned
that to me, you are perfection?

I love you, Drake."

Lucy breathed out anxiously, worried if she should mention the last three words. *Drake never mentioned them to me, but of course he does love me. I mean Drake shows it through his actions, rather than through words, but I feel the need to say it. So, I'll say it.* She wondered how he will react, because she really did love him. Smiling to herself, Lucy folded the paper and put it in her bag.

The school day finally ended, and Lucy couldn't wait to get out of here. Amy went up to her with a huge smile plastered on her face. "What is it?" Lucy eyed her skeptically.

Amy ran a hand through her hair. "What kind of friend would I be if I let you go shopping alone?"

Lucy grinned, playing dumb. "What are you trying to say?"

She rolled her eyes. "I'm saying that I want to help you out in getting Drake the gifts. Besides, I have a car, so it will be so much easier."

Lucy's face lit up. "Thank you, Amy."

She shrugged. "No problem. Besides, I still have important stuff to tell you." She winked at her.

"Sure," Lucy shook her head. "How can we forget?"

Amy punched Lucy's arm playfully as they both walked to her car. Turning the key in the ignition, Amy asked. "Where to mademoiselle?"

"À la bakery store," Lucy cleared her throat, trying to speak in French. Not waiting for Amy to reply, she mumbled. "Drake didn't call me or even message me." She swallowed back. "Do you think he's okay? Should we go check on him first?"

Amy shook her head. "Nah. I'm sure he's fine. I mean it is Drake we're talking about!"

"Yeah, I guess you're right," Lucy sighed deeply. "But I'm going to message him. See if he's really all right."

Lucy went into her contact list, pressed on Drake's number, and texted him.

"To: Drake

U didn't come to school today...are u ok? I miss u. U also have left before I even woke up. Text me back or something. Please. I'm worried."

After several minutes of driving, Amy parked her car in front of the bakery store and took a glimpse at Lucy, who looked down. "Are you okay?"

"I don't know. He didn't reply yet," Lucy furrowed her brows.

Amy patted Lucy's shoulder, trying to comfort her. "Just wait a little more. He'll answer eventually."

They both got out of the car and entered the store. The smell of yeast, cinnamon, and chocolate immediately filled their nostrils. Lucy went up to the baker and ordered. "I want a birthday cake, please. A black, chocolate cake. I want 'Happy Birthday, Drake!' to be written on it."

The baker, who was as round as a globe, nodded. "It should be done in about half an hour."

"That's great. We'll be shopping around here. So, we'll come back and get the cake."

Getting out the store, Amy asked. "Why black? It's a birthday cake not a funeral cake."

Lucy pressed her lips together. "First, it's his favorite color. Second, there is no funeral cake."

"Sure," Amy mumbled out. "Hey Lucy, I know a shop that sells cool, band tees. It's just around the corner. Want to check it out?"

She cocked her head to the side. "Okay."

Lucy walked by Amy's side who was leading the way. She couldn't stop thinking about Drake. She was starting to feel real uneasy and her concern for him was intensifying. Lucy knew that Drake doesn't really give that much attention to his phone, but still, something felt quite off to her. Amy stopped and looked behind her at Lucy who was walking slowly, taking hesitant steps. Eying the confused look on her face, Amy cleared her throat. "Um...Lucy?"

She quickened her pace, crossed her arms rather tightly, and looked up at Amy. "What?"

She sighed deeply. "It's Drake, isn't it?"

"Yes," She nodded, letting out a shaky breath.

Amy shoved her hands in her pockets. "Did you try to call him?"

"No. I'm just sc-scared that he wouldn't answer." Lucy swallowed hard, ignoring the negative thoughts that ran through her head.

"Just try. Don't immediately jump to conclusions."

Lucy rummaged through her bag, searching for her cell phone. As much as she hated carrying a big bag, it came in handy at school. Taking out her phone, she dialed Drake's number and pressed her lips together. Beep. Beep. Beep. Nothing. He didn't answer. She tried again and again, but there still was no answer. "Amy! What the hell should I do? He's just not answering! I'm going to lose it!"

She placed both her hands on Lucy's shoulders, shaking her. "Take a deep breath and calm down woman."

She pouted. "Oh Amy, do you think we should go check on him now? I mean the presents can wait..."

She shook her head. "No. I think you should ask one of his neighbors to check on him or something..." She puckered her brow. "You do know at least some of his neighbors, right?"

Lucy fiddled with her fingers. *Think. Think. Think.* She suddenly snapped her fingers together, remembering. "I know one of his neighbors. He's an old guy who pretty much knows some stuff about Drake's whereabouts. I have his number."

"Why do you have an old man's number?" Amy scrunched her nose.

Lucy rolled her eyes. "Long story." She zipped open her bag. "I think the piece of paper he gave me is in here somewhere."

"What paper?" Amy asked.

"Aha!" Lucy cried once she found what she was looking for. Holding a half torn, crumpled paper, Lucy said, "There it is."

"Good. Now call the pedophile, whoever he is. I never imagined I'd say such a thing, but oh well." Amy shrugged.

Lucy typed in the numbers nervously. "He's not a pedophile. Weird? Yes. Pedophile? Meh, I don't think so."

"Whatever," Amy mumbled, moving closer to her.

Pressing her phone to her ear, Lucy waited. "Hello?" A hoarse voice spoke.

Her eyes widened. "Um...hi Mr..." *Oh, great. I don't know his name.* "I'm Lucy, Drake's friend. He's your neighbor..." *This is so awkward.*

"Oh, hi. Is there something wrong?" He asked hesitantly. Clearing his throat, he said, "Yeah, yeah. I remember you. You're the curious cat." He chuckled, as if recalling their previous encounter just now. "The name's George by the way."

Curious cat? "Good. I was wondering if you can do me a small, little favor."

"What is it?" He asked.

"Can you knock at Drake's door or something? I just want to know if he's at home. I mean I want to know if he's okay..." Lucy's voice trailed away.

He didn't answer right away, but then he asked. "Why?"

"Because he's not taking his calls and he didn't come to school today. Just please, can you check on him for me? Because I can't be there at the moment..." Lucy ignored how desperate she sounded.

"Okay. I'll check if his motorcycle is still parked...Just a sec."

Lucy glanced at Amy who was furrowing her brows the whole time as she tried to make out what the man was saying. He breathed out. "The motorcycle's still here. I'm going to go knock...I'll call you later kiddo."

Lucy mumbled an 'okay' and hung up. She told Amy what he said and her face brightened up. "See, he's home! He's probably busy with something. I told you. Now, let's get in." With that, she pulled Lucy by her arm and walked straight through the neon-colored door.

As soon as they entered, loud, rock music was blaring in their ears. The floor tiles were black. The walls were painted a dark shade of purple, and the lighting was dim. Amy felt out of place, but Lucy had a huge smile on her face. A guy marched up to them and asked. "How can I help you dudettes?" He had a Mohawk, piercings all over his face, and sleeve tattoos. He looked like some punk guy from the 70's.

Amy giggled at the term he used as she eyed him from top to bottom. Lucy rolled her eyes at her and cleared her throat. "I'm looking for a Deaf Hamsters T-shirt. For guys. It's a present..."

He nodded and motioned for them to follow him. "So, your boyfriend likes Deaf Hamsters, huh?" He asked Amy, smirking at her.

I was the one who asked, you idiot. Amy tugged a strand behind her ear. "Um...no. I don't have a b-"

He cut her off, searching through a rack of shirts. "That's good," He winked at her and pulled out a black T-shirt with the words 'Deaf Hamsters' on it in capital letters. Lucy shook her head. "Okay. I'll take this one."

"Hey Lucy! There are guitar picks with band logos on them over here!" Amy said as she stepped towards a low shelf where they were displayed.

The guy stared at Amy while he played with his lip ring. "Stop right there."

Amy froze in her position, wondering if she did anything wrong. "What is it?"

He approached her, lifting his hand. She sucked in a breath as he grabbed a blue bandana from the top shelf above her head. He bit his lip and tied it around her head nonchalantly. "This color really suits you."

"Th-thanks," Amy smiled weakly, ignoring the tension between them.

Lucy suddenly pulled Amy away from him and asked. "While you were both drooling over each other, I chose this one. It's pretty, right?" She held the Iron Maiden pick between her thumb and index finger.

"Yep," Amy touched the bandana on her head.

Lucy sighed. "Let's go buy them now. The cake should be ready in a few..."

Lucy paid the guy, and just as Amy was about to take out her money, he said, "No, the bandana's on me."

She giggled, blushing. "Thank you."

"It's Gabe," He grinned.

"Amy," She stretched her arm out for him to shake.

"Hope you'll come back soon..." He said in a low, husky voice.

"We will," Amy waved bye and followed Lucy who was practically running out the door.

Walking side by side back to the bakery, Lucy puckered her brow at Amy. "What was going on with you two?"

She clapped her hands together. "He was flirting, duh! Isn't he cute?"

"If you think piercings and tattoos are cute, then yeah, he's cute," Lucy suppressed her laughter, as she imagined him skipping in a meadow with flowers in his hands.

"Gabe is really hot," She batted her eyelashes.

Lucy giggled at her. "Yeah, and looks like he's interested in short girls."

Amy nudged her playfully. "You mean hot, short girls."

Lucy placed the cake in the backseat of the car, smiling to herself. Amy began to drive while Lucy told her the directions to Drake's place. Lucy's phone suddenly rang. She immediately opened it with shaky fingers, her heart almost stopping. *Ugh, it's not Drake.* "It's George," Her face fell. "Hello." She answered it.

"Lucy. I don't think you should worry about him. He's fine."

"Really? That's good because I'm coming over. I'm on my way,"

"N-no! I don't think that's a good idea," He gulped nervously.

She ignored the sickening feeling that was eating her up. "Why not?"

"Because um...he's not feeling well..." He mumbled, unsure of what he was saying.

Lucy furrowed her brows, *didn't he just say that I shouldn't worry, and that Drake's fine?* "Well then I'll see for myself. Bye." Before even waiting for his response, she hung up. She really didn't want to hear what else he was going to say because she knew that he wouldn't give her the answers she wanted.

"What did he say?" Amy scrutinized Lucy's pale face.

"Nothing. Can you just please step on it?" Lucy begged, wanting to get to Drake's place so badly.

"Sure," Amy said, worried about her friend. Amy hoped Drake was all right, because if he wasn't, she'll blame herself for it. She kept telling Lucy to check on him later and that he surely was okay. She sighed, stepped on the gas pedal, and sped down the road.

Lucy fiddled with her fingers as she clenched and unclenched her jaw. The car swerved wildly to the right, the tires screeching. Amy let out a breath, gripping the steering wheel. "Which building?"

Lucy leaned in, looking through the translucent window. "The second one, over there." She pointed her finger to the tall, grey building. Amy nodded and parked her car across it.

Lucy got out of the car, took out everything she bought, and blew Amy a kiss. "Thank you, Amy. I'll call you when I get back home. Take care."

"Whoa, whoa, whoa. I'm not going anywhere. I'm going to wait for you here, okay?" Amy smiled warmly at her.

"Are you sure? I mean I'll be fine-"

Amy cut her off, shaking her head. "I'm sure. Now go!"

She took a deep breath and made her way towards Drake's apartment. As soon as she reached his door, she saw George leaning against the wall with his arms crossed. She gasped. "What are you doing outside your house?"

"Waiting for you, of course," He looked at her then looked at the bags that she was carrying. "Aww, you didn't have to."

She glared at him, not in the mood for any jokes. She lifted her hand to knock at Drake's door, but George immediately put her arm down. "I think you should visit him later. Trust me."

"What? No!" She huffed. "It's really none of your business. Thank you for your help, but I can handle myself." She knocked at Drake's door.

He shrugged. "Okay. Suit yourself." With that, he went into his apartment and shut his door.

She waited impatiently, her nervousness getting worse and worse. A sudden, loud yell came out from behind the door. "I fucking told you to stop knocking, George. Just tell her I can't see her today. Don't you fucking understand?"

Lucy's hand flew to her mouth, he didn't want to see her. She felt as if she was running out of oxygen. She felt as if she was slapped, hard. She couldn't help but blurt out. "It's Lu-lucy." And just like that, the door clicked open. She sucked in a shaky breath as Drake came into view. *Oh my God.* Her eyes widened while she stared at him, shocked. He was as pale as a ghost. His eyes were so dark; they looked black, and there were dark circles under them. His hair was wet; the edges sticking to his cheeks. He was sweating profusely. And he was breathing heavily as if he was trying to fill his lungs with air as much as he could. His lips were chapped and parted, and it seemed as if his energy was literally drained out of him. He also happened to be shirtless, but what made her take a couple of steps backwards were the red lines on his chest. It was as if someone was scratching his chest hard, correction, ripping his chest. He wasn't even able to stand for crying out loud. She felt traumatized. She cleared her throat and dug her nails in her palms. "What the hell happened to you, Drake?"

"Please leave. I-I can't explain this to you..." His weak voice trailed away.

Her heart was aching, she wanted to help him, she wanted to make him feel better, but she clearly had no clue as to what she could do. She still was freaked out, stunned, as she stared at him. "What can I do to help?" She approached him, walking in, and he moved back.

"Leaving. It would help. A lot," He mumbled, squeezing his eyes shut.

Her face fell, she couldn't recall a time when she felt as down as she was feeling now. "B-but it's yo-your birthday."

His eyes shot open and he glanced at the bags that she was carrying. He bit down on his bottom lip hard as he kept staring at them, as if just noticing them now. His eyes bored into hers. "Shit." He took a few steps towards her and placed his hands on her shoulders. "I'm so sorry. I really am. But you have to leave for your own good. I don't want to hurt you."

"I do-don't understand," She stuttered, batting her eyelashes to fight back the tears that threatened to fall.

He clenched his jaw hard, looking as pained as she was, maybe even worse. It was like he was battling with himself, with his inner demons. "You mean so much to me, you know that. I don't want you to see the monster that I am." He breathed out. "Not when I'm like this."

She tore her gaze away from his, she didn't want to face him. She knew that he wouldn't give her answers, he rarely did. Just as she was about to leave without saying another word, he pulled her by her arm. "Wait." She turned around to look at him, her body urging her to stay and help out. He asked. "What are in those bags?"

Her eyes softened. "Gifts. For you." She swayed back and forth on her feet. "I spent the whole day thinking of what to get you...Amy helped me out."

A small smile crept onto his lips as he slid down the wall and sat cross-legged on the floor. "Show me."

Bipolar much? Lucy simply listened to him, she really didn't want to argue. Besides, it was his birthday. She opened up the box to reveal the black cake. "I know you like ham and cheese, but a cake is much better on such an occasion."

He chuckled as he eyed the cake in front of him. "This looks delicious. Thank you, Loo."

"Didn't I tell you never to call me Loo?" She pouted, loving the warm, red color that was replacing the paleness of his face.

He leaned in and pulled the other bag to him. He took out the Deaf Hamsters T-shirt and smiled widely. "I love it." He then took out the pick and gave her a lopsided smirk. "You really know exactly what I like, don't you?"

She shrugged innocently. "There's a folded paper at the end of the bag. I wr-wrote it to you in class." She said as she looked at him and wondered what could possibly have happened to him.

"In class? Boy am I a bad influence." He cocked his head to the side and carefully opened it. Just as he was about to read it, he groaned in pain, his hands flying to his head. "This fucking headache won't go away."

Lucy pressed her lips together, worried about him. "Should I get you medicine or something?"

"No. I don't take meds," He said through gritted teeth.

Lucy rubbed the back of her neck, gulping nervously. "Okay-"

"Please, leave. I thought I was beginning to feel better, but I clearly am not," He stood up and tangled his fingers in his hair, pulling hard, trying to get rid of the pain.

She gasped; she has never seen Drake in such a condition. "But I can help!" Seeing him like this hurts her. Real bad.

He was literally fuming now as he clenched his fists at his sides. "Just fucking leave! I don't want you here!" He punched the wall hard and left a hole, earning a shriek from Lucy.

Letting her tears fall down her cheeks, she ran away from Drake, out of his apartment, and out of the building.

CHAPTER 17

As Lucy rushed her way out, she heard Drake cuss out loud in irritation. "Fuck!" His voice echoed through the walls. She swallowed hard and fought back the new, fresh tears. Spotting Amy's car ahead, she wiped her eyes quickly, took a deep breath, and went towards the car. She hoped her face wasn't too red, she really didn't want to talk about what happened. Once she got in, Amy's eyes widened and her mouth slightly parted. "Oh my God! What happened?" *Now I knew that my face was definitely tomato red.*

She chewed on her bottom lip. "Please I-I-"

"That bastard! What did he do? I'm going to murder him! I told you he was good for nothing!" Amy glared, fuming. If this was a cartoon, smoke would come out of her ears for sure.

"Don't start with the 'I told you so' please. I just don't know what's gotten into him today." She breathed in. "If you see his appearance, you'd freak out. I've never seen him in such a condition. I've never seen anyone in such a condition!"

Amy puckered her brow. "What do you mean?"

Ignoring her trembling hands, she mumbled. "He was sweating like crazy, his hair was wet, his face was pale as hell, he had red lines on his chest, an-and he was breathing heavily. God, I feel so confused."

Amy bit her nails as she contemplated. "Maybe he's ill or something."

"Well, couldn't he just tell me? Instead, he kicked me out! I just wanted to help!" Lucy huffed, her heart beating rapidly.

She tapped her fingers against her chin. "I'm sure Drake isn't the type of person who'd admit he needs help. Maybe he just doesn't want you to get sick because of him, or maybe he just doesn't want you to face his weak self."

Lucy looked at her through hooded lashes. "I-I don't know. I'm sure it's more than just that..." Her voice trailed away. She narrowed her eyes at her friend. "How come you're defending him? Didn't you want to murder him a few minutes ago?"

Amy rolled her eyes. "As much as I want you to have nothing to do with him, I can't deny the connection between you two. I mean he clearly cares about you a lot. I'm sure he wouldn't just tell you to leave for nothing. Just wait, he'll call you and apologize eventually."

Lucy gave her a weak smile, she appreciated Amy's attempt to cheer her up. "Thank you."

Smiling widely, Amy said, "Besides, Josh, you, and me are going to have a drink at a pub tonight."

"We are?" Lucy giggled.

"Yep. I'm not going to let you stay awake all night, thinking about your beloved Drake. We'll go have some fun, and we'll come back early. Don't worry your little head about school." Amy shook her head.

She sucked in a breath. "But-"

Amy cut her off. "No buts. I promise you we'll have a good time."

Lucy grinned. "Okay, but I don't drink, so I'll just watch you guys."

Amy let her head fall back. "Seriously? Just shut up, Lucy." She nudged her by her elbow, and started the car.

She furrowed her brows. "Wait. The car was parked in front of his place all this time? Could you drive us home already?" Her mouth fell open.

"As if you didn't know," Amy mumbled, stepping on the gas pedal.

Parking in front of Lucy's house, Lucy got out, thanked her friend, and made her way towards the door. As soon as she entered through it, her mother rushed towards her. "Where were you?"

"I was with Amy. She had to talk to me about something that's been bothering her, and as a friend I wanted to reassure her. Don't worry, I'll go to my room, and finish all my stupid homework." She faked a smile.

Natasha sighed deeply. "Well...okay. Just tell me next time. I get worried about you, you know."

She nodded her head, hugged her mother, and ran upstairs to her room. Lucy took out her books from her bag, and began doing her homework. She had to finish them, or else her mom won't let her go out tonight. Trying to figure out a math problem, she gritted her teeth and tore out the paper. She crumpled it and tossed it into the trash can. Lucy rubbed her temple, wanting to focus on her studies, but all she could think about was Drake. She swore under her breath, and took out her cell phone. She stared at it blankly, waiting for a call or a message that she was sure will never come.

Lucy was glad that her mother accepted, she felt lucky to have such an easygoing mother. However, she promised her to do a couple of chores, and that was somehow the main reason why she accepted. Sighing, she stared at the clothes in her closet. She had to look hot tonight. After trying a couple of dresses, she chose a tight, black one. She then slipped her leather jacket on, applied red lipstick, drew a winged eyeliner, and stood in front of the mirror. *Drake, you're so going to miss out.*

A loud honk was heard, and Lucy quickly grabbed her purse and made her way downstairs. She said good bye to Natasha and Chad, smiling. Just as she was halfway out the door, Chad pulled her by her arm. "Don't be late, and don't do anything stupid, okay?"

"It's like you don't know me at all," Lucy rolled her eyes.

"I'm just saying, okay?" Chad sighed.

Lucy nodded, kissed him on his cheek, and got in Josh's car. Sitting in the backseat, she said her hellos to the two. Josh smirked. "Who's going to have some fun tonight?"

"We are!" Amy squealed, excited.

Lucy bit her inner cheek; she couldn't help but feel a little bad. Drake was practically feeling like shit, and she was going out to have fun. She squeezed her eyes shut, wanting everything to be all right so badly. She hoped he was okay, and that he really didn't mean what he said to her. Just as she was about to speak to the two, her phone beeped. Taking out her phone with shaking fingers, she stared at the bright screen. It was a message from Drake. *God.* Her breath got caught in her throat as she nervously opened it.

"8:20 pm

You just can't.

-Drake-"

Lucy gulped, her breathing quickening. *What was that supposed to mean?* She quickly sent him a message, asking what he meant by 'You just can't'. Waiting impatiently, she prayed it was not what she thought it was.

Drake didn't answer her right away, and Lucy frowned, getting tenser by the minute. She sighed and averted her attention to Josh, who happened to be talking to her. "Hmm?" She asked.

Josh looked at her through the inside rear-view mirror, his brown eyes boring into hers. "Haven't you heard a word I was saying to you?"

Lucy gulped. "Um...sorry. I was thinking about something..."

Amy shot her a glare, turning around to face her. "Don't, Lucy."

Josh cleared his throat. "I said that you look gorgeous. That dress really fits you perfectly." He smiled warmly, and Amy fidgeted in her seat.

Lucy pressed her lips together. "Thank you. You look good yourself." She eyed his appearance. He was wearing a white button-up shirt with a pair of dark, blue jeans.

He gave her a lopsided smirk and shrugged his shoulders. Amy had her arms crossed against her chest, a gloomy expression lingering on her face. Lucy leaned in to whisper in her ear. "What's wrong?"

She licked her dry lips. "Nothing. I'm fine. Really."

Just as Lucy was about to question her further, her phone finally beeped. She let out a long, shaky breath, opening the new message from Drake.

"8:45 pm

You can't love me.

-Drake-"

Lucy felt as if her heart stopped beating, as if her heart was torn out of her chest. Her eyes burned, ready to let the tears pour out. *No. She wasn't going to cry, she wouldn't let herself cry.* She batted her eyelashes, wanting to push the stupid tears back. She was hurt. She was truly hurt, because she thought that after reading her poem, he would tell her that he felt the same way. She thought he'd tell her the dark secrets that he'd been hiding from her. She thought that they can finally just be. *I was wrong. He wouldn't fully let me in.* Just reading those four words made her blood boil. She's going to have fun tonight. She's going to lose herself tonight.

Josh finally parked the car in front of a crowded pub. The music was so loud, the beat pulsated throughout Lucy's body. She pushed her hair back, shook her head, and went in with Josh and Amy. They pushed their way through the shoving, sweaty bodies as the smell of smoke and alcohol permeated the place. Lucy followed Josh who sat on a bar stool and motioned for the girls to take a seat. He yelled over the booming noise. "What do you girls want to drink?"

Lucy shrugged. "Whatever you guys are taking."

Amy tapped her finger against her chin. "Order something strong, for both of us." She winked at Lucy, aware of her sudden mood change. However, she didn't want to ask her about it.

Lucy nodded shyly. She glanced around, smiling at the fact that everyone was dancing and enjoying their time. She tapped Amy's shoulder. "Let's dance."

Noticing that Josh was busy chatting with the bartender, who happened to be his friend, Amy quickly nodded. They made their way to the center, and began to dance as they both swayed their hips to the music. After a couple of minutes, Josh came up to them with their drinks. He handed the two girls their cups and yelled. "Cheers." Saying that, he gulped his entire drink down his throat.

Lucy bit her lip as she watched Amy do the same, she really didn't want to get drunk, so she did the stupidest thing ever. She sipped a little from her cup and dropped her drink on the floor. "Oops!" She shrugged her shoulders, pretending to be affected.

"It's okay! I'll get you another one!" Josh exclaimed.

"No, it's fine. I'll go get one myself." She lied. *So much for losing myself tonight.* As she marched her way to the bar, someone pulled her by her arm. Bumping against a rough chest, she assumed it was a man. She looked up, and was met by two lustful, dark eyes. "Hey there. Want to dance?"

She sighed deeply, not liking the small distance between them. Narrowing her eyes at him, she considered. *Oh, what the hell.* She nodded, saying yes. *One dance won't hurt.* He grinned wickedly as he pulled her into the crowd. He placed his arms around her waist and moved her hips from side to side. Lucy took in the man's features. He was older than she was; maybe around twenty-two years old. He had brown hair and green eyes, and he was muscular. She suddenly regretted her decision to dance with him. *What if he were forceful or something?* She shook her head, clearing such a thought. "Let's go outside, and get some fresh air. The smoke is killing me." He licked his lips rather slowly.

Lucy fiddled with her fingers nervously. "O-okay."

His face instantly brightened up as he made his way outside, making sure she was following. Lucy's purse wouldn't stop vibrating, it was her phone. She ignored it, not wanting to answer anybody, especially Drake. A victorious smile crept onto her lips as she pushed her purse back. Suddenly, the man grabbed her by her waist and pulled her into him roughly. Lucy gasped, trying to wriggle away from his tight grasp. He leaned in, his breath reeking of alcohol. "Why don't you get in my car, and let me take you on a ride, babe."

Lucy swallowed hard, her heart pounding against her chest. "Um...maybe some other time..." She forced out a smile, wishing he'd leave her alone now.

Tightening his grip on her, he spat out. "How about right now? Huh?"

She winced at the pain he was causing her, she was sure that his hand will leave a mark on her skin. "N-no. Let me go!" She twisted and turned, mentally scolding herself for being such a stupid teen.

He chuckled. "Why would I let you go? I have lots of things on my mind..." He buried his face in her neck. "That I want to try with you."

Lucy's face turned red as tears fell down from her stinging eyes. She sniffed, and tried to pull herself away from him, but it was no use. Just as his hand trailed down her back, she stomped on his foot with full force, making him yell out with pain. Turning around and making her way back into the pub, he pulled her hard by her hair, taking her by surprise. She screamed out, wanting someone to help her, but everyone was too busy getting drunk to even hear her. He fisted her hair. "How dare you fucking do that?"

Lucy squeezed her eyes shut and clenched her jaw. "Let me go, you psycho!"

"And why would I do that?" He smirked against her neck.

"Because she fucking told you so!" Someone roared, venom dripping from his voice. As the man backed away from Lucy, she whipped her head round, only to be met with dark, flaming eyes. It was Drake. She ached to see him. She didn't know how he found her, and why he was here, but she couldn't be more relieved. The man approached Drake with fists clenched at his sides. "I advise you to mind your own business, because I have a gun."

Drake chuckled darkly. "A gun? Oh, that won't help you at all." He stepped towards him. "It won't save you from what I'm about to do to you."

The man gritted his teeth as he aimed his fists towards Drake's face, wanting to punch him. Drake swiftly ducked, still smiling. He then lunged at him, and punched him several times in the face. The man wasn't able to even hit him once, Drake was too fast and strong. The man howled in torment, but Drake didn't show mercy as he continued to beat him up, watching the way blood oozed from his nose. He threw another punch against his jaw and the man coughed out blood. He wasn't able to breathe as Drake's dark orbs pierced through him. The man had a split lip, a bleeding nose, a bruised, purple eye, and was practically suffocating. Lucy couldn't utter a single word while she watched with wide eyes. Drake was about to kill him, and he didn't give a damn.

Lucy knew that she had to do something to stop all this. As much as she wanted this man to be beaten up due to the way he talked and treated her, she didn't want him to die. She didn't want Drake to have to go to jail because of her. Lucy bolted towards Drake and tried pushing him off the man who was lying on the ground, helpless, not able to do anything to save himself. Drake gripped Lucy's arm tight, his eyes burning into hers. "What the fuck are you trying to do? Move."

Lucy swallowed hard while she held his burning gaze. "No. I'm doing this for you, trust me." She looked at the man and then back at him. "I think he had enough."

Drake gritted his teeth hard, easily able to break his own jaw. "Are you okay?" His eyes softened, his thumb caressing her tear-stained cheek.

She breathed out and leaned into his warm touch. "Yes." She mumbled, new, fresh tears pouring out of her eyes. It hurts her to know that he didn't want her to love him. It hurts that he might not want her as much as she wants, needs him. All that she knew and was sure of was that she just couldn't stop loving him, ever, and she hated being this pathetic.

Drake furrowed his brows, concerned. "Why are you crying then?"

"Because of you! You're so confusing! I don't know what the hell you want with me! If y-you don't-" She licked her dry lips, cursing herself for bursting out like this. "L-love me, then why do you care if well, if some guy comes and-"

He cut her off, angry, real angry. "Stop. Stop talking like a fucking idiot, Lucy." He tugged her by her arm and led her away from the crowded place. She looked down at her feet as she walked behind him, following him. Drake stopped and turned around to face her. He wrapped his arms around her waist, pressing his head against her forehead. "Oh, Lucy." He let out a breath, his plump lips so close to hers, Lucy wanted him to close the distance between them so badly. She ached for his kiss. Pushing her against the wall, Drake pulled her body to his hard. "I can't believe how naive you are." Smoothing her hair out of her face, he clenched his jaw. "You really have no idea what you do to me, do you?"

Lucy looked at his troubled face with wide eyes, not knowing how to answer his question. When he noticed that she wasn't going to say anything, he continued. "You drive me crazy with want, Lucy." He tightened his hold on her. "I'm sure you know that already." Drake tilted his head and took her by surprise when he pressed his cold lips on her neck. He ran his mouth up and down the length of her neck and goosebumps formed everywhere on her heated skin. She sucked in a shaky breath as he slowly spread her legs open with his knee, and desire coiled inside her. He flicked his tongue against the sensitive skin below her ear, teasing her. "Oh, the things I want to do to you. I want to feel you, all of you, Lucy."

Lucy gulped, she was both excited and stunned. She knew that he was somehow distracting her. He didn't answer her question yet and she wasn't going to let him win. She slightly pulled away from him, feeling her heart clench against her chest. "Answer me, Drake. I want a real, honest answer."

Drake was fuming, not liking what she just did. His eyes darkened, and that meant he was outraged. "You want an answer?" He dug his teeth into his bottom lip, taking a couple of steps backwards. "Well, good luck in fucking finding one." He yelled, his nose flaring. Just as Lucy thought he was going to leave, he raked his hand through his hair. "Go home."

Who does he think he is to order me around? He can't even say the words I love you. She clamped her eyes shut, ignoring the pain that suffocated her. Pulling herself together, she turned around and walked away, not wanting to argue with him anymore. Lucy wanted to go home for sure, this was one terrible night. She took out her phone and dialed Chad's number. She didn't want to call Amy or Josh, because if they really did care about her absence the slight bit, they would have at least contacted her. They probably were too drunk or doing the dirty or something.

Lucy huffed and waited for her brother to answer; but there was no answer whatsoever. Lucy pouted and was obliged to call a cab. *Curse not having a car.* After a couple of minutes, the cab arrived. Sighing gratefully, she got in and sat in the backseat. The taxi driver looked at her through the inside rear-view mirror and smiled. "Where to?"

Lucy's eyes widened once she noticed who was driving. It was Drake's neighbor. "George? What are you doing?" *That man gets stranger and stranger.*

He chuckled. "I'm doing my job as you can see."

Lucy puckered her brow. "I didn't know you worked as a taxi driver."

"Well, now you know," He winked at her and repeated his question. "Where to?"

She gave him a weak smile and told him her address. Looking out the window, she tilted her head up, and stared at the shimmering stars. She took in their warped shapes in the vast blackness. She felt so down in the dumps. Just as she thought the silence was about to eat her up, George spoke. "You know, you mean the world to Drake."

Lucy whipped her head round and looked at him, gaining her full attention. "Yeah, right." She really didn't want to talk about him.

George shook his head. "I want to tell you something." He cleared his throat. "I have been Drake's neighbor for a while now, so I kind of know how that mind of his works. He maybe doesn't tell you how he feels about you every day, but he sure as hell shows it. You just have to wait a little, he'll spit it out eventually. He's just scared of losing you. He did lose a lot of people in his life. He has no one he can rely on and trust." Swerving the car to the right, he said, "Just be patient with him. No matter how tough he seems, he's actually as fragile as ever."

Lucy gasped, feeling warm on the inside. "How do you know all this?"

"Let's just say I'm one hell of a curious neighbor," He chuckled, his eyes focusing on the road.

Lucy giggled. "Thank you, George." She sighed deeply, remembering the day he cried in front of her and told her what he had faced as a kid.

CHAPTER 18

Lucy knocked and knocked on her front door, but no one answered. She furrowed her brows in confusion as she took out her keys, opening the door. She stepped in, her eyes searching the dark, empty house. *Where is everybody?* Lucy gulped nervously, taking in the eerie silence. She entered Howard's room, and realized that he also wasn't here. Just as she was about to turn around and walk out the room, she spotted a crumpled piece of paper on the nightstand. It was a note, a note from Chad. As she read, she noticed that the handwriting was somehow illegible, it was obviously written in a hurry. It said,

"We're at the hospital nearby. Meet us there as soon as you read this."

Hospital? Lucy felt uneasy, trying her best not to panic. She hated hospitals, and she didn't want anything to do with them. She rushed outside, her eyes scanning the area, hoping George was still there. He wasn't. Lucy dialed his number quickly, her phone almost slipping out of her hands. As soon as he answered, she told him to come pick her up, and she made sure to tell him to come here straight away.

"Faster!" Lucy mumbled, clutching the seat belt in her hands tightly.

"I'm driving as fast as I can!" George exclaimed, stepping on the gas pedal even harder. He hoped there were no cops around, or else he'd be in so much trouble.

Lucy took quick, deep breaths and squeezed her eyes shut, trying to calm herself down. However, George's loud voice made her eyes snap open. "We're here!"

Feeling her heart hammer against her chest, she paid him, and got out. She ran inside the hospital, almost knocking out one of the nurses passing by. Lucy dialed Chad's number, hoping the line wouldn't be out of service or something. She went up towards the receptionist and asked which room they were in. The receptionist, who had a stern look on her face, motioned to the fourth room on the left. Thanking her, Lucy made her way there, feeling her steps become wobblier by the minute. She entered through the door hesitantly. Chad was the first to notice her enter. He looked up at her, his face red and tears were pouring down his face. Natasha then glanced at her, crying her eyes out, as her body slightly jerked every time she wept.

Lucy eyed the empty hospital bed, swallowing hard. "What's going on?"

Natasha looked down, burying her face in her hands, while Chad spoke, his voice coming out raspy and hoarse. "Howard is dead."

Lucy's eyes widened in horror. "What? How?"

"We didn't address him the whole day, we were watching TV in the living room. Natasha then went into his room to bring him his dinner, and he wasn't moving, wasn't speaking. We thought he was sleeping, but he wasn't actually br-breathing. So, we rushed our way here, thinking that maybe he had a chance to l-live or something." Chad sucked in a shaky breath. "We've only been here for less than an hour."

Lucy didn't move a muscle, she simply stood there, glued to the floor. She knew that they were both crying out of shock, especially Chad. Howard wasn't a good father nor was he a good husband. However, Lucy couldn't help but feel pity for him. She didn't cry, she couldn't. She was just totally stunned. "Did the doctors know the reason?"

Chad shrugged, wiping his tear-stained cheeks with a tissue. "No. They said it was unknown."

She raised her brow, stepping closer to Chad. "Unknown?"

He chuckled sarcastically. "Yes, can you believe that? What kind of doctors do we have these days?" Bending and pushing his mother's hair back out of her hidden face, he continued. "First it was the murdered bodies; the doctors did not know the cause of their death, correction, who was the cause of their death. And now, it's the same with Howard."

Lucy dug her nails in her palms hard. Chad had a point. She knew all along that there was something unusual happening, but never did she relate it to the person that kept popping in her head, haunting her. Deep inside, she knew, she had a feeling as to who could be the reason behind all this. However, no way in hell was she going to share it with anyone. She was going to keep it to herself, until she knew the truth, the whole truth. Lucy pressed her lips together, staring at her mother who has finally straightened up and grabbed three tissues. "It's okay mom, he's in a better place..." Her voice trailed away.

"Better place?" Chad shook his head. "He's in hell."

Natasha's eyes widened at Chad as she parted her trembling lips. "Shut up! He was changing, and you know it."

Chad's nose flared. "Don't you think he was a little too late?"

Lucy mouthed a 'stop it' to Chad, she knew that he was truly hurt. After all, they both didn't have a good relationship with their father, and he had never treated them as his own children. He certainly had never treated them in a caring and fatherly way ever. While other dads were enjoying their time with their kids on Sundays, their dad was busy reprimanding them, telling them how worthless they were, and of course, making sure he was the only one satisfied. Lucy sighed deeply, remembering the words that made her and Chad upset the most. 'You shouldn't have been born, you were both a fucking accident!' That was what he always said, reminding them that he truly didn't want them.

"Lucy?" Chad breathed out, snapping her out of her trance.

"What?" She cleared her throat.

He rubbed his temple, trying to get rid of his headache. "Tomorrow's da-Howard's funeral, okay?"

Natasha nodded her head rather quickly. "Yes. We contacted the church, the priest..."

Lucy fiddled with her fingers nervously. Last time she had been at a funeral was when her grandfather died four years ago. All she remembered was that she never really wanted to attend one ever again. Chad blinked twice. "I think we should head home now...it's getting really late." He helped Natasha up, as Lucy followed behind.

As soon as they arrived home, Chad and Lucy immediately took Natasha to her room, making sure she got some sleep. She was obviously exhausted. Lucy then marched up to her own room, and let herself fall forward on her bed. With her face pressed against the sheets, she screamed at the top of her lungs, her screaming muffled. She fisted the sheets tightly with both hands, wanting to cry, to feel the release, but she just couldn't shed any tear. She felt completely numb. *Drake. Where are you when I need you?*

Lucy yawned, stretching her arms. She had fallen asleep last night without even changing into her pajamas. Blinking her eyes to get accustomed to the bright light that was seeping through her window, she got up slowly. She wasn't feeling so well. Lucy made her way to the bathroom and looked at herself in the mirror. Her eyes widened as she combed through her wild hair and washed her face with ice-cold water.

"Lucy! Hurry up and get dressed!" Chad yelled from downstairs.

She sucked in a breath, memories of yesterday came crashing back. Lucy pulled herself together, marching her way to her closet, and choosing a black outfit. People usually wear black to show their sadness and mourning, but she was just wearing black for the sake of wearing it. She really wasn't that upset about losing her father, and that fact kind of worried her. Settling for a black, tight top with black, skinny jeans and black high heels, she felt sort of Goth. After checking her appearance in the bathroom mirror one last time, she got back into her room only to be met with a pair of intense, dark, blue eyes. Lucy gasped, her hand flying to her chest. "What the hell are you doing here?"

Drake took a couple of steps towards her, eying her from head to toe. "I came to see you."

Lucy breathed out. "You have to stop scaring me like that." She crossed her arms tightly. "What do you want anyways?"

Drake furrowed his brows, not pleased with the tone she was using. "I wanted to say...sorry." He clenched his fists at his side. "Sorry about last night."

Lucy's mouth fell open, Drake rarely apologized. She took a deep breath, trying her best not to forgive him so easily. He looked breathtaking in his leather jacket that clung to his body so perfectly. And those eyes; their icy blueness invoked a feeling like she was being dragged into a river of frozen emotions. His fiery, red locks fell onto his face, and he was clenching his jaw as he stared at her, tempting her. Nodding her head, she whispered. "I have to go."

Just as she turned around, Drake grabbed her by her arm roughly, pulling her to him. "Don't ever avoid me. We both know it kills you to turn away from me." He leaned in, his manly cologne engulfing her. "Just like it kills me."

Opening her mouth to speak, Drake stopped her by cupping her cheeks in his hands and kissing her urgently. He kissed her hard and fast, wanting to taste her so desperately. Lucy trembled in his arms, kissing him with as much passion and want. Drake stroked her lips with his tongue, and Lucy wrapped her arms around his neck. He then thrust his tongue inside her mouth and raised her arms above her head. She whimpered against his warm, wet lips as his hands trailed up her torso, pushing up her top to reveal her black, lace bra. He groaned, his eyes darkening. He gripped her tightly by the waist and kissed down her neck, her collarbones, and in between her breasts, savoring her soft, heated skin. Lucy moaned, curling her fingers in his hair, and lifting his face up to hers. Drake captured her lips again in another deep kiss, not seeming to get enough of her.

He slightly pulled away, pressing his lips against the tip of her ear. "You're all mine."

Lucy nodded her head quickly, burying her flushed face in his hair. She could hear both their hearts pounding against her ears. Breathing in his intoxicating scent, she closed her eyes, succumbing to his warmth. Drake stroked her hair softly with one hand, and with the other, he held her to him possessively. "You're going to Howard's funeral, right?"

Lucy looked up at him, her eyes searching his. "You know?" She gulped nervously. "Is there something you're not telling me, Drake?"

Drake stepped backwards, releasing her. He ran his hand through his hair, pulling at its ends. "I-" He stopped, suddenly gritting his teeth. His muscles flexed as he dug his fingers in his palms hard. "Fine! I'm the one who killed that bloody, fucking father of yours."

Lucy blinked, slowly taking in the information. She knew that Drake had killed him, she knew it all along. "Why? Why so...suddenly?"

Drake pressed his face into his hands, irritated. "I had mentioned it. He deserves to die."

Lucy sighed deeply. "Drake-"

He cut her off, clamping his eyes shut. "It's better to kill a sinful person rather than to kill an innocent one." He swallowed hard, his eyes boring into hers.

She furrowed her brows, drowning in the power that his eyes held. "What's that supposed to mean?"

Just as Drake was about to answer, Chad yelled out again. "Aren't you done already?" Lucy heard him mumble out in a lower tone. "Girls. We're going to a damn funeral, you know!"

Lucy crossed her arms, glaring, as she yelled back. "Calm your tits!"

A smile crept onto Drake's face while he puckered his brow. He then pressed his lips together in a tight line. "I'm going to leave." He headed to the window. "I'll be there at the funeral."

"Wait!" Lucy wanted him to explain to her what he meant, but instead of begging him to answer, she chose not to. Knowing Drake full well, he wouldn't answer her anyways. "You're leaving through the window?"

Drake stared at her worried expression, chuckling. "I came in through the window, and I'll leave through the window." He gave her a lopsided smirk and jumped out instantly, making Lucy run towards the window to check if he was okay.

Lucy tried blocking out her mother's weeping. Natasha wouldn't stop crying as she held several tissues to her face. Chad was standing beside her, patting her back in reassurance. Lucy simply stood there, eying her surroundings. The sun shone brightly on the dusky, pink roses that were placed on top of the casket. A few people wearing black stood with their heads down, facing the front. Howard wasn't considered to be a loved person, which is why he didn't have many friends. Lucy looked up at the priest who was standing beside the casket with a pitiful look on his face. He was clearly waiting to see if there were more people coming before he said his prayers. *I wonder if he knew what an awful person Howard was.* Sighing deeply, Lucy waited for Drake to come and rescue her from this dark, gloomy atmosphere. But then again, Drake was a dark person himself.

"We gather here today to celebrate the life of Howard Brown, who has now returned to his home with our God, the Father," The priest spoke, beginning his speech.

Lucy rolled her eyes, he was definitely not with God now. She averted her gaze, not really wanting to listen to the priest; and that is when her eyes landed on a familiar figure. A wide smile instantly took over her miserable expression. He was wearing a black suit with a tie. He looked very classy, especially the way his long hair was tucked back. *Since when did Drake own a suit?* Lucy parted her lips as she stared at him. Drake winked at her, smirking. As he walked towards her, Lucy sucked in a breath and ignored the warm feeling that was growing stronger and stronger inside her.

Drake stood right in front of her, his hands in his pockets. "I've come here to whisk you away on my noble steed." He referred to his parked Harley Davidson as he faked a British accent.

Lucy giggled, puckering her brow. "You're rather charming, Sir Drake. However, you do know that I certainly cannot leave, even if I want to." She bit her lip, trying to sound British as well.

Drake grinned mischievously. "British suits you so well, my darling," He ran his tongue across his bottom lip and snaked his arms around her waist, pulling her to him urgently. Lucy's cheeks reddened and her heart drummed in her chest.

A clearing of someone's throat caused them both to slightly pull back from each other. "Are you seriously doing this, you guys? We're at a funeral, and the priest is standing right ahead. Control yourselves," Chad whispered, sighing.

Drake's pupils dilated as a low grunt escaped his light, pink lips. "Hello to you too."

Chad nodded his head, forcing out a smile. "Thanks for showing up. Although, I reckon you're not such a fan of the man."

Drake gritted his teeth. "I showed up for Lucy, you idiot."

Lucy tugged at Drake's sleeve, wanting to get his attention. Just as Chad was about to answer, Natasha came into view. She threw herself at Drake and hugged him tightly. "Oh, you came! Such a sweet, sweet boy, you are."

Drake almost choked on his breath, he was definitely far from 'sweet', but he simply smiled at her, taking in her puffy, red face. "Of course I did."

She slowly let go of him, straightening up, and focusing on the priest's words. Lucy glanced up at the priest too, only to notice that he had a horrific look on his face as he looked in their direction. She furrowed her brows, whipping her head from side to side, wanting to know who has caught his attention. It was Drake. She fiddled with her fingers, hoping that he would stop staring at him. Drake did look like 'bad news', so she wasn't that surprised.

Natasha's voice interrupted her thoughts. "Could you please go get me some more tissues, dear?" She sniffed.

Lucy shook her head. "Sure."

Making her way towards the church, Drake spoke loudly. "Hurry back!" He earned a couple of glares from a few people as he raised his hands in surrender.

Lucy giggled, quickening her pace. She searched for the toilets as her heels clicked against the floor tiles. It was very silent; she was able to hear her own breathing. Finally finding the stupid toilets, she hurried inside, and that was when the door slammed shut. Lucy gasped out loud. Not being able to react, she was pressed against the wall in a very familiar position. She swallowed hard, looking up at two grey eyes. It was Bernard. "What do you want?"

He smiled widely, his hair and beard seemed whiter than they were the last time she saw him. "Why I came here to give you some advice."

"I don't need your advice! If you came to warn me about Drake again, well then, it's no use, because I'm never going to stay away from him." Lucy huffed.

Bernard sighed deeply, covering her mouth with his hand. "I know I know. That's why I'm here."

Lucy had a puzzled expression on as she stilled in his grasp. He took a deep breath, eying her. "I noticed that you're still with him. So I just want to say, and do listen very carefully to what I'm about to say. Let Drake suffer. In order for him to be free, he should suffer and feel the pain."

Lucy twisted and turned, outraged by what he just said. She bit down hard on his middle finger, causing him to remove his hand instantly. "What the hell are you saying?" She yelled.

"You'll understand on your own once you complete the puzzle. You have a lot of missing pieces," Bernard shook his head as he made his way out the door.

"Where are you going? I need answers! What do you know about Drake? Tell me," Lucy blurted out, her patience running out.

Bernard slightly opened the door. "I'm not telling you anything. My advice was enough. Though, I hope you listen this time."

Lucy clenched her fists at her sides as she watched him walk away. *What kind of advice was that? All that he kept telling me was bullshit, that's what it was.* She ran a hand through her hair, cursing under her breath. She'll have to keep this to herself, as much as she wanted to tell Drake, she really didn't want to have to ruin his mood. He seemed rather content today, and she ought to keep it that way. Besides, Drake shouldn't have to deal with a low-life like Bernard. Grabbing a bunch of tissues, Lucy got out. She'll have to find out what Bernard meant by herself, if his words did mean anything, that is.

CHAPTER 19

Once Lucy came out of the church, she immediately spotted both Amy and Josh, talking to her mother. She narrowed her eyes, *why are they here when they practically forgot about me the other night?* Giving her mother the tissues she asked for, she marched up to them, crossed her arms, and cleared her throat. Amy whipped her head round and looked at her, giving her a pitying look. "Oh, hey Lucy. We're really sorry about your dad-"

Lucy cut her off, frowning. "How did you guys know?" Drake was shooting daggers at Josh who quickly stopped ogling Lucy when he noticed the look of rage on Drake's tense face.

Amy bit her bottom lip. "The news spreads pretty quickly here. Besides, I tried calling you-" Amy stopped, noticing the hurt in Lucy's eyes. "Is this about the other day? Look, we're sorry." She drew nearer to her, whispering in her ear. "We were so drunk, and you know what that led to. I'm just truly sorry that I sort of didn't notice you weren't there and all."

Lucy shook her head. "Whatever. I'm just happy for you guys, I guess." *I just don't think he's the serious and dedicated type,* was what Lucy wanted to say to her about Josh, but preferred not to.

Josh ran a hand through his hair as he took a couple of steps away from Drake. Outstretching his arm for Lucy to shake, he mumbled. "May your father rest in peace."

Lucy smiled faintly and glanced at Drake who was scrutizing her intently. She involuntarily cringed, wondering why he looked so distant. "What's wrong?" She asked in a low tone, only for him to hear.

"You're hiding something," He said casually, his intense eyes boring into hers.

Lucy gulped, *was I that obvious?* "What could I possibly hide?" She instantly hid her hands behind her back, to avoid fiddling with them.

Drake sucked in a breath. "Babe, I know you by heart. Do not lie to me."

Lucy's heart fluttered as she opened her mouth to speak, but Chad interrupted them, just like he did this morning. "Lucy! Any last words you want to add before we bury the casket?" He asked, picking up a shovel and walking towards the casket.

Lucy dug her nails in her palms, what could she say? Chad knew how much she disliked him as a father, so why even bother asking her about such a thing? Feeling embarrassed and under pressure because of the people who were gawking at her, waiting for her reply, she answered with a hesitant 'yes'. Cursing, she walked up to the front, thinking of a nice, decent thing to say. Lucy breathed out, looking right at Drake, who nodded his head rather slowly, urging her on. "I know that my dad, Howard, is now in peace. I know that he's going to be missed a lot, because he was there for us all the time. I just want to say that we all will never forget him." Lucy blurted out, as a word kept popping in her head. *Lies, lies, lies.* Shaking that damn thought off, she went back to Drake who was smiling mischievously at her.

She ignored all the sympathetic looks that the people gave her as she focused her attention on Drake. "What?"

He wetted his lips with his tongue. "You're a rather pretty good liar. I shouldn't underestimate you."

262

Lucy rolled her eyes, hiding the smile that was threatening to break free. "Well, what do you expect me to say?" She pouted.

Drake clenched his jaw, gently reaching out and stroking her bottom lip with the tip of his finger. "Do not pout, love."

Lucy leaned in, smiling warmly at him. She felt her heart constrict as she wished that he would tell her he loved her, she yearned to hear those words from him. In fact, she wondered if he'll ever say them to her. She wanted to shout out, to yell out and say how much it hurts her. But instead, she sighed miserably and averted her attention to Amy who had looped her arm through hers. "May I borrow her for a little while?"

Drake nodded, expressionless, and Lucy was dragged away from him. Amy swayed nervously on her tiptoes while she eyed Lucy. "I'm ready to hear everything you have to say to me, but first, I owe you by telling you what happened that night."

Lucy scrunched her nose. "Um...I really don't have to know about the details of your-"

Amy blushed as she cut her off. "I wasn't going to!" Clearing her throat, she said, "When you left to supposedly get a drink, Josh and I, well, we sort of had a lot to drink and he began to say weird things about you-" Her face fell.

"What do you mean?" Lucy frowned.

"He said that you are such a hot girl and he'd bang you anytime," Amy fiddled with her earring. "I don't remember the rest of the things he said, but I do remember that he said he hated Drake so much, he'd kill him if he could..." She pressed her lips together. "He was drunk! So, I didn't really take what he had said seriously. I just kissed him to shut him up, and you know what follows a kiss..."

Lucy's eyes were wide open as she stood there looking shocked as ever. "That's horrible Amy! How could you let him take your virginity after what he admitted? Are you asking to be played or what?"

Amy glared. "I told you, he was drunk. He probably even said your name by mistake."

Lucy sighed deeply, she knew that there was no use arguing with her. Amy really liked Josh, and there was nothing she could do about it. So, she simply nodded her head and said, "Good luck with him. I hope he appreciates you."

Amy shook her head. "Enough about me. How's Drake? Did he confess his feelings yet?"

"Yeah, right," Lucy muttered.

"Maybe you should play hard to get, you know. Stop throwing yourself at him!" Amy winked.

"I don't do shit like that. Besides, I am not throwing myself at him." She flipped her hair.

Amy giggled. "You do know that he didn't stop staring at us all this time."

Lucy's mouth fell and she slightly looked over her shoulder to notice Drake's powerful gaze fixed on them. *Typical Drake.*

"You know, he sucks at hiding his feelings." Amy chuckled. "To be honest, I'm actually jealous of the relationship between you two. I wish Josh would give me a quarter of the attention Drake gives you."

"Are you serious now? Did you forget all the times he avoided me or what?" Lucy puckered her brow.

"Yeah, but still. He's crazy about you, you blockhead," Amy shrugged.

Yeah, and I'm going 'crazy' because of him.

Lucy watched everyone leave as they all offered their sincere condolences to them. Lucy sighed, stepping closer to Drake. He was holding her firmly against his side with one hand and twirling her strands around his fingers with the other. Wrapping her arms around his waist and resting her head against his chest, she ignored the glares that the priest shot her as he made his way inside the church. Lucy frowned, wondering why the priest seemed to dislike Drake's presence. Drake rested his hand on Lucy's lower back, forcing out a smile. "I'm going to have to leave now. I'll see you tonight."

Lucy slowly drew back from him, narrowing her eyes. "Tonight?"

Drake nodded with a mischievous smile. "We're going to go on a ride." He licked his lips slowly. "Be ready at 8 p.m. sharp."

Lucy blushed slightly. "Aye aye, captain."

Drake furrowed his brows while he shook his head with a smile. He kissed her cheek slowly yet tenderly, his hair falling onto her face, and then he walked away.

Arriving home, Lucy made her way upstairs. Just as she was about to close her bedroom door, Chad cleared his throat out loud, wanting to get her attention. "Lucy, I want to talk to you about something."

Lucy puckered her brow and went down the stairs. She stood right in front of him. "What is it?"

He motioned for her to come with him, turning on his laptop. "I've been doing a little research. I got curious as to what dad's case was. I mean why doctors didn't know how he died. We've all been hearing on the news about the recent deaths, and that not one doctor knew the reason behind those deaths. Sure they knew that they were killed, murdered, but how? They don't know. So, surfing the internet and searching here and there, I found something. Something really interesting."

Lucy took a seat beside him, intrigued by what he was about to say. Chad ran a hand through his short, messy hair. "I found similar news on a couple of sites."

"What do you mean?" She asked.

He rolled his eyes at her. "I mean that this bizarre case is not just occurring here in this town, but also had occurred in other towns. It started in one town, stopped happening there, then started in the next town, and then in the next, and so on. What I'm trying to say is that this case of murder is not new at all."

Lucy gulped nervously. "If it happened in several towns before, then why doesn't anyone find out what's going on already?"

Chad tapped his fingers against the table. "I think...I think they're scared. They're scared to know who, in other words, what is killing those poor, innocent people."

Lucy chuckled tensely. "Did you just say 'what'? You don't think it's an animal that-"

Chad cut her off, speaking in a lower tone to make sure not to wake their mother up, who was sleeping on the couch. "Not an animal, Lucy. I think it's more than that."

Lucy's mouth fell open. "You sound crazier than dad. What the hell, Chad? Please, don't start talking nonsense."

Chad gritted his teeth. "I'm not talking nonsense! I really do think it's something of the sort, or else how can you possibly explain what the hell is going on?"

Lucy bit her lower lip, thinking. "It could be a really smart, scratch that, a super smart person. Or maybe a group of people who-"

"Seriously, Lucy?" Chad rubbed his temple. "No matter how smart they are, I'm sure they can't hide what they used to kill those people from doctors and police officers. I mean, the doctors have tried almost everything, and it was no use!"

"What if they haven't tried everything? What if the doctors are hiding something themselves? What if the police officers are hiding something as well?"

Chad had a puzzled expression on his face as he urged her to continue. She swallowed hard. "Maybe, like you said, that they're scared to know. But maybe they already know and they don't want us, the citizens, to know. What if they think that it's better to keep it hidden and just move on?"

Chad nodded his head with a smile. "Maybe." He turned off his laptop. "But we don't know for sure, and I don't think we even can. Maybe we're just overreacting, exaggerating."

Lucy shrugged, standing up. Chad looked up at her. "Nevertheless, we should all keep our eyes open."

She shook her head in agreement, and went back to her room. No matter how odd and intimidating the situation was, Lucy was not scared, not even a little. Knowing that she had Drake, she felt safe. Lucy smiled, opening her closet to pick out something decent to wear tonight. She pushed the dresses back at the end of the closet, and took out a pair of ripped, skinny jeans and a white T-shirt. Drake was going to take her on his motorcycle for sure, and she had to wear a suitable outfit for it.

After getting herself ready, Lucy went to the kitchen to drink some water. "Where are you going?" Chad asked, eying her from top to bottom.

"With Drake," Lucy beamed.

"Don't you think you should reduce the amount of times you spend with him?" Chad raised one brow.

"Don't you think you should mind your own business? I'm sorry but Drake is the only reason...the only reason I'm happy." Lucy confessed shyly.

Chad huffed, leaving the room. The sound of a motorcycle's engine was heard, and Lucy rushed towards the door and opened it. "It's Drake! I'm leaving!"

Chad rolled his eyes. "Yeah yeah."

Stepping outside, Lucy marched up to Drake. He had just parked his Harley Davidson and was now looking at her with piercing, dark, blue eyes. Pushing his wild hair back, he smirked at her. "Hey babe." He outstretched his arm for her to take.

Lucy placed her hand in his and was pulled up behind him. He slightly turned around to face her. "Press your body hard against mine, because I'm not going to go slow."

Lucy involuntarily shivered all over at the way he just spoke. She wrapped her arms tightly around his waist and pressed her front to his back. She felt his whole body tense as he clutched the handlebars firmly. She sighed deeply, ignoring the sudden warmth that engulfed her insides. Drake whispered out hoarsely. "I can feel your body shivering." He slightly parted his lips. "Shivering with want and desire."

Flushing tomato red, Lucy sunk her teeth in her lower lip. Just as she was about to say something, Drake pulled away in a spray of rocks.

Lucy slid even closer to him due to the way he was driving. Drake was, as usual, driving very fast. Lucy clamped her eyes shut to avoid the wind that was tearing at her face, making her eyes water. She huffed and lightly smacked his back, wanting him to slow down. Drake simply squinted his eyes at her through the rear view mirror and gave her a sly, devilish smirk. He ignored her. She knew darn well that he was doing it on purpose, he enjoyed teasing her a lot, a whole lot. Smiling to herself, she decided to tease him as well. She wasn't going to hit him or yell at him, no, she knew exactly what to do. Lucy slowly slid her hands under the front of his shirt, and smoothed her palms up his toned chest. Drake stiffened, clenching his hands hard against the poor handlebars until his knuckles turned white and his muscles bulged. Lucy smirked in triumph as she ran her fingertips over his stomach, tracing soft circles around his navel. Chills shot down his spine as he gritted his teeth and pulled the motorcycle abruptly to a stop. "Lucy." He warned, enraged.

Lucy batted her eyelids, forcing herself not to giggle. "What?"

Within seconds, his fingers were knotted in her hair and her head was tipped back roughly, his dark eyes boring into hers. "Don't play games with me. You know damn well what I'm capable of."

Lucy swallowed hard, wondering why he got so furious over this. "I didn't do anything wrong."

Drake averted his gaze. "Do you like perverted thoughts, Lucy?"

She puckered her brow, confused. "Huh?"

He grasped her hand and brought it to his lips. He sucked her finger into his mouth, and swirled his tongue around the tip. "That's what I want to do to your whole body. I want to taste every inch of you." Pulling away slowly, without removing his fixated stare on her, he mumbled. "I think of you naked in my bed, in my arms, and under the covers. I'm a fucking sick, psycho who wants to fuck you whenever I get the chance. But I don't let that happen, and do you know why?"

Burning tingles exploded throughout Lucy's veins as she gawked at him with wide-open eyes, and shook her head in a no. Drake's eyes drank her in, his hands trailing down her waist and resting on her upper thighs. "I don't let that happen because I care about you. I don't want to taint you, I don't want to corrupt you." He sighed deeply.

Lucy looked away and crossed her arms firmly against her chest. She was sick and tired of the way he thinks. She loved him, and she didn't care if he took her innocence or whatever. She wanted him, she wanted to be with him, and she couldn't wait any longer. So, she merely gave him a faint smile and urged him to start his motorcycle. Noticing her frustration, Drake didn't speak another word as he revved up the engine.

Lucy got off Drake's Harley, and took in her surroundings in awe while they both entered the restaurant. It was a fancy restaurant. A man in a white tuxedo greeted them at the door, and escorted them to their seats. Inside, the lights were dimmed and both candles and flowers decorated each table. Classic music was playing and some couples were dancing. Long, embroidered curtains decorated the stationary windows. The black, granite, floor tiles were so unblemished that Lucy was able to see her reflection through them. She had never been to such a restaurant before. She certainly didn't expect Drake to bring her to a place like this, it wasn't the type of place he'd enjoy going to. "This place is amazing, Drake."

He smiled warmly at her. "I knew you'd like it. Change is good."

Lucy pressed her lips together. "Not all the time." She hoped he understood what she meant. Once he slightly clenched his jaw, she knew he actually did.

"Here are your menus. Tonight, I'm your waiter." A man about the age of twenty stood right in front of them. He motioned for the name tag on his white chemise while he handed them the menus.

Lucy scanned the menu hopelessly, while Drake stole glances at her, chuckling. "I'm as confused as you."

After a couple of minutes, Lucas, the waiter, came back. "What would you like to order?"

"We'll have the broiled seafood combo," Drake winked at Lucy.

The waiter nodded, and just before he left, he smiled at Lucy. "I must say, you're not dressed in fancy clothing but you look breathtaking. I hope you enjoy your time here."

Lucy thanked him awkwardly and looked back at Drake who was boiling with anger as he tried his best not to burst out. "He better watch it, or I'll break that jaw of his so hard he'll never be able to smile again."

Lucy sighed, hiding the fact that she enjoyed it when he was jealous. "It was just a compliment."

Drake glared at her, his eyes becoming even darker. "And did you enjoy that fucking compliment of his?"

Lucy bit her inner cheek. "Maybe."

Drake drew nearer to her, so near, she could feel his hot breath hit her cheek. "You're going to regret saying that 'maybe'." He dipped his hand between her thighs and rubbed his palm against her sex, taking her by surprise as she blushed furiously. Lucy gasped and involuntarily placed her hand on top of his, not wanting him to stop. Drake parted his lips and let out a long, deep breath, rubbing her even faster. "Say you're mine."

Lucy moaned softly, afraid someone might catch them. "I'm yours."

Drake chuckled darkly as he slowed his pace, and watched her pant and squeeze her eyes shut. "Say it louder. Louder, Lucy."

"I'm yours!" She blurted out, squirming away from his grasp, not wanting to give in in front of all those people.

Placing her hand on her warm, red cheeks, Lucy tried to avoid Drake's heated, lustful gaze, but failed miserably. "You look so hot right now. Fuck." Drake curled his fingers in his hair and tugged hard.

Lucy instantly crossed her legs, wanting to get rid of the throbbing between her thighs. She simply sat there with a shocked expression on her face, she had never experienced this before, and she wanted much more. Drake gave her a lopsided smirk as his black pools studied her intently. He knew that he couldn't control his want for her anymore, a little bit more of her begging, and he'd lose it. He wouldn't be able to tame his needs no longer.

CHAPTER 20

As soon as the waiter came with their meals, Drake shot him a dark, cold glare, which practically screamed 'watch it'. Lucy bit her bottom lip hard, not wanting to giggle at the enraged Drake in front of her. Her eyes widened the minute they landed on the steamy dish that she was supposed to eat all by herself. Shrimps and slices of fish decorated the middle of the plate, and on the sides rested a couple of lemon slices and oysters. Lucy breathed in, inhaling the scent of the sea. "Do you expect me to eat all that?" She motioned to the plate with raised eyebrows and a faint smile.

"You should. I want my girl healthy," Drake narrowed his eyes at her, watching her.

Nodding her head, Lucy looked at him warmly. "Thank you," She tapped her finger against her lips as she watched him dig his fork in the mushy fish. "You know, I thought you only ate ham, cheese, and peanut butter, but I guess that's not true." She giggled.

"Nah, I only prefer the peanut butter. I only get the ham and cheese in case you come over to my place. But I guess you could say that these three are my favorite," He winked at her.

"Are you saying that if I don't come over, you only eat peanut butter?" Lucy mumbled, confused.

"Yep," Drake popped the 'p'.

"You're, how do I say this, bizarre," Lucy pressed her lips together, not knowing what to say.

Drake burst out laughing as he squeezed his eyes shut. "Took you long enough to notice." He sucked in a breath. "Being bizarre is the least trait I'm worried about." His eyes darkened suddenly.

Lucy sighed deeply. *Who would only eat peanut butter every day anyways? He was messing with me that's for sure. He always does.* Running a hand through her hair, she opened her mouth to speak, to change the subject, but Drake spoke first. "Do you think I'm a killer, Lucy?" He asked softly, in a low tone, almost in a whisper.

Lucy's mouth fell open at the drastic change of subject as she eyed him peculiarly. "Why are you asking such a question?" She swallowed hard.

"Because I never got an honest answer from you," Drake took slow, deep breaths.

Lucy stared at him, dumbfounded. He seemed as though he wanted her to say 'yes'. Just as she was about to blurt out an answer, the loud shattering of dishes got both their attention. Lucy whipped her head round, gawking at a waiter who accidentally dropped the plates on the floor as he gaped intensely at Drake with a look of horror on his face. He looked pale as if all his energy was drained out of him. Sweat was dripping down the sides of his face and he struggled to breathe. Lucy stole a glance at Drake who was clenching and unclenching his fists with irritation. She took several nervous gulps, wondering what the hell was going on. Slowly, Drake averted his gaze from the panicked waiter and looked back at Lucy. "Eat. Your food will get cold."

She picked up her fork, and started playing with her food, pushing it back and forth on her plate. "What just happened?"

Drake grimaced. "What do you mean what just happened? A clumsy waiter just dropped the dishes he was carrying. He's probably new here."

Lucy fiddled with her fingers. "I'm serious, Drake."

He pushed his hair back, fidgeting in his seat. "How should I know?"

She crossed her arms against her chest. "Drake..."

"Stop saying my fucking name! He's scared of me, don't you see? He practically shit his pants for crying out loud," Drake rubbed his temple and dug his fingers in his palms, trying to control his wild temper.

Lucy leaned in, resting her elbows on the table. "The question is why was he scared of you?"

Drake rolled his eyes, chuckling darkly. "Because I can end anyone's life instantly. No one would even know."

She froze, her breath getting caught in her throat. "What are you trying to s-say?"

Drake's pupils dilated, instantly making his eyes look black. "I know what you're trying to do love, but I'm not going to say anything further. So whatever you conclude, keep it to yourself." He leaned back in his chair.

Lucy clamped her eyes shut, then quickly opened them. "Then I'm going to have to talk to that clumsy waiter."

Moving her chair and standing up, Drake quickly pulled her down by her arm. "You are not going anywhere." He gritted his teeth, his blood boiling with anger. If it were a cartoon, smoke would come right out of his ears for sure.

"I just want to ask him...something," Lucy muttered, trying to free her arm from his hard grasp.

He let go of her, burying his face in his hands. Lucy glanced at him one last time before she rushed behind the waiter who went inside the restaurant's kitchen. Ignoring the part of her that was tugging at her, wanting her to go back to Drake and soothe him, she went inside. Lucy searched the room for any sign of him, and just when she spotted him, a man with a stern look on his face cleared his throat. "You're not supposed to be here, ma'am."

Ma'am? Seriously? She faked a smile. "I just want to um...give my cousin his...house keys. He forgot them at our place..." She motioned to the clumsy waiter who was just ahead of her as she smiled once again and walked towards him. As soon as the guy saw her heading his way, he bolted towards the other direction. "Wait! I want to ask you something!" Lucy said hesitantly.

He stopped abruptly and turned around. "If h-he sent you here, tell him I-I-"

"No, no," Lucy cut him off. "I just want to ask why you acted that way when you saw him. Answer me, and I promise I'll leave you alone..." She gave him a faint smile. "I'm just curious, that's all."

278

He breathed out, looking behind her, as if making sure Drake was not lurking around. "I'm sorry, but I can't tell y-you."

"Please...I have to know," She whispered, almost begging him.

Taking a deep breath, he licked his lips slowly. "I watched him kill someone."

Lucy was hardly breathing, her hand automatically flying over her chest. It was like everything was moving around her rapidly and she was motionless in the middle of it all. She pressed the heels of her hands into her eyes until she saw nothing but sparkles, she did not want to believe what she had just heard. Noticing the look of horror on her face, the waiter mumbled out. "It's not what you think."

"What do you mean?" Lucy took quick, deep breaths, wanting to squeeze the words out of him.

The waiter shoved his sweaty hands in the pockets of his apron, Lucy knew just how nervous he was, but he was sort of good at hiding it. "Let's go talk somewhere private. The kitchen's too crowded." Lucy shook her head rather quickly and followed him. "By the way, the name's Ray." He smiled a little.

She smiled back, ignoring the sickening feeling that had crept upon her. Once they stopped at the very end of the kitchen, near a door with a 'Do not enter' sign on it, Ray sucked in a shaky breath. "It was around 1 am, my friend and I were quite drunk, we were heading home after having a really good time at a pub nearby." He cleared his throat, swallowing. "I was too drunk to actually focus on my surroundings, I mean, to what was going on. One minute I was walking with my friend, the next, he was screaming his lungs out."

Licking his dry lips, he continued. "A thief, a burglar, whatever you want to call that sad excuse for a man, wanted to take advantage of our vulnerable states. So, he attacked my friend and tried to rob him. However, my friend wouldn't let go of his wallet as he struggled with him, pushing him back. I simply froze in my position, not being able to grasp what's happening right in front of me. I was yelling and begging the man to stop as he constantly punched and kicked my friend. I wanted him to let go of that stupid wallet – the burglar had a gun." Ray breathed out. "That is when he came along."

"You mean Drake?" Lucy asked, eying him intently, anxious to know what he'll say next.

Ray nodded, speaking in a lower tone now. "He appeared out of nowhere and instantly, in the blink of an eye, ripped the man off my friend. He threw him to the ground so easily as if he weighed nothing." Choking on his own breath, he coughed. "He actually saved us. But the part that my mind can't comprehend is the way he killed the burglar."

"The way?" Lucy swallowed back, her eyes widening.

Ray shook his head. "I didn't get to see much since I was panicking and focusing on running away, but I do remember him placing his hand on the man's chest and pressing down. I remember the man choking and suffocating as his eyes widened and his breathing stopped. I don't know what happened next, but I knew darn well that the man was indeed dead at that moment." Ray dug his fingers in his palms, opening his mouth to speak.

"That's enough," Drake's authoritative voice suddenly barked out. Lucy whipped her head round, her eyes meeting his dark, cold ones. Ray flinched, trying his best not to scurry away from him. "Lucy, come with me." Drake said through gritted teeth.

Lucy looked at Ray then back at Drake, hesitating. "I said, come with me now." Drake repeated, his tone slightly getting higher as he forced himself not to lose control of his temper. Lucy quickly nodded and followed him. Once they arrived at their table, Drake motioned for her to sit down, his gaze locked on her. Lucy sat down and wondered what he was going to tell her. The softened expression on his face proved that he was going to tell her something that was rather unpleasant. "Eat your food. I don't want to have to watch you faint or something," Drake muttered, his eyes distant, and glistening dully.

"I don't have anemia, you know," Lucy rubbed the back of her neck.

Drake chuckled bitterly. "It wouldn't be because of that, love. But because of what I'm about to tell you. So eat already."

Lucy's eyes widened as she instantly raised the loaded fork to her mouth and put the fish inside, chewing. Drake was staring blankly at the plate in front of him, battling with his inner thoughts. "So now you know that I killed someone."

Lucy looked up to meet his stare, clearing her throat. "But you did it to save someone, you killed a bad person, Drake."

He huffed, annoyed. "You think one could easily kill another person if one hadn't done it before?"

Lucy gulped nervously. "You told me that...Earl made you kill when you were young, I'm sure it does explain your actions. It wasn't the first time..."

Drake licked his lips slowly, inhaling deeply. He looked like a shark that was ready to pounce on its prey. "Please don't say that fucking name." He rubbed his temple roughly. "Remember when I told you that Annie and Scott took me in after Scott almost ran me over with his car?"

Lucy quickly shook her head and sat up straight, feeling internally ready for whatever he was going to further say. "Yes, and they had a son called John."

Drake forced a smile. "Good girl." He clenched and unclenched his jaw, squeezing his eyes shut. "I was living with them for about one week. One whole week of love and care that I have never received in my life before. They bought me new clothes, they fed me until I was full and satisfied, they gave me my own room, and they even told me how happy they were that they got to meet me. I thought that it was going to be the beginning of a brand new life. That I would never again face what I previously faced – that I would never see Earl again." He shuddered. "But I was wrong. So wrong." Letting out a shaky breath, he continued. "Earl found me all right. He ruined my so-called fairy tale."

Lucy was scanning Drake's countless face expressions as she waited for him to form the words he wanted to say. His eyes were soulful, flashing with deep, concealed emotions that surely were foreign to Lucy. Drake pressed his hand against his stomach. "You know when that feeling deep inside of you, right in the core of your whole body, screams out to you that something bad is going to happen, that something is not right." Drake's eyes were glued to Lucy's as he uttered.

She fidgeted in her position, involuntarily leaning in. "Yes." She mumbled, craving to know more about his past.

"That's exactly what I felt when I went out to dispose a garbage bag," Drake sighed deeply. "Scott was feeling a little sick that day, and Annie was busy with the chores. So, I was helping out with the house, and was asked to throw the garbage away. A kid, around my age, passed by me. He was crying his eyes out as he stared at me with his big, brown eyes. Me being sympathetic, I asked him what was wrong. He told me that his cat was stuck in a tree and he couldn't get it down." Drake dug the tines of the fork in the palm of his hand. "I know, that was foolish of me to believe him, but he looked so down, I couldn't help but fall for that stupid lie of his. I followed him all right. I remember thinking about how far that tree was as we kept walking and walking. I began to feel as though I did the stupidest yet biggest mistake ever."

Drake pushed the tines of the fork even harder in his hand. "Just as I wanted to go back, a rough hand was pressed against my mouth and I was being tugged back with full force. I was slammed against the brick wall, facing Earl's fuming, sinful eyes. I have never seen so much evil in a person's eyes before. He snarled at me, his voice dripping with venom. 'You fucking ran away from me you little bastard, but I'm not mad at you. I'm proud of you. You wanted to impress me by getting along with the Mitchell's.' I was confused as to what he meant, but I figured it out when he continued. 'The Mitchell's are one of the richest family in this town, I'm sure you know that so far. I want you to stay under their roof, but take advantage of their trust in you. I want you to steal the wife's jewelry, and whatever you think is worth stealing. Oh, and I want you to kill the boy.'"

Drake let go of the fork as it tumbled to the floor, his breathing ragged. "I remember how frightened I was at that moment. I was trembling, shaking all over. I felt so sick, so suddenly. And when he handed me a gun, I vomited, I threw up all over Earl's shirt. Earl cursed under his breath, saying how he knew that I would react that way, so he told me he had another plan for me. 'The Mitchell's have a pool, and their boy cannot swim without his inflatable armbands, so I want you to push him in when he's off guard, and let him drown. Make sure the parents are busy.' I remember nodding my head, pretending to be okay with his atrocious idea. I just wanted to get away from him as fast as possible, and I did. As I ran, I heard him yell out from behind me. 'Don't forget to do as I say, or I will kill you, Drake. I will make you suffer so badly, you'd wish you were fucking dead already.'" Drake's lips were parted as he instantly took out his wallet, placed the money on the table, and stood up.

Just as he was about to speak, Lucy stood up as well, and literally threw herself at him. She wrapped her arms securely around his waist, burying her face in the crook of his neck. Drake's eyes widened as he ignored all the stares that they received, and pulled her to him even closer. He tightened his grip on her, trapping her against him. He pressed his soft lips on her left cheek and ran his hand up and down her back soothingly. Lucy released a pleasant sigh while warmth engulfed her. Pulling back slowly, Drake cradled her face in his hands, touching her forehead to his. "I'll tell you what happened on our ride back home." Drake whispered, his lips inches away from hers. Her eyelids sank shut as she tried to calm her pulse. Just like that, the warmth and safeness that she felt due to his closeness was sucked away as soon as he moved back.

Lucy followed him out to his Harley, watching him climb up. Outstretching his hand, he pulled her up behind him. "Thank you for everything," Lucy said, smiling a little.

"It's nothing, love," Drake revved up the engine, and drove them away. Once they reached the highway, Drake stopped the motorcycle due to the red light. He huffed, waiting impatiently for the green light to pop up already. Taking Lucy aback, he muttered. "I wasn't able to do it."

Lucy averted her gaze from the old man in the red car next to them, and looked at Drake with curiosity. "What?"

"I couldn't kill John, nor could I steal from Annie and Scott," Drake explained. "When I went back home that day, I wasn't able to look them in the eyes, to face them. When John wanted to go to the pool in the afternoon, I felt as if my throat was constricting, as if oxygen was running out. I just couldn't hurt him. Afraid of what I might do, or of what I might be forced to do, I ran away from their place at night when everyone was sleeping. I just couldn't risk causing hurt to anyone, especially to people who actually cared about me." Drake started his motorcycle again as soon as the red light vanished.

"Did Earl find you?" Lucy asked, dreading the answer.

"Oh, he found me all right. He always did," Drake spat out, his mood drastically changing as he increased his motorcycle's speed. Lucy clutched onto him, sliding against him hard. Her hair was fluttering in the wind, blowing into her face, and blocking her vision. "Do you know what he did Lucy? He was the cause of what I am, of the monster I became." Drake drove so fast, tears flew out of Lucy's eyes. "When he knew that I didn't fulfill the task, he brought the gun to my face and threatened to kill me. Oh, but he didn't, instead he lifted it and-"

Just like that, tires squealed against the pavement and a loud car horn rang in their ears. The world turned into a series of snapshots as reality merged with the impending.

CHAPTER 21

Lucy slowly fluttered her eyes open. After bearing complete darkness, it was a relief to see light – lights again. Lucy furrowed her brows as she examined the round light bulbs above her. She squinted her eyes in attempt to sharpen the blurred images before her. Taking in her surroundings, she noticed she was in a white color scheme bedroom. Out of the blue, an old woman, apparently a nurse, hovered over her, smiling. *How come I didn't notice her in the room?* Lucy cursed under her breath as soon as she realized that she was in a hospital. Memories crashed back in her head like a tidal wave; a car crashing into them, Drake almost flying off the motorcycle. *Drake. Where is Drake?*

Noticing the way Lucy jolted up in bed, the nurse spoke. "Calm down dear. You're in good hands."

Lucy's eyes couldn't hide the look of fear they were portraying. "Where's Drake? What happened? Is he okay? How am I okay?"

The nurse slightly parted her lips. "You mean the boy who was with you? Such a strong, brave lad." Lucy gasped, clutching her shirt tightly. "From what I understood, he saved you. He was fast enough to protect you from the crash. He said he covered you," The nurse continued.

Lucy gulped back slowly, not seeming to remember all the minor details that occurred. *How was he fast enough? I remember that he almost flew off his Harley himself, so...how?* "Wait. Where is Drake? I need to see him," Lucy's eyes began to water as the feelings of shock, panic, and insecurity overcame her.

"Just calm down, he's fine-"

Lucy instantly cut her off. "But you said he c-covered me...are you sure he's okay?"

"Yes, he is. You were both unharmed. You just fainted, and he, well, he was checked for injuries, but he had none." The nurse smiled happily, her eyes closing; she looked like she had taken a high dose of medication or something. *Wasn't she shocked that he wasn't injured at all by the crash? That they both were perfectly fine?* Lucy fiddled with her fingers nervously as she sensed that something weird was happening. "Do you know by any chance where he is?" Lucy asked again, urgently wanting to see him, to talk to him.

"I'll go check if he's still waiting for you outside," The nurse moved towards the door. "The poor guy was waiting for you this whole time, he didn't leave, didn't even go eat or drink. He was just sitting on the bench right outside the room you're staying in, waiting for you to wake up." Opening the door, she mumbled, almost to herself. "He was so calm about all this...it's like he knew that you'd be okay." She shrugged, saying 'oh well' and went out the door.

"Wait! How long was I out?" Lucy's voice trailed away, realizing that the nurse was long gone.

After a couple of minutes, the door creaked open, revealing Drake, who literally looked as though he came back from the dead. Lucy gasped out loud, remembering the day she came to surprise him on his birthday, remembering his features, his whole eerie appearance. He almost looked exactly the same as he did that day. He was as pale as the color of marble, and his energy was sucked out of him. He was sweating like an open faucet, and his eyes were as dark as a black cat roaming the night. Not to mention that his breathing was so heavy, it was like he was having an asthma attack. Lucy involuntarily squealed as she jumped out of bed, not minding her current, weak state.

Stumbling towards him, she wrapped her arms around him, steadying herself. "I thought you were o-okay...what happened to you, Drake? Please tell me..." Lucy blurted out, forcing herself not to shed any single tear. It hurt her to see him that way, especially because she had never seen anyone in such a condition before. She just wanted answers. Complete, honest answers.

"Go to bed and rest," Drake squeezed her arm a little, slightly pushing her away from him, towards the bed.

"I don't care about rest right now! You look...awful! And I have not even one single clue as to what is going on! What really happened? Start spilling," Lucy breathed out, anger and confusion lacing her voice.

Drake's eyes widened in surprise, Lucy had never burst out like that. She usually was somewhat patient when it came to getting answers. He wanted to argue with her about the 'looking awful' part, but he was too worn-out to bother teasing. He rubbed his temple with the heel of his palm, trying to maintain normal breathing. "A car crashed into us; the fucking driver shouldn't even have a driver's license. What a piece of shit. A bastard that's what he is. I should have fucking ripped his-"

"Drake," Lucy cut him off, sighing. "I get it, he's a bad driver."

He gritted his teeth, trying to stay put and not lose control. He was in no state to chat. Just as he was about to speak, Lucy mumbled. "The weird nurse said that you protected me from the crash. How?" Her eyes glinted, staring at Drake's two vacant, black pools.

Drake knocked the wooden chair beside him, causing it to fly across the room, and crash against the wall. It broke into three pieces. "I couldn't let you die! I'm fast and strong, Lucy. When we crashed, I sped towards you and covered you. I received all the damage. You simply fainted because of the shock that overcame you." He paced back and forth. "If I didn't do what I had to do, you could have died. Fuck. I wouldn't have lived if anything bad were to happen to you." He said the last part in a very low tone, almost in a muffled whisper.

Lucy heard it though. She gulped back nervously, ignoring the sparks that ignited within her. She wanted to ask what he meant by fast and strong; sure, Drake was indeed fast and strong, but she knew darn well that he didn't mean it in a typical way. She wanted to ask him why he wasn't harmed. She wanted, once again, to ask what exactly happened to him. But, she didn't ask either of those, instead, she probed timidly. "Why?"

Drake knew exactly what she meant. He sucked in a deep breath, his temper bubbling up. "Because I fucking love you, you foolish girl!"

Not waiting for a response, Drake captured her mouth in a punishing, hungry, wet kiss. Lucy moaned out loud, threading her fingers in his hair, clawing his shoulders, and pulling him to her just as eagerly. Drake let out a throaty groan as he dug his fingers into the small of her back, caging her against him. He stroked his tongue against hers roughly, desperately. Lucy clamped her eyes shut as she felt herself melt against his hard body, as she felt her entirety be filled with lustful heat and desire. Engulfed by his heavy breathing and soft hums, Lucy sucked his wild tongue that was impatiently exploring her mouth. She slowly yet urgently rocked her hips against his, not seeming to control her need anymore. It was very obvious, the erotic, heated tension in the air around them.

Drake slid his wet lips down her neck, peppering a trail of kisses across her collarbone and in the valley of her breasts.

Grumbling, he instantly ripped the first buttons of her shirt, wanting to gain full access of her round, small breasts. His eyes darkened and a boyish grin took over his lips as he stared at her so openly, with triumph. Lucy blushed furiously, her emotions scattered everywhere. Drake yanked up her bra and cupped her left breast in his hand. He wrapped his warm tongue around the other, pleasuring her in ways she had never experienced before. Lucy's breathing quickened as she further dug her nails in his flesh, suppressing a loud yell. Drake kneaded and caressed her firm globes, pulling her nipples lightly. Lucy let out a long, weak moan as she involuntarily bucked her hips forwards, right against him. She could feel just how big and hard he was.

Drake gritted his teeth as he felt her growing want for him. Spreading her legs open, he positioned himself in between her, running his fingers up and down her thighs teasingly. Lucy's breathing quickened even more and she wrapped her legs tightly around his waist. Pulling him to her, she didn't hesitate when she slightly lifted his shirt and pressed her lips to his toned stomach. His muscles twitched against her soft lips as his intoxicating, manly scent filled her, consuming her. He tugged at her hair, pushing it back while he watched her with wide-open, dark eyes. She kissed her way up, and swirled her tongue against his nipple. With a groan, he pulled her head back and crashed his swollen lips against hers, mumbling huskily. "God, how much I fucking love you." Breathing out agonizingly, he repeated. "I love everything about you, all of you, every little inch of you." He buried his face in the crook of her neck, inhaling frantically. "You're mine, Lucy. Plant those words in that head of yours. Bury those words deep within you. No one, I fucking repeat, no one will ever take you away from me. I will kill for you, know that, believe that. I'm not a merciful guy, Lucy. Especially when it comes to you." He sucked in a breath, panting.

Lucy barely touched her lips to his as she tightened her hold on him, her pulse thudding wildly. Their intense gazes connected. They were both in their own kind of twisted world, in their own

290

dark yet passionate bubble. Lucy hummed, smiling softly at the gorgeous face in front of her. Looking at him now, she was at rest, knowing that he himself was hers. "I love you too, Drake."

He smirked widely, cupping her face and squeezing. "I know that, love." His eyes pierced through hers, in a warning way, but that look was instantly washed away.

And just like that, the door swung open, startling Lucy. "Uh...excuse me b-but..." The nurse stuttered as she eyed the position that the two were in. She cleared her throat. "Intimacy is not allowed in here." Drake rolled his eyes at the nurse, and chuckled at Lucy's flushed face. Pulling her up to him and covering her, he muttered, clearly annoyed. "What is it?" He raised his brow, impatiently.

The nurse smiled widely, as if they didn't just break a rule. "Well, since Lucy woke up from her eight-hour sleep, she is okay to leave now. That is if you think she should-"

Drake cut her off. "Yes, she's going to come with me. Thank you."

Before anyone could say another word, Lucy gasped in shock. "Eight hours?"

"You've been out for eight hours..." Drake glanced at her, a sympathized look present in his eyes. "But you're okay, love. I wouldn't let anything happen to you, ever." Furrowing his brows, he whispered, "I mean it from the dark depths of my cold, black heart."

Lucy blinked, reaching out and touching his cheek. "Your heart is not black nor cold. Your heart is red, warm, and pumping with life." She smiled faintly. "I can feel it, I can hear it when you hold me against your chest. It's always pounding, drumming in a fiery, welcoming manner."

Drake stilled, fighting the urge to rip all her clothes out of his way and claim her as his. He wanted to devour her entirely, he wanted more and more of her. She was his undoing. He knew that Lucy could very easily tear his heart into bits and pieces. She was all he ever cared for, and she was his. And because she was his, he wanted her to know that she has fallen in love with a monster. He blurted out in a throaty whisper. "Lucy, I have no soul. I am soulless."

Lucy breathed in slowly, her eyes narrowing slightly. "What do you mean? I don't understand." She spoke indistinctly.

Drake pushed his disheveled hair back, tying it in a low, loose bun. "It means what it means." Noticing the confusion further fogging her face, he cleared his throat, mumbling. "Earl didn't shoot me as I expected, he lifted the gun and hit it against my head with full force. I dropped to the floor, losing my consciousness." He stared at Lucy long and hard before continuing. "Pitch-black darkness overtook me, flooding my senses. Coldness held me in a death grip. I did not see any single ray of light, didn't feel any trace of warmth. I remember thinking that it was the end for me; that I was going to die. That was until some sort of a shadow came into view; I felt evilness ravishing the air around me. And as the shadow drew nearer and nearer, I was stripped bare of anything resembling the idea of hope. Just as I was ready to succumb to the dreadful darkness, the translucent yet grayish shadow spoke."

Drake bore his eyes into hers, taking in her stunned yet rather calm demeanor. He blinked slowly, digging his teeth into his bottom lip, his voice becoming a little raspy. "It hissed like a slithering snake, telling me that I have two choices. As it circled me, it spoke again in that snake-like tone, making me shudder all over. 'Give me your soul and I shall let you live. Keep it, and you will wither and die.' I was so terrified; I was young and just wanted to get away from that…that thing. So, I agreed. I gave that shadow – that pure force of maliciousness, my soul. In an instant, the shadow placed its cold, transparent fingers against my heart. And just like that, I felt life, light, bliss, and hope get sucked out of me. And just before I regained my consciousness, the shadow sneered. 'Don't forget you are soulless now. But on the bright side, you can feed on others.' Saying that, it disappeared, and I woke up with a gasp." Drake rubbed his face and his temple, groaning. He didn't dare to look at Lucy, not wanting to see what was taking over her pretty face; he was too afraid to know.

Looking up at the dull, white ceiling, he gripped the door handle very tightly, it would surely break if he kept applying such pressure. "When I blinked my eyes open, I thought that this was all a dream, but I was wrong, because I felt different. I felt empty in ways that cannot be explained. I felt...lifeless. And the first person who came in sight, was the person I detested with every ounce of what was keeping me alive and breathing. I felt so much hatred, so much loathing, that I didn't think twice when I jumped and attacked him. That I didn't know what the hell was going on when I felt him suffocate beneath me. Didn't know that it was me who was slowly taking away his pathetic life. I killed him. But that was not just it. The way I killed him was not normal, was not human. It was too easy, too quick." Drake pressed his fingers into his eyes, trying to push back the excruciating tears that were threatening to fall down like a gushing stream.

He screamed his lungs out; pain, hurt, and agony evident in his loud yet vulnerable cries. He felt arms wrap around him from behind, comforting him. He pressed his lips together, swiftly turning around, and pulling Lucy to him urgently. Burying his red, wet face in the crook of her neck, he said in a muffled whisper. "You're still here. Why?"

"I will n-never leave you. I can't," Lucy dug her fingers into his back, swallowing back the bitter taste in her mouth.

Drake tangled his hands in her hair, tugging at the soft, blonde strands. "I'm a killer. I have killed a whole lot of people. How can you love a killer, Lucy?" He clamped his eyes shut, dreading the look of disgust that will cloud her big and bright eyes.

Lucy didn't notice that she was sobbing herself. Sniffing quietly, she inhaled deeply. "Because you can't choose who to love. The heart has a mind of its own." She chuckled sadly, her eyes glinting. "I felt the negative energy whenever you were around, whenever I was near you. All this despondency, and yet I felt warm and safe with you. I am yours Drake; as you have always said. I want to mend you, help you, and love you. That's why I'm here."

Drake cupped her cheeks, planting a delicate kiss on her nose. "I never thought that I could be able to love anyone after what I have become, after all I have done. But then you came along, and confused the fuck out of me." He sighed. "However, no matter how much I want to become a better person, it's just...too late for me. I have already caused a lot of sorrow and grief."

"It's never too late, and you know that. You can change...change your ways. You just have to open up a little more to me and I'd be able to understand, to help out." Lucy fiddled with her fingers nervously.

Drake cursed under his breath. "There are a whole lot of things you don't know about. I'm afraid that if I tell you, I'd put you in danger."

Lucy squinted her eyes at him. "I'm not scared. You're here."
Letting out a long, shaky breath, she asked, her voice slightly
cracking. "Let's start with simple questions. Why and how did
you kill all those people?" She licked her lips slowly. "I know it
was you. I knew it all along, but I just...I just couldn't accept it,
couldn't digest it."

Drake's eyes morosely searched the dull room they were in.
"Before I further answer any of your questions, let's fucking get
out of here."

Lucy's eyes widened as she whipped her head from side to side,
looking around, as if forgetting that they were still in the
hospital. Nodding her head in a hasty manner, she followed
Drake out the door. She quickened her pace once she realized
that he was halfway into the long corridor.

"I want you to be at the Golden Oak Medical Center as soon as
you can, please," Drake's voice echoed through the hall as he
spoke with, apparently, a taxi driver.

Lucy scrunched up her nose as she stepped towards Drake's stiff
figure. "Aren't we going on your motorcycle?"

"Are you insane? Of course not. After what happened, I'll never
take you with me on my Harley again." Sighing glumly, he
mumbled. "Besides, it's in the garage. It needs a little repairing
here and there." He shook his head in dismay as they both stood
outside, waiting. Lucy looked up at Drake, eying him from the
corner of her eye. He was involuntarily clicking his tongue,
staring blankly ahead. His lips were pouting while he continued
that weird tongue-clicking. Lucy hummed, wondering how such
a gorgeous-looking guy who happened to be sweet, protective,
caring, funny, charming, and as vulnerable as ever, had no soul.
Lucy gulped, the air thickening around her. But then again, not

everybody saw Drake the way she did. Nobody trusted him the way she did. Nobody really wanted to give him a chance, they would never be able to discover how humane and down to earth he actually was.

His thick, dark lashes that outlined the shape of his eyes fluttered as he slowly blinked, turning around and facing Lucy. She had a look of confusion mixed with admiration plastered on her face. "What is it?" His mouth eased into a smile.

"You're angelic," The words flew out of Lucy's mouth. She gasped, not really wanting to say that out loud. Her cheeks slightly reddened after realizing that he will now think she was obsessed with him; that is if he hasn't thought so already. He always caught her staring.

"I-I expected you to say a lot of things, but that wasn't one of them, at all," He chuckled, wiggling his brows. "It's weird that you think I'm angelic. Please do tell me the traits that so outstandingly portray me as this, well, angelic guy that you can't seem to stop staring at." Drake grinned, humor dancing in his narrowed eyes.

Just as she rolled her eyes, and was ready to speak, a loud car horn rang in their ears. Averting their attention to the cab parked right next to them, Drake said, "There's the taxi driver. I'm really glad they exist here on this world, what would we do without them?" He smiled widely, striding his way towards the awaiting car. Lucy pressed her lips together, murmuring in a low tone, only for her ears to hear. "You know, if that big secret of yours was that you were bipolar, I wouldn't have been shocked at all." She shook her head, climbing in the car herself.

After getting in and putting her seat belt on, Lucy furrowed her brows at Drake's calm demeanor. Following his gaze, her lips parted as soon as her eyes landed on none other than George. "You again?"

Drake cleared his throat annoyingly. "Yeah, he always follows me around." He rubbed his temple. "I fucking told you I'm not part of any cult."

Lucy burst out laughing as George grinned at them both through the inside rear-view mirror. "I work as a taxi driver, how many times should I tell you? It's completely normal to stumble upon me every now and then." He shrugged innocently.

"I still think you're following me," Drake grumbled, pressing his head against the closed window.

Lucy shoved the thought of 'George appearing so often' to the back of her mind, and focused on the fact that Drake was actually taking this pretty calmly. Drake bit the inside of his cheek. "You know I can sue you for stalking, but I won't."

George made a 'huh' sound as he licked his lips. "You know I can sue you for stealing my guitar, but I didn't."

Confusion clouded Lucy's features while she thought this over. "Ah, so let me get this straight, Drake stole your guitar and you um...happened to forgive him? And then taught him how to play it?" Her voice trailed away.

Drake shook his head frantically. "I did not steal the guitar. I was going to return it after I finished practicing. That's what I always did. I returned it back. But you happened to come back early from wherever the hell you where, and you caught me."

"Aha! So you admit to stealing it more than once!" George snapped his fingers, seeming to enjoy Drake's reaction.

Lucy sat back, getting herself comfy. God knew how long this ridiculous conversation will last. "I did not fucking steal it, you moron!" Drake's voice boomed in her ears as he leaned forwards.

George sighed deeply, switching his gaze to Lucy. "Now, instead of getting him arrested for stealing, I actually let him have my precious guitar, and I taught him how to play it."

Drake clenched his jaw. "You mean you gave me some of your advice; I already knew how to play the guitar." He gave him a lopsided smile, and Lucy couldn't help but mentally 'aw' at it. It was clearly the most genuine lopsided smile he ever wore.

"Yeah, but admit it, they helped you a lot," George held his head high, smiling like an idiot.

Lucy's heart instantly warmed as soon as Drake's eyes wrinkled at the sides and he laughed. He laughed heartily as if what George said was the funniest thing ever. Lucy beamed, his happiness rather contagious. It was nice to know that he had George. They somehow liked each other's company, and that was rather obvious. "So since when were you guys...guitar buddies?"

"Whoa, I wouldn't call him my buddy-"

Drake was quickly interrupted by George who enthusiastically said, "About 5 years."

CHAPTER 22

Whoa, five years? Lucy looked at Drake, then back at George, waiting for some sort of objection, but there was none. Drake had his face buried in his hands, sighing dramatically. "That long? Jeez, how did I tolerate you?"

George chuckled. "Oh, cut the crap. You know darn well it was five years."

Lucy smiled to herself, recalling the first encounter she had with George. He didn't sound like he knew him, *I remember him saying that Drake was really strange, and that I shouldn't follow him. Maybe he just wanted me to stay away from Drake, since he was a rather withdrawn kind of person.* She shrugged, opening her mouth, and spilling out what she just thought of. George slightly turned his head around to look at her. "As you have noticed by now, Drake hated having any company. So, I was um...how do I say this?" he paused, clicking his tongue. "I always got rid of anyone who asked to see him."

Lucy pouted, glancing at Drake, who was staring at her with just as much intensity. He smirked, pulling her to him as he wrapped one arm around her waist. His warm fingertips lifted her chin until she met his eyes. "Even though I pushed you away, I always wanted you around. You flickered something deep inside me to life."

Her smile was so genuine, her eyes glinted, making the blue in them more vibrant. Drake slowly pulled back from her, his eyes widening in horror as he stared through the window. "That's him!" He yelled, rage evident in his voice.

Lucy furrowed her brows. "Who?" She looked at the man Drake was glaring at with so much hate.

"The fucking driver that almost killed us!" Drake blurted out, asking George to stop the car immediately. When he did, Drake got out, rushing towards the man like an eagle diving towards its prey. He harshly grabbed the man by the collar of his shirt, taking him by utter surprise.

"How could you fucking drive off like that after almost killing us?" Drake spat out, his eyes were two black holes, daring the man to defy him.

"Yo-You trying to scare me? You're just a teen with feminine hair," The man chuckled, obviously trying to shield his growing fear.

Drake widened his eyes in shocked disbelief, and then squinted them, as if trying to read through this foolish man who was asking for a death wish. He clearly didn't know what Drake was capable of. Pressing his knuckles into his throat, and hearing the slight rasp of material ripping; Drake sneered. "Oh I will not only manage to scare you, you fucker, but I'll also make you beg me to spare your life." He let go of his collar, only to tighten his grasp on his throat, chocking him. Drake slammed him hard, so hard against the wall, the air was knocked out of the man.

The man clamped his eyes shut, managing to mumble out. "Are you going to kill me? Well then just do it, you'll finally get caught, you heartless asshole!" The man winced and cried out in pain after Drake grabbed a fistful of his hair and hit his head twice against the wall. "You killed a person so dear to me...it is not wrong to almost kill someone so dear to you too."

Drake furrowed his brows, finally remembering who the man was. "Your so-called dear friend was a drug dealer who not only sold drugs but women. He fucking deserved to die and so will you." Spitting in his face, Drake whispered hoarsely. "And what you just said is going to cost you your life, goddammit!" And with that, Drake showed no mercy at all. Whatever pity or sympathy he felt was completely gone. He now understood that this man did try to kill them, and it was no mere accident at all. The idea that he was trying to harm his Lucy made him go berserk, made him show his true, brutal self.

Drake repeatedly punched him in the face causing blood to flow from both of his nostrils. "Damn you to hell." The man coughed up blood, and slowly slid down the wall, weakness consuming him.

"I'm already damned," Saying that, Drake crouched and pressed his throbbing hand onto the man's chest, his eyes piercing through the man's vacant stare. The man shivered and choked, unable to breathe as his eyes widened to the extent of almost bulging out.

"Stop! You're going to kill him!" Lucy yelled out, making her way towards him with her mouth hanging open. Her eyes scanned the man's state with shock and horror. "H-how are you d-doing that? W-what are you doing?" Lucy referred to the unrealistic way he was sucking the life out of the man. "Dr-Drake." She took tentative steps backwards.

"He deserves to die. He's a bad man, Lucy," Drake's eyes were fixed on the man as he pressed his hand even deeper into his chest. Drake's hair flowed, almost turning redder as the now dead man took his last, frail breath. "He killed a lot of people...I'm glad I got rid of him."

Lucy gasped, almost tripping as she kept a good distance between her and Drake. "But yo-you killed a lot of people too...you shouldn't die, you should have another chance. Just like that man should."

Drake clenched his jaw. "Well, he's dead now, and I don't regret it."

Standing up, he approached Lucy, but she took another step back. "Drake, you said yourself you didn't want to be like this. Why do you keep on killing people? You should stop, you have to. How else would you become this better person you want to be?" She not only witnessed Drake kill a man, but witnessed how easy it was from him to end someone's life. By simply pressing his hand into a person's chest, and staring into the eyes of that person – it would lead to an instant death. This proved to Lucy that he was truly made to kill. She didn't imagine or consider it to be that easy when it was confirmed that he was the mysterious killer. Being in such a situation made it hard for her to think, hard for her to take in what just happened. She needed time to think this through. "I-I'm sorry, Drake," Lucy squeaked out, tears pouring down her face. "I need to...I-I have to go home." Turning around, she ran.

George yelled out from the car. "No! Don't follow her Drake."

Drake stopped in his tracks, sighing deeply as he rubbed his aching temple. "Fucking hell." He cursed, slamming his hand against the hood of the car.

George jumped in his seat. "Hey! I need this car!" Noticing Drake's troubled and disturbed expression, he said, "Don't worry too much, she just needs a little time. You do know that, don't you?"

"Of course I do," Drake huffed. "I'm just fucking scared that she'll realize that she's better off without me. Without a killer like me."

302

George snapped. "Stop it. A couple of minutes ago, you had this I-have-no-mercy act on and now you became a pussy?" Drake glared at him, his breathing quickening. "What I'm trying to say here is that calm down. Everything will work out, just try to control yourself. Control yourself boy."

Lucy was pacing back and forth in her room, her head throbbing from all the thinking. She knew that it was stupid of her to run away like this, but she just couldn't stay. She couldn't quite decipher what just happened before her very eyes. But now she knew exactly what Drake could do. And when she came to think about it, Drake was the one she was terrified of all along. She was afraid of the brooding killer on the loose, when he was actually right in front of her, almost always with her. She laughed ironically. However, she somehow always knew it was him, and he knew it too.

Then suddenly, Bernard's words popped into her head like a slap in the face. *Let Drake suffer. In order for him to be free, he should suffer and feel the pain.* Lucy's eyes widened; even though she didn't understand what he really meant, it sort of made more sense now. Grabbing her phone off her nightstand, she dialed Drake's number. After several seconds, Drake answered in an alarmed whisper. "Lucy? You okay, love? I'm sorry-"

Lucy cut him off as warmth slowly spread throughout her body and relaxation crept in at the sound of his voice. "It's fine. It's just that…I think I have an idea."

She heard Drake's breathing quicken at the other end of the line. "And what might that be?"

"First, I'd really like to know who Bernard is, because I actually think he wants to help," Lucy stated, crossing her fingers.

Drake's tone changed to one of irritation. "Fine. I'll be there in five."

Lucy smiled and fisted the air in triumph.

The sound of tiny rocks rattling against the window, made Lucy furrow her brows and get up. She opened her window, and a giggle escaped her lips as she stared down at Drake who was climbing his way up. "You know, you could have just entered through the door." Lucy pressed her lips together.

"I really am not in the mood to fake smiles and have chit chats with your mom and Chad," Drake murmured throatily.

Sighing, she sat on her bed, patting the empty space beside her. Drake hesitantly stepped towards her and sat down, his hands buried in his pockets. "So, you want to know who Bernard really is." Drake paused, his narrowed eyes raking her face. Lucy nodded quickly, involuntarily leaning in.

"Remember that Godforsaken shadow that I told you about? Well, Bernard is sort of the opposite. He's a good guy. A weird yet good guy. However, he hates me." Drake rolled his eyes, chewing on his bottom lip. Taking in Lucy's rather perplexed expression, he continued. "Remember when you followed me into the forest and saw me speaking with him? He wanted me to stop killing, to reduce killing at least. He was the one who banned me from heaven. You see Lucy, I am stuck here. When I die, I don't go anywhere. I have no soul, and that is why I will forever remain roaming around the earth with nowhere to go." He was now harshly chewing his lip, his head shaking in frustration.

"What if that is not true? What if you can have your soul back? Maybe that's why Bernard keeps showing up out of nowhere, and giving me these advises of his," Lucy suggested, her wide-open eyes gleaming with hope.

Drake huffed. "That's impossible."

"No it's not. You just have to listen, and stop killing-"

Drake cut her off, standing up. "Lucy, I kill in order to live. I feed on the souls of those I kill. That is the only way I can remain alive. And if I stop, even for a little while, well, you know exactly what happens to me. You've seen the side effects twice already." He blinked back the tears as he clenched his fists so hard, his knuckles ached.

Pale face, drained energy, pitch-black eyes, excessive sweating, and heavy breathing, all those awful, dreadful features came flooding into Lucy's head as she gasped out loud. But then it hit her. "Oh my God. I now completely understand what Bernard was trying to tell me!" Noticing the way Drake eyed her, she explained. "You should suffer in order to be free. Drake, you should face the effects of not feeding on others." Lucy clapped her hands together, whispering under her breath. "I'm a genius."

Drake's face fell, looking straight into her eyes. "Lucy...If I don't feed at all. I will die."

Lucy swallowed back, her heart pounding erratically in her chest. "But what if you don't die, Drake. Maybe, sacrifice is truly the answer. I mean, you said it yourself. Bernard is a good guy." She clamped her eyes shut and felt bitter bile rise up in her throat.

Drake tapped his finger against his lips, his brows furrowed in concentration. "Okay." He bluntly replied.

"Okay what?" She asked, leaning in even closer.

He drew closer to her, his nose almost touching hers. "Okay I'll stop killing, and we'll see what happens." Smiling faintly, he'd do anything to make sure that bright, wide smile will always be etched on those lips of hers.

Lucy's eyes widened with sheer delight. She threw her arms around him and hugged him with all her womanly strength. Drake chuckled, pretending to suffocate. "That's a little bit too tight, don't you think?" He sucked in several breaths.

"Oh, shut up," She pressed her lips against his urgently, taking him by surprise. With a groan, he slid his tongue inside her mouth, gliding it against hers. He broke the heated kiss briefly. "You're getting quite bold, aren't you?"

Lucy blushed. Opening her mouth to speak, Drake pushed his tongue back inside her mouth, smirking against her lips. He tangled his hand in her hair, turning her head to the angle he wanted, deepening the kiss. Lucy moaned, her nerves set on fire. "I love you." She breathed out, meeting his intense, lustful eyes.

"I love you too, angel," Drake murmured huskily, brushing his thumb against her flushed cheek.

Lucy smiled genuinely, warm tingles erupting within her, spreading all over her like a plague.

Drake kept his eyes focused on the white, dull ceiling above him as he lay sprawled on Lucy's bed. He was so lost in his spiraling thoughts that even Lucy's words were muffled, muted. Drake knew that he agreed not to kill for one reason only, and it was to keep Lucy satisfied and hopeful. He knew that he wouldn't have his soul back. It was one crazy notion. Not killing would be futile, it would not only weaken him, but kill him. Nevertheless, he would not argue nor oppose her. Drake wanted her content, even if it will risk killing him. Cursing under his breath, he raked his hand through his long, red locks, and hoped. For once in his entire existence, he actually hoped. He wanted Lucy to be right; he craved that her words were true. Succumbing to Lucy's feathery touch, he blinked, bringing his attention back to her.

The raw torment in his eyes shocked her, sliding her hand down his side to rest on his thigh, she asked. "Are you okay?"

Drake nodded, placing his large, warm hand over hers. "I am." He met her bright gaze, clearing his throat. "I want to tell you something." Lucy inhaled sharply as she searched his pale face. His eyes darkened, burning with fierce intensity. "When my infatuation for you grew, until my need to possess you nearly reached the degree of insanity, I stopped killing the way I always did."

Ignoring the jolt of heat that ran through her core at his rather lascivious words, she gulped, asking. "What do you mean?"

"I stopped killing innocent people, Lucy. I only killed those with gruesome sins. I think that was a rather good thing, to get rid of people who don't deserve to live. As I spent time with you, I realized how wrong my actions were, and decided to right them by at least ending the lives of those who know no good," He breathed out, his tongue darting out to lick his rather dry lips. "That's when I decided that Howard, your so-called father, should die."

Lucy swallowed back, understanding his way of thinking. "But now, you're not going to kill anyone, right?" Lucy wanted an affirmation of some sort. She wanted to make sure that he really wouldn't, since he truly believed that what he just admitted to doing was right, and it wasn't.

"I won't," He half-smiled. Standing up, his expression hardened, his gaze remaining fixed on Lucy. "When are you going to start packing?" He asked, enjoying Lucy's shock.

"Packing?" Lucy asked, a puzzled expression settling over her features.

Drake moved closer, standing right in front of her so that he was towering over her. Lucy pressed her lips together in a tight line, not being able to ignore the pull she felt whenever he looked at her like that – with his piercing, dark, blue eyes. "You're going to come live at my place. You don't expect me to stay without food and suffer the side effects all alone, now do you?"

Lucy shuddered at the word 'food'. Ignoring it, she said, "Right." She walked towards her closet, her mind quite foggy due to the effect he had on her. She opened it and stared at the rack of clothes in front of her.

She could feel Drake's presence behind her, mere inches away. She felt the faint warmth of his breath on her neck as he whispered. "Make sure to pack the sexiest lingerie you own." He brushed her hair away, revealing a side of her neck. His eyes were fixated upon her fair, white skin. Planting an open-mouthed kiss there, he groaned. "I'm warning you from now, Lucy. I won't control myself, I won't be able to. I'm going to take away your virginity so swiftly, so easily, just like I take...souls away." Lucy shivered, his dark words warming her, overwhelming her. Wrapping a strong, possessive arm around her waist, he buried his face in her neck, his hair falling over his face. "But I promise you, I'll make you feel so good, so fucking good."

Lucy's legs felt like jelly. Involuntarily leaning back, Drake suddenly moved away, taking the warmth with him. Lucy almost tripped, glaring at his back. "What are you doing?" She huffed, blushing red.

Rummaging through a folded pile of undergarments, Drake pulled out a black, lace thong. "Didn't know you wear such sexy panties." A mischievous grin was plastered on his face as he looked at her then at the thong that he held so casually.

"Give me that," Lucy gasped, her cheeks becoming even redder as she snatched the thong from his hands. Drake turned back around, looking through more of her undergarments. "Pack this one," He threw a pair of red panties at her. "And this," He threw another one. "Oh...damn...and this," And just as he threw the pair of blue panties, Lucy caught it, furrowing her brows. "Hey! Ever heard of privacy? I know how to pack my own stuff." She chewed on her bottom lip, watching him stand up and face her.

He smirked, amusement dancing in his eyes. Raising his hands in surrender, Drake made his way to Lucy's bed. He sat down, crossed his arms, and puckered his brow at her. Smiling to herself, Lucy opened a rather big, black bag and began packing all the necessities. She made sure she brought her razor, which was the most important item at the moment. As she packed, Lucy felt Drake's stare burning into her back. Instantly turning around, her widened eyes were locked with his dark, lustful ones. "W-what?"

Drake clenched his jaw. "Nothing...it's just that you were putting on quite an interesting show." He swallowed, licking his lips. "Just don't sway your hips like that."

Lucy's lips parted. *Why was he so hormonal today? Not that he usually wasn't, but still.* "Really? How am I supposed to move and pack? Am I supposed to walk as still as a machine?" She clicked her tongue, eying his lopsided grin. "Stop looking at me like that."

"Like what, Lucy?" He asked, grinning even wider if that was possible. He was enjoying her priceless reactions.

"Never mind," Lucy rolled her eyes playfully, turning back around to finish up.

"You know...lifting up your jeans could definitely help. Your black underwear's showing," He chuckled darkly, taking in her now flushed face. Her mouth was hanging open as she pulled up her jeans, feeling rather embarrassed.

Blinking at him, she narrowed her eyes, a smile tugging at her lips. Drake's chuckle died as he curiously asked. "What?"

"You might want to tame that," Lucy motioned at the bulge in his pants, giggling with her hand over her mouth.

Drake's pupils dilated as he clenched his jaw, and remained silent. Completely silent.

CHAPTER 23

"I'm going to um...have a sleepover..." Lucy said to her mom and Chad as she fiddled with her earrings and nervously switched her weight from foot to foot.

Natasha averted her attention from her knitting, a hobby she had engaged in ever since Howard died, and looked up at her daughter with a curious expression. "At Drake's?"

Chad almost stifled at the sound of Drake's name. "I like that boy. He attended Howard's funeral even though they both weren't on...good terms. Such a forgiving person he is." Natasha said, resuming her knitting. Lucy suppressed the urge to ask her if she was being sarcastic, or if she was joking. She realized that her mother truly had no clue about how Drake really was. "Don't stay too long though." She added, her nearsighted glasses sliding down the bridge of her nose as she tilted her head down.

"I won't," Lucy hesitantly mumbled, hastily pressing her lips to her mom's cheek and rushing towards the door to open it. Drake was already outside, waiting for her with her bags.

"I'm assuming it went well," Drake said huskily, eying the wide grin on her face. Lucy nodded, knowing that it would have since her mom was quite naive. She slowly looked around, confusion clouding her features. "Um...how are we going to go to your place?"

"By flying of course," Drake smirked, outstretching his hand for her to take.

Lucy pressed her lips together in a tight line, trying to fathom if he was joking or if he could actually fly. Noticing her blank expression, Drake's smirk widened, a faint dimple appearing on his cheek. "Come on, I don't have all day." He stepped closer, his hand reaching out for hers.

Lucy gasped loudly, her mouth agape. "You seriously can fly? Oh my God, why didn't you tell me?" She squeaked, her fingers instantly intertwining with his.

Drake chuckled, amusement lacing his deep voice. "Do I look like superman to you?" He squeezed her hand, his chest rumbling as he kept laughing at how gullible she was. "Or better, peter pan? Wait till I get some pixie dust baby. I'll sprinkle some all over."

"Oh well excuse me for 'believing' a guy who has no soul, and can do things no human can," Lucy rolled her eyes, huffing.

Just as she tried to remove her hand from his grasp, he gripped her hand even tighter. "I'm going to carry you all the way to my place." Drake pulled her to him, crouched, and lifted her up on his back without any effort as if she weighed nothing. "Hold on tight; I'm fast." Licking his lips, his pink tongue darting from right to left; he added. "In everything."

Lucy's face flushed as she wrapped her arms tightly around his neck, and her legs around his waist, avoiding his now dark, intense eyes. "Good girl." He breathed out hoarsely. "Oh, and you might want to close your eyes; the wind is not going to be so friendly with my speed." Clutching Lucy's bags with his hands, adrenaline surged through him as he took off at a fast pace.

As Drake ran faster and faster, Lucy held onto him tighter, her face buried in the crook of his neck. Her shirt sleeves were flapping against the wind. And her hair was flying around wildly, she was sure it would be tangled up in knots when they arrive. Despite that, she couldn't help but giggle out loud; her dopamine levels skyrocketing due to the abnormal speed, and due to the way the wind seemed to carry her. Nuzzling her face in Drake's hair, his alluring, masculine smell invaded her senses. She felt his essence pulsing through her veins as her heart beat accelerated; relishing this extraordinary moment.

"That was amazing," Lucy grinned brightly, her teeth showing. Drake's lips curled into a smug smirk as he leaned against the door frame, watching her. Setting her bags in Drake's room, Lucy rushed to the bathroom, and immediately glanced in the mirror. "Shit," She cursed, her hands flying up to her hair. She grabbed a brush and quickly ran it through her tangled locks, biting down on her bottom lip to try to lessen the pain. Groaning, she said, "Next time, tell me to have my hair tied up."

Drake snickered at her struggle with taming her hair. "Come here," He gestured for her to move closer to him. Sighing deeply, Lucy made her way towards him, and puckered her brow. He gave her a lopsided smile that always seemed to do strange things to her insides. Removing the brush from her hand, he turned her around, and gathered her hair in one hand. Drake began to brush her hair slowly as he slightly held the strands from the roots in order to brush the ends without hurting her scalp. He tipped her head back as he raked his hand through her hair, smoothing out the tangles. Lucy involuntarily moaned softly, the feel of his skillful fingers in her hair was beyond soothing. She automatically leaned further back against him every time he brushed his fingers against her neck. Her body was pressed to his front, and she chewed on her inner cheek and sucked in a long breath once she felt something hard against her behind.

314

Drake groaned, his eyes rolling back in his head at the feel of her cushioned against his hardness. His fingers tightened on her hair as he pushed his hips forwards, and pressed his pink lips right under her ear. "Move baby." Lucy didn't seem to hear his words clearly as she remained in his arms, her eyes clamped shut. "I said move," Drake repeated, gritting his teeth, wanting to control himself. Moving away with embarrassment flitting across her now flushed features; little did she know, Drake had so many plans for her during her stay.

"Let's watch this one," Lucy tapped her blue-manicured finger against the DVD she was holding.

Drake rolled his eyes when he read the title of the movie 'Trembling Lily'. "Not that movie." Crossing his arms, he groaned. "It's pathetic."

"No it's not!" Lucy defended, her hand pressed against her chest. Glaring at her, he shrugged, sitting back on the sofa and letting her do whatever she wanted. He watched her place the CD in the DVD player, excitement evident in her features. Lucy grinned widely once the movie started and quickly plumped herself down next to him.

"Can't we watch an even older movie?" Drake mumbled, his voice dripping with sarcasm as he stared at the opening scene. "I mean 1990 is still fresh."

Smiling slyly at him, Lucy said, "You're mocking the 90's? Really?" Her eyes twinkled mischievously. "Your long hair and your style scream 90's." She giggled at his blank expression;

knowing full well that he was not going to come up with a comeback, because what she said was truth. Drake grunted, a small smile on his lips. Reaching out with a strong arm, he pulled her closer to him. Drake smirked once Lucy laid back against him, letting her head rest on his shoulder.

Lucy's vision blurred, the last scene of the movie now unclear through her half-closed eyes. The sound of the characters' voices became distant and muffled as sleep was slowly overcoming her. *Thud. Thud. Thud.* Lucy woke up with a jolt. Terror seeped through her as adrenaline burned a fiery course through her veins. She was on full alert. Whipping her head from side to side, she wanted to know the source of the loud, booming noise. It sounded like objects were falling down – like objects were slammed against the walls. And suddenly, the noise stopped. Lucy rushed towards the kitchen, her feet thundering underneath her. Leaning on the counter, her eyes widened as she took in the chaos in front of her. The table in the middle was broken. The fridge was open and food was sprawled all over the floor-tiles. Drawers and cupboards were ajar; half of the utensils were scattered on the floor. The chairs were in different corners. The curtains were torn. And Drake was sitting in the middle of this evident havoc, his elbows were braced on his knees and his face was pressed into his palms. He was shaking; terribly. His clothes were sticking to his skin, his breathing heavy and labored.

Lucy pressed her now dry lips together, her heart slamming against her rib cage. "What happened?" She asked hesitantly, dreading the answer.

"I can't do this," Drake spat out, removing his hands from his face and looking up at her. Terror was etched into every line of his face. His dark eyes seared through her, begging her not to say anything; not to soothe him. He didn't want her to try to comfort him, he knew that her words wouldn't help. What he was currently feeling was nothing compared to what he would feel, to what he would face later on. His inner demons were tempting him, drawing him away from that tiny, glowing light he thought he had in him. Sinking his teeth in his bottom lip, he groaned loudly. No – no matter how strong the dark impulse was, for her, he'd fight. He'd try to no longer be tainted. He'd try to win this time.

Drake quickly stood up and left the room. Lucy's face contorted in fear. "Where are you going?" She yelled, bile rising in her throat.

Within a few seconds, he returned with keys in his hand. "Take them," Drake said, grabbing Lucy's arm and placing the keys in her hand. "I want you to lock me in my room."

"Wait, what?" She asked, utterly confused.

"You heard me," He sighed heavily. "I don't want to have to go outside. I don't want to have to kill." He felt too hot so he instantly pulled off his shirt and threw it on the floor.

Tearing her eyes away from his mouth-watering upper body, she gazed at the keys in her hands. "But even if I lock you in, you can easily break the door...or the window," She was feeling fidgety on the inside, uncertainty eating away at her.

Drake ran a hand through his disheveled hair. "I'll do my best not to." Stepping closer to her, he cupped her cheek and smoothed his thumb down the side of her face. "And don't open the door even if I scream or cry out. Open it only when I tell you to."

Lucy took several nervous gulps. "But, I can help-"

Drake cut her off, shaking his head. "No. I need some time alone at the moment..."

Lucy nodded, her fingers trembling. She understood him. Drake didn't like to appear vulnerable. She knew that he'd want to confront himself on his own, well, for now at least. Following him to his room, she watched him enter through the door. As she closed it, he did not glance in her direction, not even once. After Lucy locked the door, she slid down the wall and hugged her legs to her chest. *Please let everything work out*, she chanted in her head.

Drake lunged forwards, a knife clutched tightly in his hand. A blank look was etched on his face as he ignored the high-pitched screams that escaped the woman's lips. She was shaking terribly, her teary eyes searching his face for any sign of sympathy. There was none. In an instant, he attacked, stabbing her over and over, watching the blood spatter. Her screams were slowly quieting, her body now lying limp on the floor; right next to the other two dead bodies. A ghastly feeling twisted in my stomach as I forced myself not to vomit. Stepping back, I accidentally hit someone – something. I whirled around only to be met with a grayish, transparent shadow. A sudden feeling of oppressive malevolence engulfed me, threatening me. My legs were shaky and I was feeble in the knees as I tried to move away. "Drake never told you that he killed Annie, Scott and John?" The shadow hissed.

"N-no, you're lying, he'd never-"

"Oh, but he did," Approaching me, its black eyes bored into mine. "You can't save him, Lucy. He can't be saved."

Lucy jolted awake, her heart racing wildly. She whipped her head from side to side, realizing that she was still on the floor right outside Drake's locked bedroom door. She must have fallen asleep and ended up having a horrendous nightmare. She sucked in a shaky breath, *it was just a nightmare, that's all it was.* Still, she couldn't quite get rid of the apprehensiveness she was feeling. Pressing her hand against her chest, she quickly got up. She unlocked the door and pushed it open without hesitation. *What did really happen to the three? Drake never mentioned anything about that.*

Her question was completely wiped out of her mind as soon as she was met with Drake's torturous, black eyes. Her mouth was hung open while her eyes took in Drake's nakedness; Drake was naked. His skin looked so white and untouched, he resembled a mannequin. Tentacles of warmth spread across her skin, heating her entire body. Swallowing hard, she instantly averted her attention from his length, and boy was he...huge. Lucy stepped back, startled, and almost stumbled over her own feet. "I-I didn't know you we-were uh..." She paused, nervously pointing her finger at his perfectly-sculpted body. Drake's shoulders rose and fell as his breathing quickened. His blank expression twisted into that of desire, and it consumed his every feature. Lucy didn't know she was holding her breath until she gasped out loud at the view of his erection. *Maybe I shouldn't have barged in here like that.*

"You fucking asked for it, Lucy," Drake dug his teeth into his bottom lip, drawing blood. Lucy's heart pounded erratically, her feet planted on the floor as she watched him approach her slowly and steadily like a predator. He swiftly grabbed her and pushed her down onto his bed. He climbed on top of her, his hands holding his weight on either side of her head. "I want to bury myself in you. I can't control it any longer. I want you."

Drake pressed his forehead against hers, his eyes searching her shocked ones.

"I've been wanting you to do that ever since I laid my eyes on you, you fucking idiot," Lucy breathed out, her hot breath fanning his parted lips. As soon as those words escaped her mouth, he urgently pressed his lips against hers. Lucy entangled her fingers in his long locks, gently pulling at the roots as she pushed her hips towards him. Drake ran his hand down her sides, and then slid his hand right under her shirt, ripping it off her. A smirk curled his lips while he unclasped her black bra, and got rid of it. Lucy sucked in a shaky breath as soon as he had her left nipple in his mouth. He swirled his tongue around it as his other hand kneaded her right breast. She moaned, her fingers trailing down his chest and resting above his hardness. Pulling away, he slowly removed her skirt, kissing at the exposed skin.

"You're so beautiful, so...delicate," He murmured, spreading her legs wide open. Lucy whimpered as he buried his face in between her thighs, and plunged his tongue into her. He lapped her clit, nipping and sucking. She writhed underneath his hold, her soft moans filling the room. Just before she could no longer control the waves of pleasure that threatened to take over her, Drake removed his lips from her now red clit. He shifted his weight, positioning himself between her spread legs. He locked his eyes with hers as he stroked his length, enjoying the dazed yet lustful look on her flushed face. And just like that, he thrust his massive erection into her; her scream heaven to his ears. Drake's deep growls vibrated against her back while he looked into her passion-glazed eyes. She dug her nails into his shoulders as he slightly pulled out and then quickly slammed back into her, causing her whole body to shudder. She moaned and his pace quickened, the feel of him filling and stretching her entirely made her eyes roll to the back of her head. She wrapped her legs around his torso tighter, and chewed on her bottom lip, the slight pain dissipating. Drake gripped her buttocks and pressed her harder against him – Lucy's hips meeting his every thrust.

"Drake," Lucy whimpered, throwing her arms around his neck. He panted softly against her ear and plunged even deeper inside her, their glistening bodies shaking. "I'm going to-"

"Shh," Drake whispered, pushing her wet hair back and watching her eyes widen. A scream left her lips as her body shook with wave after wave of pleasure; Drake's own intense release following as he came inside her.

Drake let himself fall forwards on his bed. His face was buried in the crook of Lucy's neck, his arm placed around her waist. "I love you," Lucy inhaled heavily, her lips pressing against the top of his head.

"Me too, love," He smiled against her, his eyes clamping shut. Lucy's rhythmic heartbeat was what he last heard before unconsciousness overcame him.

"As cliché as it might sound, I'm really glad that you decided to move to this town or else I would have never met you. I know you moved from town to town – Chad and I found out about the killings in other towns the other day. You-" Lucy's voice trailed away once she realized that Drake was not really listening to what she was saying. Her brows furrowed as she straightened up and inspected his face closely. "Drake." She breathed out hesitantly, removing his arm from around her and placing it at his side. The hair at the back of her neck stood up as she shook him gently, hoping that he was only sleeping. However, she knew that Drake was definitely not sleeping because he didn't wake up yet. Her heart raced, pounding fiercely within her chest while she shook him harder. "Drake," She yelled out his name over and over, but it was of no use at all. He just didn't wake up. Lucy stumbled out of bed in abject fear, almost falling off, realizing to her instant horror that Drake might be...dead. "No, no, no," She chanted, begged, without seeming to take a breath.

Digging her nails into her palms, she slowly drew nearer to him. She pressed her head against his chest, and was able to hear a heartbeat. She let out a long, deep breath of relief and mentally told herself to calm down. *It will be fine.* Lucy hurriedly grabbed her phone; she had to get help pronto.

The first name that popped into her head was George. She bit her bottom lip hard as she dialed his number and waited for him to answer. "Hello," His gruff voice came from the other end of the line.

"George, it's me Lucy. I need your help. You have to come over right now," She panted.

There was a brief silence before he spoke again. "I'm coming." He hung up the phone.

After a couple of minutes, there was a loud series of knocks at the door. Lucy flung the door open, grabbed George's arm, and pulled him towards Drake's bed. "He's...unconscious." She admitted, her voice shaky. As George scrutinized Drake's state, she expected him to yell at her for not calling an ambulance. She expected him to quickly take action and maybe check his breathing or his blood sugar level. But he took her by surprise when all he did was stand still and mumble out. "I have seen him in such a condition before; about two years ago."

"What?" Lucy asked, confusion swirling in her head as she absentmindedly leaned in. If he had seen him in such a state before, it meant that Drake has indeed previously tried to stop – tried to be better.

George rubbed his temple, frowning. "He had the same well...symptoms. I'm going to call them symptoms since I don't know what the hell they really are. Paleness, excessive sweating

– the red lines on his chest; he tends to involuntarily do that to himself when he feels he has no control." He paused, pulling at his white mustache. "I took him to the hospital that day, but it was useless."

"How did he recover then?" She asked, impatience coating the words.

"By himself. He woke up the other day, and was feeling better than ever. I didn't understand it. I still don't understand it. But I say, we wait. As you have noticed, Drake is not what I'd call...normal." He sighed deeply. "I still haven't figured it out yet."

Wait. George didn't know that Drake was soulless? Her eyes widened, *but how come? If he had known him for all these years, shouldn't Drake have trusted him or maybe felt the need to tell him? George was a bizarre, old man; surely he would have understood or something.*

Lucy's glassy eyes were fixed on Drake as she watched his chest slowly rise and fall with every breath he managed to take. She drew in a breath of air sharply, her lips trembling. "Did he tell you anything about his past?" She asked out of nowhere.

George puckered his brow. "Not really. All he did tell me was that a family raised him when he was younger and had no one."

"Annie and Scott?" Lucy narrowed her eyes at him, hoping he knew something new – something recent about them. "Do you know if they're...still alive?"

"I'm sorry dear, but I know nothing of the sort," He sighed deeply. "May I ask, why is it that you're asking? Why is that important at the moment?"

She rubbed the back of her neck, hesitant. "I don't know." It was that nightmare that she had; she wanted to make sure that it was completely false. "I guess I was only just wondering."

George had a questioning look on his face as he spoke under his breath. "Can't you check online or something?"

Lucy beamed, a grin stretching her lips. "You're right." *If they were still alive, wouldn't Drake have still been in contact with them? Why else would he not, considering that Earl was no longer a threat?*

He interrupted her thoughts, saying. "You can use my computer. I'll stay here and watch Drake."

"It's okay. I'll just use my phone," She launched the web browser and typed in their names. Scrolling down all the links that popped, her eyes widened and her breath got caught in her throat once she reached the following title. 'A family of three had been saved unusually'. She clicked on it, waiting. The page loaded, and her eyes quickly scanned the words written.

On Wednesday, March 13, 2016 Annie, Scott, and John Mitchell were in a tragic car accident. Two cars had crashed, leading to the death of Andrew Lewis, who was driving the Honda. However, the family who would have thought to be dead as well, had miraculously yet unusually survived the incident. How? It is unknown...

Lucy blinked twice, pushing her phone back into her pocket. Drake saved them. They were still alive. Swallowing hard, she gasped. It was also two years ago. The same year when he last fell unconscious.

CHAPTER 24

Lucy was panting, panic building inside her like an unstoppable snowball. She wasn't able to think straight. Her heart was beating uncontrollably as her brain started firing out negative thoughts like a machine gun. *What could I do? I don't even know what I should do to help Drake!* The arguments in her head kept adding up as she tangled her hands in her hair and allowed herself to cry. Tears burst forth like water from a dam, spilling down her face. She felt the muscles of her chin tremble like that of a small kid. Her vision blurred as she stared at Drake's unconscious body.

She felt a hand rest on her shoulder in reassurance. "You know, I haven't really been honest with you." George sighed in defeat, his heart aching at the sight of her. She looked so broken.

Lucy sniffed and rubbed her nose as she gave George a confused yet curious glance. His lips formed a tight line before he said, "I work with Bernard. But I'm not like him. You see, Bernard doesn't really like Drake because of what he has done, but I do. I sympathize with Drake and I actually want to help him, that's why I have always been around."

Lucy's mouth fell open, gasping. "What do you mean you work with him? What are you two?"

"You could say that Bernard and I are angels. We never had to leave the heavens before, but Drake is a serious case, and he's one of his kind. That's why we were sent here to watch him. My intentions are different from Bernard's except for the fact that we both want what's best for him." George pinched his temples, taking a great pause. "I shouldn't be telling you this; but I think you have the right to know. However, that's the only information I'm willing to share with you. Humans are not supposed to know of all this."

Lucy was at loss for words. She did know deep down that something was off about George; she was just glad that he was trying to help Drake all along. "Thank you for entrusting me with this. I won't tell anyone." Her eyes continued to drip with tears for she wasn't able to stop her crying. "What will happen to Drake? Is there nothing we can do to save him? I will do anything but please-"

"There's nothing we can do, Lucy. I'm so sorry," George cut her off, his voice full of pity.

She swallowed back hard, refusing to believe this. "No! There must be something! Maybe if I go find Annie and Scott, maybe they can help! Or if I find his dad who left him when he was twelve, maybe that will help...I c-can get the families of those he killed to forgive him or-" She stopped; speaking was becoming harder as she sobbed hysterically. She felt like a hollow shell. Lucy stumbled towards George and gripped his shirt with both hands pleadingly.

He removed her hands that were digging into his chest and pulled her to a chair and seated her. He crouched down and managed to say. "We can't do this-"

"Why not?" She interrupted him, her lips trembling with hurt.

"Because it's absurd! Annie and Scott can't do anything, they're just going to be as sad as you. His father was never there for him, why would he care now? And as for the families...there are over hundreds. To even find them is ridiculous..." He breathed out, shaking his head. "I know you want to help but it's just no use."

Lucy knew he was right but she just couldn't sit there and watch Drake die. She stood up, rushed towards Drake, and sat next to him. She gently caressed his cheek, pushing a hair strand away from his face. Tracing her fingertips against the softness of his parted lips, her hand trailed down to his and held it. She squeezed his hand and hoped he would be fine. He looked so peaceful. With the shaft of light from the window illuminating his pale face and lending his porcelain skin a frail transparency, he looked like an angel.

"You might be actually right, he does resemble an angel when he's harmless like that." Lucy whipped her head to the source of the voice and glared. It was Bernard, who always seemed to pop out of nowhere.

"You. What do you want?" Lucy asked weakly.

"I came to tell you that you did well. You followed my advice." He smiled sincerely. She furrowed her brows, her hand still clutching Drake's. "He must suffer in order for him to be free. The suffering is over, and now he belongs to us."

Lucy clenched her jaw, her nose flaring. "What do you mean? I won't let you hurt him!"

"You've got it all wrong. I'm not here to hurt him. I'm here to set him free." Bernard admitted, smiling faintly.

George drew nearer, and stood next to Bernard. "Lucy, Drake is not breathing anymore. He allowed himself to suffer, and he's going to have to die."

"No! No! No!" Lucy begged, she couldn't bear to lose him. "It's all my fault. I shouldn't have listened to you!" She burst out, and held onto Drake. She wrapped her arms around him tight and buried her face in his chest. She did not feel any heartbeat. Her crying was muffled as she tangled herself around his body. "Please..."

"On contrary my dear, you have saved him. He's going to have his soul back and he's going to heaven. He is no longer banned because he sacrificed himself for the sins he has done and he did the right thing. His life span is different from that of a human's. So would you rather he live on long after you are dead, alone and without a soul...?" Bernard said.

Lucy let his words seep into her mind. Drake was going to be free. "But I'll never get to see him again." She whimpered.

"Yes, you will. You will in the afterlife," George reassured her, approaching her.

As soon as Bernard lifted his hands, Drake's body was lifted too. Lucy gasped with shock and stared at Drake's floating body. His fiery, red hair was glowing and was flying wildly. His body was hovering right above her. "It's time for us to take him to heaven where he belongs." Glancing at Lucy, who was staring in stunned surprise, he said, "You will get to have one final word with him before we take him."

Lucy's heart leapt out of her chest with happiness and relief. "Oh my God. Thank you so much!" She began laughing, her tears spilling down her face and she could taste the saltiness of them.

"I didn't know you were that happy about my death," A familiar voice, that she yearned for, said. Lucy instantly turned around and was met with Drake's open arms. He flashed her a wide, warm smile as she jumped into his embrace. He wrapped an arm around her shoulders and pulled her close. Lucy hugged him tight, her body melting into his. Despite the heaviness in her stomach, it fluttered at the feel of him. Sinking into his warmth, Lucy squeezed him even tighter. She felt like the world stopped still on its axis and it was only him and her. She did not want the moment to end. Her worries dissipated and were replaced with hope. She felt him brush her hair back lightly as he leaned in and kissed her. The kiss was slow and soft, comforting Lucy in ways that words would never be able to. His hand rested below her ear, his thumb caressing her cheek as their breaths mingled. She ran her fingers down his spine, pulling him closer until there was no space left between them. "Thank you so much for everything." Drake breathed against her lips. Lucy smiled, a tear falling down her rosy cheek. "Don't ever cry. I want you to smile. I want you to be happy always. Even now. I might not still be here, but I will protect you and watch over you. You have been my angel on Earth, and it's time I be your angel in the heavens." He wiped her tear away with his thumb and touched his nose to hers, earning a giggle from Lucy.

Drake slowly pulled away and held her hand. "I love you."

George and Bernard were already gone, and Drake was floating even higher now. He was about to leave her. "I love you too." She cried out and watched him fly higher, her fingers slipping from his. Drake's lips stretched into a radiant smile as he floated away from her until she couldn't see him no more. At that moment, the sun shone brighter than ever. He was her sun.

Three years later

"Be careful, Blake," Lucy said and watched the young child run around in the meadow, giggling and making silly faces. His shoulder-length, red hair was flying everywhere as he kept sprinting in circles. He was a happy, carefree kid.

"He looks just like his dad, doesn't he?" George said as he glanced at Lucy, who was watching her son attentively.

"He does," She beamed, her heart slightly stinging. She missed him, but wherever she was, she felt his presence surround her and Blake.

"He has your eyes though," George pointed out. Lucy nodded and sprinted towards her son, ready to catch him. He ran even farther, laughing loudly, not wanting his mom to catch him.

George has been there for Lucy ever since she got pregnant. Drake did not want her to be cared for by her brother and mother only. That is why George was here.

As Lucy and Blake played together, she knew that someday they will be both reunited with Drake.

Acknowledgments

First, I would like to thank God for all the blessings. Thank you for helping me go through the difficult times and still be able to stand strong.

I would like to thank my family, friends, and my boyfriend for the endless support. The completion of this book could not have been possible without you.

Thank you to the people, whose names may not all be mentioned, for all the assistance given.

90430872R00198

Made in the USA
Middletown, DE
23 September 2018